D1795953

THE KENNEDY EFFECT

MICHAEL J. FOY

ALTERNATE REALITY PRESS

The Kennedy Effect
Copyright © 2009 Michael J. Foy

ALL RIGHTS RESERVED

No part of this publication may be reproduced, stored in a re-trieval system, or transmitted, in any form or by any means (elec-tronic, mechanical, photocopying, recording, or otherwise) without the prior written permission of both the publisher and the author. The scanning, uploading, and distribution of this book via the Internet or via any other means without the permission of the publisher is illegal and punishable by law. Please purchase only authorized electronic editions, and do not participate in or encour-age electronic piracy of copyrighted materials. Your support of the author's rights is appreciated.

PUBLISHER'S NOTE

This is a work of fiction. Names, characters, places, and incidents either are the product of the author's imagination or are used ficti-tiously, and any resemblance to actual persons, living or dead, business establishments, events or locales is entirely coincidental.

Published by Alternate Reality Press
A subsidiary of Publishing Search Solutions
http://www.publishingsearch.com

Printed in the United States of America

ISBN-13: 978-0-9841053-0-4

ISBN-10: 0-9841053-0-1

Cover Background Image Credit:
NASA/JPL-Caltech/L. Cieza (Univ. of Texas at Austin)

Acknowledgments

I wish to thank Steven Plotkin, Research Director at the JFK library, for his reading suggestions in researching John F. Kennedy, the man and president; G. Miki Hayden, author of the alternate-history cult novel *Pacific Empire*, for her encouragement and invaluable wordsmithing contributions; Jennifer C. Harris, director at Plymouth Public Library, for her support of new and upcoming authors.

Last, but not least, I want to thank my wife, Sharon, for her patience and judgment in creating the right impression.

Michael J. Foy

This novel is for those President John F. Kennedy inspired with his wit and intelligence and who still wonder at what could have been ...

And for all those lesser-known Kennedys, including my mother's family, who persevere and survive in obscurity.

"The tendency to turn human judgments into divine commands makes religion one of the most dangerous forces in the world."

—Georgia Harkness, theologian

Prologue

The minds of an entire race followed the progress of its probe into the young solar system. So vast were these minds that they could split their concentration in nearly limitless divisions and monitor their various works across space-time. Now, they perceived a revolving disk of debris surrounding a newly ignited sun. The accretion process had already begun, with perhaps four, possibly five, rocky worlds to be formed.

The probe valued nothing more greatly than sentient life, and this system held promise due to the size of its sun, the amount of material available, and the likely orbits of still-forming planets. The development of intelligence would take time, however, as the ongoing, violent creation of these worlds so far left too hostile an environment for organic existence. Another billion or more years would be needed.

The probe completed its survey and prepared to leave, but not before depositing a presence that was also a catalyst for life. The system was now seeded with life's chemistry. Only time and the mechanism of random chance were required to produce a biological structure capable of spawning some form of self-aware being with intelligence. Once that being sprang from the primordial slime, the catalyst would protect it from competitors.

Even given their highly prospective minds, the catalyst's creators could not know their device would play a part in threatening survival across multiple realities, universes unguessed at in the imaginings of these beings. That lack of vision, however, would not be a deficiency in the sentient species that these founders coaxed and sponsored. In a mere four-and-a-half-billion years, the experiments producing this young species would spawn a conflict to pit parallel universes against each other. These new multiverses would face a threat from the most dangerous weapon ever to be devised. The mind of Man.

PART I

Incursion

CHAPTER 1

Summer 1960

Under a full moon, a tour bus glided about twenty feet above the ground. The top half of the bus was mostly glass, allowing panoramic views of the woodland from every seat. Inside, the vehicle was comfortably appointed with high-cushioned chairs for the well-paying tourists. Outside, bright moonlight turned the foliage several shades of silver as summer breezes caused the branches to gently sway. The cabled course followed a path that was mostly clear of tree limbs yet was tight enough that the tourists could have touched the leaves had the windows been open. On certain occasions, a swaying branch might momentarily intersect with the bulk of the bus, but the leafy appendage would pass through, as ethereal as fairy dust.

Eventually, the bus emerged into a clearing, a manmade clearing that the locals called a "back yard." The vehicle continued on and into the house, passing through the walls and other solids as easily as it had passed through the forest. Inside, two teenage boys at their respective desks poured over some books, unaware that they were being observed. In a separate bedroom, a girl chatted on a dial telephone in a most animated manner as she lay on her bed. The tourists noticed books untouched on her desk.

"Not as diligent a student as her brothers," commented the tour guide at the front of the bus.

The vehicle continued on its circuitous route around a typical suburban neighborhood. At times it climbed above the houses, while at others, it descended to observe the residents indoors. After a lengthy series of indoor excursions, the guide encouraged questions from his group.

A boy spoke up with one inquiry. "What's holding the bus up?"

"A very thin bucky cable reinforced with other elements that the engineers could tell you about better than I. Suffice it to say, we owe a form of carbon molecule for our suspension."

Another boy raised his hand and was acknowledged by the guide. "Why can't the people see us?"

"Good question—but again, physicists might best explain that. All I'll say is that we're slightly out of phase with their universe. While their reality proceeds according to a certain wave form, we're a couple of degrees ahead or behind it. Our engineers tell me that if we were any less removed, our presence could be detected as a shadow or ghost image.

"We're now entering another single family home. Due to the father's odd working hours, the family eats later than the norm. Here we'll be able to observe family dining in this America in this reality."

As the bus passed through walls, the tourists found themselves in a primitive kitchen where a family of five sat around a table laden with food. The passengers marveled at the decor. Strangely, a large white, metal cube with a control panel—a washing machine—sat in the kitchen. And the table had a small metal skirt that hung down a couple of inches from the eating surface. The surface itself was smooth, blue in color and looked as if it had metallic flakes embedded in it.

An electric fan rotated left and right, creating a breeze on what must have been a hot summer night. The passengers, of course, were unaware of the exact temperature, since they were ensconced in a comfort-controlled cable bus.

The father sat wearing a sleeveless T-shirt and drank a beer as he listened to his son's story of a schoolyard game. His wife sat at the other end of the table and wore what the tour guide called "rollers" in her hair.

Soon the bus passed through another wall to the outside, where drying garments hung from clotheslines on a porch.

As the back of the bus emerged from the interior, the guide noted that most of the tourists were engrossed in the living habits of the locals. Amateur anthropologists all, he thought, and smiled to himself. Of course if truth be told, his own fascination with this society was why he'd signed up for the job in the first place. The setup seemed so primitive in comparison to his own, and yet it ran quite smoothly in its own barbaric way. Here was a family calmly enjoying each other's company in a world filled with war and disease and injustice. Amazing what the human soul could tolerate.

For all of that, however, mathematical models indicated a future in which most of these ills would be conquered. The guide reasoned that faith and patience must truly be in abundance here. If the course of this society's evolution remained undisturbed, he knew those qualities would be rewarded.

April 1961

In his Back Bay Boston neighborhood, Rick Gerard sat at a stool sipping his coffee between puffs of a cigarette while he watched the black-and-white television up in the corner of the cafe. Absent-minded at first, the agent from an alternate Earth became more alert as something on the news focused his attention: an address to the nation about Cuba by President Kennedy.

"This administration plans to take responsibility for its mistakes," Kennedy said, referring to the recent Bay of Pigs disaster.

Rick sat open mouthed for several moments after the speech was done. He fumbled for something in his pocket and withdrew a small metallic device about the size of a cigarette lighter. Regaining his composure, he looked around to see if anyone had witnessed his actions before shoving the device back into his pocket. He then threw some change on the counter and ran out the door. In a secluded alley, he brought the device back out, pressed a few buttons, held it up to his mouth, and began a conversation.

"Did you just see the news?" queried Gerard.

"Yes, we've known for a while," Proconsul al-Rahiim replied.

"Well, what do you make of it?"

"We aren't sure yet. We're running the figures again, but every model indicates that Kennedy should've provided air support for the Cuban exiles."

"I'll tell you—when I heard that he didn't, I had to check to see if I was in the right place. It was the perfect opportunity to oust the Communists from their backyard," offered Gerard.

"The only thing I can think of is that the new administration wasn't keen on the old Eisenhower strategy. Our agents even told us that the Navy had been briefed to intercept the invasion force and turn it back, as a contingency plan. I still don't get it, though.

The Bay of Pigs should at least have been a military success if not a political one."

"Why not political? Castro has no support here."

"We're talking world politics, Rick. The United States' respected position would be undermined if they were proven to be behind a successful invasion."

"Is it any better for an unsuccessful one?"

"Point taken."

"Do you think we have a rogue infiltration? A case of tampering?"

"The way this parallel reality fits... Or rather doesn't fit into the others now, I'd say that's a strong possibility. Another rogue agent, after all the safeguards," mused al-Rahiim. "It seemed like we had a handle on our people. Now, we might have to intervene with a correction."

"You mean you'll send a cleaner here?"

"I don't know yet. Maybe as a last resort if we can't make some sense of this."

The agent didn't want to hear about an intervention but could imagine it was coming. An intervention entailed all kinds of risks to his own reality, but if tampering was proven, his people would have no choice.

"Will we need to evacuate?"

"No. At least that's what the word is now. Even tourism is continuing."

CHAPTER 2

September 20, 1961

Barney Hill laughed at the joke he shared with his wife, Betty, as he drove along the dark New Hampshire highway. The White Mountains surrounded them in familiar yet pitch black silhouettes. Their headlights carved into the night to reveal the road but very little else. Returning home to Portsmouth, New Hampshire, they relived their vacation in Montreal. The couple, of mixed race, favored Canada as a destination since the locals there didn't reproach the white woman simply because she was with a black man.

While he entertained pleasant memories, something finally broke into Barney's consciousness. In the distance a light had been hovering in the sky for a good portion of their trip. Only now did it register with him. It had probably gotten a lot closer in the last few minutes, too.

"Betty, you see that light back there?"

She turned around and looked at the road behind her.

"No, I mean up in the sky," Barney said.

"Yes, Barney, now I see it. Is it a plane?"

"I don't think so. Its flying is too erratic."

They watched the thing a little longer and noted that at times it would swing wildly across the sky.

"I've only seen spotlights do that, but it looks more solid than one of those," said Barney as he slowed the car to a stop.

"Barney, what are you doing?" she asked in a concerned tone.

"I just want to take a look." He got out of the car and peered skyward. "I don't know, Betty. I've never seen anything like it before."

After a while, he became bored, got back in the car, and started again for home. Betty kept her eye on the light.

"Barney, I think it's following us," she said with a quaver in her voice.

Barney could tell his wife was afraid, and even though he felt alarmed himself, he feigned a calm demeanor.

"I don't see it anymore," said Betty at last.

"It's in front of us now," Barney informed her.

He stopped the car and left the engine running. Remembering a pair of binoculars he kept in the back seat, he grabbed them, got out of the car, and trained them on the light. What he saw challenged his powers of reason.

"I don't believe it! I don't believe it! This is ridiculous!" he shouted in a frenzy.

Through the binoculars, the light revealed itself to be a flying craft of some sort. Figures on it moved beyond a double row of windows, and Barney had the distinct impression that they weren't friendly. Even more disturbing, however, was the feeling that they were trying to communicate with him without the use of words.

An eerie sensation played along the boundaries of his perception. *Come closer,* it said. *We won't hurt you,* it assured.

Barney ran back to the car as Betty, now in near hysterics, observed him from the passenger seat that she'd never left. Barney got in and slammed the door closed.

"They're going to capture us," he shouted and raced the car down the road.

The light had gone, but that didn't make the couple feel any safer as they continued to speed away. Suddenly, Barney and Betty heard what seemed to be a loud note from a tuning fork.

"How are they doing?" asked the alien captain of the vehicle that had appeared to the Hills.

"They're semi-conscious, sir," stated the doctor.

"Well, let's get our samples and get out of here. And let's do it quickly, shall we? Before their kind suspects tampering."

November 14, 1961

On yet another formal occasion, the Kennedys demonstrated their knack for social engagement as Maestro Pablo Casals entertained a White House audience with his mastery of the cello. It was a new era for presidential interaction, a happy time in spite of the ongoing cold war. The president proved that one could enjoy national life while trying to solve its most vexing problems. The country was upbeat, optimistic about the future.

In spite of the Bay of Pigs fiasco, Kennedy still enjoyed broad support at home. Internationally, however, reaction proved a mixed bag. Friends outside the country who knew the young president were confident in his inestimable skills at diplomacy. Adversaries, however, were drawing their plans to test his will.

CHAPTER 3

August 1962

The icy mantle reverberated under his feet causing some puzzlement to the new arrival. A midday sun in a cloudless sky cast a blinding glare off the blue-white surface of the ice floe. The landing area was not supposed to be like this. His point of insertion was intended to be remote but not a frozen wasteland. Where was he? Perhaps someone had miscalculated elevation or planet rotation. In any case, he was better off here than at some point underwater or even underground for that matter.

The thudding vibrations increased in frequency and intensity, and finally it occurred to him to turn around. A large male polar bear was nearly atop him.

The stranger's movement was just quick enough to avert the full force of the pounce, and instead of being crushed under the weight of the animal, he was knocked to one side. The bear soon straddled him, however, its claws shredding a jacket that was already inadequate.

Oddly enough, the claws didn't penetrate the skin. The beast seemed puzzled as it sniffed at the man. Ultimately then, it lost interest and ambled away. Rising, and none the worse for wear, the man stared after the predator. He removed a pair of sunglasses from his pocket, seemed to get his bearings from the sky, then turned and walked south.

With his shredded jacket blowing in the breeze, he continued on an inexorable march. In spite of the frigid conditions, he offhandedly noted that Arctic Canada presented a myriad of islands, only some of which could be seen above the ice. They weren't invisible as much as simply flat. The highest elevation of some of the peaks he'd seen might have been only fifteen feet above sea level. As far as animals went, only the polar bear made an appearance, although the man was sure the area teemed with seals, fish, walruses, and maybe even whales. A short distance under his feet, under the ice, was surely enough meat and blubber to keep whole villages of Inuit alive and healthy. He, on the other hand, felt unconcerned about strategies of survival. His constitution would sustain him at least as long as it took to get to civilization.

Eventually, the traveler came upon a hunting party of Inuit. They seemed quite fixated on a small area of the ice that looked no more significant to the walker than any other part of the unending whiteness. As he got closer, though, he realized that they had discovered a seal's breathing hole. For all he knew, he could've passed hundreds without noticing them. He was sure that the natives' keen senses were honed to notice the subtle differences in the ice indicating a hunting opportunity. When the Inuit heard the man's approach, they angrily turned around and put their fingers to their lips in the universal sign for silence. Apparently, he was jeopardizing the hunt. He immediately stopped in his tracks.

Two of the group of five still squatted by the hole as the other three stood guard—no doubt checking for polar bears. Two of the three who had motioned the stranger to be quiet turned back to the hole, while the third couldn't help but stare at the man who was dressed suicidally for the climate.

Within minutes, the primary hunter, with a lightning fast flurry of spearing activity, struggled to haul a seal up onto the ice with the help of his mates. All interest in the stranger disappeared as they bent to their task. The walker was free to move on and make all the noise he wanted. Eventually, within the hour, he came to a body of water.

A Narwhal swam instinctively along a route that led it to its feeding grounds. Had the animal any more than a dull curiosity, it might have checked its advance as it spied a man swimming. The whale must have previously observed swimming polar bears, walruses, and seals, but surely not a swimming man, and certainly not one that didn't wear protective covering. The interloper swam with machine-like strokes, never varying his tempo, and apparently unperturbed by the water temperature.

Dragging himself ashore near a human settlement, the man went through his start-up procedure. Nanoprobes the size of a gnat escaped his body, one from under each of his shoulder blades. Immediately upon their exit, the skin resealed, hiding any evidence of their passage. The probes orbited for a moment and then cloaked themselves to veil their existence.

Data soon streamed into the visual cortex of the man's brain. The microrobotic devices now functioned as virtual third and fourth eyes and an effective early warning system in case of danger. The interloper not only enjoyed a genetically designed constitution, but nanorobotic enhancement—the hovering microsentinels being only part of the technology at his disposal. Assured that all his resources were operational, he resolved to continue south.

Finally, after a long trek in the chosen direction, the interloper settled into a comfortable room at the Chateau Frontenac in

Quebec City, Canada. The man, who now called himself Jack, gazed out his window at the mighty St. Lawrence River. Some revelers on the boardwalk below laughed and cavorted in the moonlight. The lilting French accents floated up to Jack as he eavesdropped.

After a few moments Jack closed the drapes and turned off some of the lights. Putting his sunglasses on the bed, he fumbled in his jacket pocket. After finding what he was looking for, he withdrew a small device about the size and shape of a nine-volt battery. He plugged the cord that trailed from it into his glasses and turned a small thumbwheel on the unit. With his glasses on, he further manipulated the device by pressing the thumbwheel as he scrolled through numbers and letters that showed on the inside of his glasses. Satisfied that he had found the address he wanted, he took off the glasses, watched them, and waited. Within a few seconds, a shimmering image appeared above the sunglasses and resolved itself into the form of a man from the chest up.

"Hello, Jack," the image said.

"Good evening, Proconsul al-Rahiim."

"I heard that you had some trouble with the portal. Any ill effects?"

"None other than the delay. But I've got to tell you, I didn't believe my colleagues who said they were pressured to cover up problems with the portal. After finding myself in an Arctic wilderness, though, it has occurred to me they might have been right."

"Former colleagues, Jack. And now that you work for us I assume I can trust you to keep those messy details out of the hands of your friends in the press."

"Those journalistic instincts are hard to ignore, but yes, you can rely on my discretion."

"For your personal information, it may interest you to know that we've dramatically decreased the frequency of those little accidents. Pretty soon we'll have the problem licked altogether."

The proconsul's statement made Jack wonder how frequent the little accidents had been. Now that he had a taste of the portal's fallibility, he remembered some of the rumored horror stories. People materializing under hundreds of feet of water for instance.

The proconsul continued: "I regret we had to pluck you out of a profession you enjoyed, but I hope you appreciate that anyone could be called on at any time. Just depends on the history and the people involved. This mission suggested you for obvious reasons."

"Understood. But to be honest, I considered this profession before journalism. At one time I chewed over politics too, so I don't feel put upon. And as a matter of fact, I'm eager to satisfy my own curiosity about this reality."

"Really? You? Politics? But why am I not surprised? Anyway, you have some other documented tendencies that I hope you'll at least try to keep in check. Any questions at this stage?"

"None so far."

"Good. Now I'd like you to report to Rick Gerard in Boston. He'll be able to set you up with a more permanent residence, along with all the documentation you'll require. Good luck and if you need to contact us, you know the protocols."

The image of al-Rahiim dissolved into nothingness, just as a knock came at Jack's door. After putting away the device, Jack opened the door and greeted the young lady standing there.

The first time he'd seen her in the lobby, she'd reminded him of Angie Dickinson. He'd wondered if she'd be willing to help him explore his fantasies about actresses. Giving in to this urge, he struck up a conversation with her. His uncanny way with women had the desired effect, and she agreed to a date with the stranger. Prompted by his strong libido, Jack wondered if he might find any other actress look-alikes around. A look-alike Marilyn Monroe might be particularly intriguing.

"You're early," he said.

"There's a show near the city wall that I just found out about," she replied with a French accent. "I didn't think you'd mind starting your tour of Quebec a little earlier."

"Good idea. This stranger to the city wouldn't want to miss all it has to offer. Particularly with such a charming tour guide."

The girl smiled knowingly.

For the last several years, Rick Gerard had enjoyed a comfortable existence in Boston in a Commonwealth Avenue apartment. His neighborhood was upscale and conveniently located near the attractive Boston Common and Garden. A representative strip of grass from these landmark parks ran down the center of the wide street providing both greenery and shade from the well-established trees. This piece of land was called the Commonwealth Mall, and Gerard often walked it to the park where he enjoyed feeding the ducks and other water fowl that swam around tourists on their Swan Boat rides. His work demanded little enough of his attention that he could afford complacency. Indeed, his waistline had expanded as a result.

Today, however, his attention was focused on a *Boston Globe* newspaper page. An article talked about the latest strangler victim, Ida Irga, a seventy-five-year-old woman. Police Sergeant James McDonald described how he'd found her splayed out in an obscene parody of an obstetrical position.

Gerard's thoughts, however, were soon interrupted by the doorbell, and he opened the door to a tall, rugged-looking man.

"Hello, Rick. I'm Jack," said the visitor.

"So you're the cleaner?" asked Rick.

The man nodded.

"Where the hell have you been? Al-Rahiim said you'd be along days ago." Rick grabbed Jack and pulled him in the door, then shut it quickly so their next comments wouldn't be overheard.

"The portal administrators thoughtfully arranged a tour of the Arctic. Ever been north of Hudson Bay?" Jack said facetiously.

"What? Are you all right?" Gerard asked as he looked the newcomer up and down for evidence of injury.

"I had a run in with some wildlife, but suffice it to say the creatures found me unappetizing."

"I'll bet. Well you seem none the worse for the cold. Is that due to your enhancements?"

"Remarkable technology. And it's getting better all the time. I wish the portal locator worked as well. Anyway, the enhancements almost make the selection and training seem worthwhile."

Rick imagined himself going through the rigors of the process Jack referenced and decided he was just as happy being ordinary.

"I don't want to know how you managed to get here without money or ID. But let's see if we can make you legal."

Rick walked over to a roll-top desk and extracted cash and papers. As Rick did that, Jack noticed the headlines on the paper Rick had been reading. There were cigarette burns on it from Rick's ill-chosen habit, but Jack could make out the topic.

"The Boston Strangler is still at large?"

"Seems so."

"Strange character. Makes me wonder if that's not the result of tampering too."

"This Earth is quite a bit different than ours, Jack. It's tough to mathematically model down to the level of solo lunatics. My guess is he's normal for this reality. Just another Jack the Ripper."

"I suppose so."

Rick handed the new documentation to his guest. "Jack, you said 'the result of tampering too' when you saw the newspaper. Does that mean that tampering has been confirmed?"

"I'd rather not say right now, Rick."

"Well, the fact that you're here must mean they're taking the possibility seriously."

"All I can tell you is that they see a high probability of an international crisis occurring very soon. Beyond that, you'll have to draw your own conclusions."

"I just hope that the council knows what it's doing. I've become used to this universe and would hate to see it snuffed out of existence."

"I wish this was the only reality at risk."

A couple of days later, Jack walked toward the brownstone building where he'd met Rick the first time. As expected, he needed another infusion of cash. Setting himself up in this society had been an expensive proposition so far. Renting apartments and buying cars, although on the cheap, still had taken most of his stake. Now, with that done, however, his requirements would be more modest.

It was night time but Jack could clearly see Rick on the front steps talking with two men. All of a sudden, one of the men punched Rick in the stomach, doubling him over. Jack ran the rest of the way and intercepted the men on their way down the stairs.

"That wasn't nice what you did to my friend," he said.

The men looked at each other and grinned. "Tommy, did you hear that?" said the light-haired man to his companion. "Maybe Rick's friend here would like some of the same treatment?" He reached into his pocket.

Preternaturally fast, Jack grabbed the man's arm at the same time he delivered a kick to Tommy's solar plexus. Now the light-haired man was bent over on his knees while Jack held his straightened arm with the hand and wrist at an upturned angle. Brass knuckles lay on the ground. Probably what he was reaching for, guessed Jack.

Tommy couldn't even catch his breath enough to writhe in his apparent pain.

"Jack, I'm okay," called Rick since he must have noticed Jack getting ready to deliver a further blow.

Jack released the kneeling man but not before he administered a kick to the ribs.

"This is your lucky day," said Jack to the thug, and then the cleaner backed away.

Tommy had at least recovered his breath enough to rise, although he was still stooped over.

"C'mon, Whitey," said Tommy. "Let's get the hell out of here."

The man called Whitey looked up from the sidewalk and glared at Jack, who returned his gaze with no trace of emotion other than a clinical curiosity about the damage he'd done. Both thugs hobbled away.

"That Bulger is a wild one," said Rick when Jack arrived at the top of the steps. "Some day he'll make headlines with his temper."

"Whitey Bulger? He has a brother, doesn't he?"

"Yeah. Billy Bulger. But it's hard to believe they have the same parents. Billy's a good kid. Terrific civic sense. Always active in the community. On the other hand, you just saw the type of people Whitey hangs out with."

"I remember that from my training. Billy may go far in politics according to the models we ran. Wasn't Whitey the one who hit you?"

"It doesn't pay to joke with him. I just commented on his new haircut. Thinning hair, you know. And then bam! Before I knew it, I was trying to catch my breath. When I saw you confronting them, I was afraid you might kill them."

Jack stared at Rick a moment. "Do you think cleaners are predisposed to that?"

"I've heard you have a flexible moral code when correcting a penetration into another universe."

As soon as Rick said that, his facial expression changed, and Jack could see that Rick regretted those words. Jack also sensed that Rick wondered if he'd just put himself at risk by revealing his lack of naiveté. Was Rick privy to his last-resort option, too? Jack suspected that might be the case. But what could he do? Anyway, it was an option that Jack hoped would not be necessary.

"Let's get inside," suggested Jack.

Moments later, Jack exited the brownstone with a fresh wad of cash. He was surprised to find that the money came from an organization that boasted Whitey Bulger as a member. *I suppose the underworld economy is the best place to get untraceable cash*, he reasoned.

Whitey knew his boss by only one name, Mr. Winter. And Mr. Winter was not pleased. One thing you didn't want to do was displease this mobster with the Irish temper. Returning without the jewels they'd been sent for was bad, but at least they hadn't paid out the money they carried. More importantly, though, in Winter's mind was the issue of humiliation. Whitey considered lying about his encounter with Rick's friend but decided not to risk the truth getting back to Winter by other means.

"Beaten up by one guy?" Winter yelled in a rhetorical way. "Did anyone see this?" he asked further in a non-rhetorical fashion.

"No one but Rick and Tommy, Mr. Winter," said Whitey who looked at his companion for confirmation.

Winter walked around his desk to come face to face with Whitey, who folded his hands in front of himself. As Winter approached the two men, he exhaled through his teeth. When he finally spoke, he seemed to be calmer.

"Boys, if we're going to be good at this business, we have to be respected. Even by business partners like Rick. You understand that, don't you?"

"Yes, Mr. Winter."

"If we lose respect, how do you suppose we get it back?"

"By setting an example?"

"Very good," said Winter, pretending to be impressed. "How would you set an example in this case?"

"By paying back the one who did this."

Winter merely stared, not uttering a word. Then without warning he slapped Whitey hard across the face. "Then what the fuck are you still standing here for?"

Whitey returned to Rick's house to ask Rick how he might get hold of this Jack. No one answered the doorbell or the persistent knocking, however, so after checking to see that he had no witnesses, Whitey broke a pane of glass with his hand wrapped in a handkerchief. Reaching in, he opened the door and entered the building.

Whitey checked all the rooms and satisfied himself that Rick wasn't home. Whitey had been inside often enough to know where Rick kept things. He then entered a room with a roll-top desk and riffled through Rick's papers. Not knowing Jack's last name, however, made his task difficult in spite of finding the files.

Painstakingly, Whitey scanned each index card looking for the first name "Jack." There were five. Fortunately, only one lived in Boston, Jack Fitzgerald. Of course, the others might have been visiting but odds were that the Jack he'd met lived locally. If not, he'd track down the others later. Whitey jotted down the address and left.

Near Fields Corner in the Dorchester neighborhood of Boston, Jack Fitzgerald left his recently rented first-floor apartment, opened the front door to the three-decker house, and walked toward his car parked on a side street. Across Adams Street, the owner of the small convenience store waved as he swept the sidewalk. Doyle ran the store from the basement of one of the three-story homes. On that side of the street, basements were on the ground level as the homes were built on a hill that ascended steeply. Years before, a prior store owner must have specially extended his basement to the sidewalk by cutting into the hill. The store front was quaint and peculiar all at the same time.

It was a clear day. Now out on the street, the microsentinels that invisibly orbited Jacks body indicated no threats—at least in their range. But then a shot rang out from across the busy street. Amazingly, Jack moved fast enough so that the bullet's downward trajectory missed his head and instead entered his body from the back. Moving left or right, he might have escaped altogether, but even with his enhancements he misinterpreted the sounds due to the echo of the houses and cars. He had inadvertently run along the path of the bullet.

His crumpled body lay in a heap on the sidewalk. A woman, walking with a bag of groceries, screamed as a pool of blood spread out from the victim. Twisting around, Jack tried to locate the source of the shot. On the second floor porch across the street he noted a man with a rifle. He recognized Whitey Bulger's friend Tommy before passing out.

Whitey and Tommy Meet with Rick

Whitey Bulger returned to the brownstone where Rick lived. Pleased with himself now that a wrong had been corrected, Whitey wanted to apprise Rick of the example that had been made of Jack. Respect would be restored, and Mr. Winter would be satisfied.

Tommy was with Whitey and seemed eager for the meeting. Whitey guessed the other man wanted to boast about his marksmanship.

The pane of glass that Whitey had broken to gain entry last time had been repaired. He rang the bell, hoping that Rick would be home. After a third try, he resigned himself to leaving just as someone finally came to the door. It was Rick, fumbling to put a pair of strange looking glasses in their case.

"Whitey?" Rick exclaimed. "I thought our meeting was next week."

"It is. I just wanted to be the first to deliver some news."

Rick, sensing that meant something illegal, ushered the two men inside.

"What have you got for me?"

"Just wanted to let you know that your friend Jack won't be around anymore."

Whitey watched Rick for a reaction he could take satisfaction in.

"How do you mean?" asked Rick in a suspicious tone.

"Jack was involved in a little accident this morning. A shooting incident, I hear." He turned to his companion and grinned.

Rick looked back and forth between the two of them. "You don't know what you've done," said Rick as he fell into a chair and shook his head.

"Nobody fucks with the Winter Hill group," yelled Whitey at a startled Rick. "If he was part of our diamond pipeline you better find a replacement. Or Jack will have company."

"You can't know what you've done. I hope for your sake he shows some restraint." That wasn't the reaction Whitey expected. He wondered if Rick understood that his friend was dead.

Earlier That Day

An ambulance, sirens blaring, screeched to a halt near the collapsed man. A gurney appeared out of the back as the crew worked efficiently to get the injured man inside. At first glance his chances didn't look good. The man was unconscious, shot in the back with no exit wound. He had lost a lot of blood and carried a bullet somewhere in his chest. With the shooting victim secured, the ambulance raced to Carney Hospital.

The emergency room doctors faced a grim prognosis. A punctured lung, massive blood loss, and possible brain damage did not bode well for their patient. They couldn't even extract the bullet without killing the man due to where it had lodged. All they could do was try to stabilize him, which they did, though his vital signs were very weak. Moving him to intensive care, they waited for the inevitable news.

A few hours later, with the emergency room somewhat calmer, the administrator, Doctor Pascal, went upstairs to check on the shooting victim. The doctor was surprised that he hadn't heard of the man's passing by now. Did he dare hope that the patient could survive? The nurses, dutifully conducting their business, recognized the doctor and ignored his entry into the unit.

Inside, Pascal found Jack's bed. It was empty. The covers were pushed aside as if someone simply had gotten up to go to the bathroom. Pascal was about to call to the nurses when he noticed something lying on the sheets. Stepping closer, he picked it up to be sure his mind wasn't playing tricks. It was a bullet, a spent bullet judging by the deformation. The same bullet they'd seen on the X-rays?

"Nurse, was Fitzgerald moved?"

The nurse working at the next bed looked over as if she wasn't sure she'd heard correctly. "No," she started to say. "Why would ... ?"

She noticed the empty bed. "Strange. I never saw anyone come in for him. I've been here the whole time."

Pascal went to the head nurse at the desk. She'd noticed the exchange between Pascal and her nurse.

"Have any patients been removed from this room?"

"No, Doctor Pascal."

With bullet in hand and an old memory, he asked another question. "Did anyone... any man leave this room?"

"I thought I saw an orderly about an hour ago. For some reason I didn't think to ask him where he was going."

"Could you describe him?"

"Sure. He was..." The nurse hesitated. "Um. I can't..."

"That's okay, nurse. Never mind."

"I better get someone to find this patient."

"Nurse, if I'm right in what I'm thinking, you won't find him. Not only that, no one will be able to describe him either."

In spite of Pascal's advice, she started to dial the phone. Walking back to his office, Pascal recalled a similar, strange incident. Twenty years before, during his tour of duty in the South Pacific, he'd treated a wounded sailor for severe shrapnel wounds. The man had been near the engine room of the destroyer *U.S.S. Farragut* when it was struck by a torpedo. The sailor was so badly torn up that the young doctor marveled the patient was still breathing. All Pascal could do for the man was to make him as comfortable as possible in his last hour. Or so he thought.

Miraculously, the man's vital signs strengthened in that hour. Several hours later the sailor got up and dined with the crew in the mess hall. Not knowing this, the doctor went to check on his patient, but all he found was a bed full of jagged metal. Shrapnel, he thought. It was as if the sailor's body had ejected the foreign material on its own. But how? Time for a talk with this special sailor.

Attempting to track the man down, the doctor was forced to wonder if he'd imagined the incident. His questions to the crew about this medical miracle man yielded blank stares. A Lieutenant Carstairs was the only one who could even confirm that there ever was such a crew member.

"Crewman Ross? Sure he was here. I remember the men calling him Frank. Short for Franklin," said Carstairs.

"Well then, half the boat's been pulling my leg. I can't get anyone to tell me that he existed, never mind that they served with him."

"Wishful thinking on their part perhaps?" conjectured Carstairs.

"How do you mean?"

"Ross was strange. It was almost like he was afraid of getting too close to people. Friendly enough to work with, but it didn't go any farther than that. Never established real relationships. Also if he ever made eye contact with you, it was almost like a personal invasion."

"What?"

"Yeah, sounds a little weird, doesn't it, but it's hard to explain. It happened to me once, and the next thing I knew I was on the bridge. Didn't remember walking there, but there I was."

Perplexed by Carstairs account, Pascal had gone back to his office and stared at the shrapnel that had come from Ross' body. At least this physical evidence proved the doctor wasn't crazy. This stuff had been in a man's body. Eventually, Pascal placed a piece under a microscope. It looked like ordinary metal. Increasing the magnification, however, he was startled at what he saw. A small colony of what could only be described as living metal microbes moved across his field of view.

Catching his breath, Pascal increased the magnification to the maximum, but by this time the particles had either moved or evaporated. His last glimpse suggested microscopic mechanical devices except they were more than that. They seemed to act with intelligent coordination. That made them what... some kind of miniature robots?

Back in the present, Pascal still held the bullet in his hand from the Dorchester shooting victim. It would be interesting to put this under a microscope. See if it looked the same as the shrapnel that came out of Ross's body twenty years ago. The doctor rushed to the closest lab in the hospital that he knew had a microscope.

Jack Fitzgerald knew that he owed his life to his nanobotic enhancements. Even with his genetically engineered constitution, he doubted he could have survived the considerable damage caused by the bullet otherwise. Possibly he might have recovered but certainly not so soon and with no ill effects. The little robots expelled the bullet and worked with his own biosystems to heal the wound with incredible swiftness. The locals at the hospital must view this as a miraculous happenstance, he thought. They would, that is, if they could remember. Now on to the task at hand.

Skulking in the shadows, Jack waited with a patience that would be the envy of a stalking lion. A lion, however, didn't harbor the malevolence that Jack felt toward his quarry. This was not just about survival, although eliminating interference from a potential foe figured in his mission. Jack also wanted revenge, and revenge was not beyond the purview of a cleaner if the quarry was deemed insignificant enough to the local reality. Any incident involving his would-be murderer would simply be seen as part of the current mob wars in Boston.

At last Jack spied the marksman, Tommy, walking to his apartment. The South Boston street was devoid of foot traffic, and only an occasional car passed by. Perfect, thought Jack.

Whitey Bulger woke to some insistent knocking at the front door of his home. As usual, he was covered in sweat that resulted from nightmares. Had he understood the consequences, he would never have volunteered for the CIA-sponsored LSD experiments a few years before. At the time, however, in his Atlanta prison cell, Whitey would've done anything to reduce his time.

The continued knocking prompted him to get up. Opening the door, he immediately recognized his partner, Tommy, lying face up on the floor. Strangely, though, he also lay stomach down. His head was completely twisted around. So gruesome was the image that Whitey thought he was still in the throes of an LSD nightmare. His wakefulness was confirmed, however, when the frozen expression on Tommy's face made Whitey wretch.

PART II

The Readymade War

CHAPTER 4

Early September 1962

Jack watched the black-and-white TV in the mirror while the chatty barber cut his hair. The news was about Vietnam. A U.S. military council had been established there, and Jack knew that an escalation with more troops would follow. Making a mental note, he fumbled in his pocket for a tip while the barber brushed him off after finishing up.

After leaving the barber shop, Jack walked slowly along the sidewalks in Hyannisport, Massachusetts and pondered his mission. Though he tried to plot his strategy, he became distracted by the various characters in this America. The passersby cavorted about in strange period fashions as they enjoyed the pleasant late-summer day. Men sported Bermuda shorts and women wore flowery sun dresses. Almost all wore dark sunglasses, while a small portion of the population dressed as weekend, civilian sailors. A breeze carried the salty tang of the nearby ocean where several sailboat captains pitted themselves against the heavy swells.

Further along the street, Jack heard Frank Sinatra's voice ring out from a radio or a 45 record through an open window. As he passed the house he came upon a group of teenagers cavorting nearby in the sand. Their red and white convertible had the top down allowing the car radio to drown out Sinatra with strains of the song "Duke of Earl."

Leaving the beach area and continuing his sightseeing in town, Jack couldn't help but note an elegant lady who passed in front of him after conducting some business in a store. A man in a dark suit took a package from her and opened the door of a limousine waiting at the curb. The brunette had thick hair neatly cut to shoulder length and wore a green dress with stockings and high-heeled shoes. She also wore sunglasses and long white gloves and sported a pillbox hat.

Jack had the distinct impression the woman had come from church just prior to running her errands, so to spite her piety, he pictured her wearing just her undergarments and stockings. He desired her but he also recognized her as the first lady. Strange, he thought, that the president was rumored to have strayed with such a provocative companion.

He continued to walk toward his car.

"Jack!"

Even before Jack turned around, he knew he would find Father Herlihy waving to him. Well acquainted with the priest's voice, he didn't need the microsentinels to identify the speaker. The priest, who jogged toward Jack, wore his black street clothes with the obligatory white collar.

"Hello, Father."

"I missed you at church today."

"I know. I just got back in town."

"I wasn't looking for a reason, Jack. It's just that you've become popular with the rectory staff and they were asking for you. I think they were worried."

"I'll be sure to inform them when I leave again," he said without a hint of sarcasm.

"Such a serious man. Don't you derive any pleasure from life, Jack?"

"I do, Father. It's just that I'm preoccupied these days. That's why I was out of town and that's why I may be leaving again soon."

The priest studied him for a moment before answering. "Well, whatever you lack in humor you make up for in secrecy," he said in a half-joking manner. Then in a more serious vein, he added, "I'll hate to lose our newest and most curious parishioner."

The priest seemed to have something else on his mind, but he stood and thought for a moment longer before speaking.

"From the first time I met you, I gathered you were not unschooled in the ways of the Church, yet you questioned the staff and me as if it was all new to you."

Jack nodded slightly. "Let's just say I've been brought up in an environment that celebrated the progress of knowledge over the culture of mythic traditions. The way people in this community practice their faith fascinates me."

The priest blanched at that, and Jack could tell that his ill-advised answer had inspired a cavalcade of new questions. Before the priest could ask them, however, Jack excused himself abruptly and made for his car.

September 12, 1962

President Kennedy spoke at Rice University. Those in the press were tipped off that the speech would outline a bold new initiative and chart a challenging new course for the nation's scientists. In spite of the heat, the president seemed quite collected as he worked toward his conclusion. Those behind him, however, hoped he would adhere to his promise made at the beginning of the speech and keep his lecture short. After condensing the last 50,000 years of mankind's history for his audience, Kennedy shared his awe at the speed of progress and the resolve of men determined to achieve that progress.

"William Bradford, speaking in 1630 of the founding of the Plymouth Bay Colony, said that all great and honorable actions are accompanied by great difficulties, and both must be enterprised and overcome with answerable courage. If this capsule history of our progress teaches us anything, it is that man, in his quest for knowledge and progress, is determined and cannot be deterred. The exploration of space will go ahead, whether we join in it or not, and it is one of the great adventures of all time, and no nation which expects to be the leader of other nations can expect to stay behind in this race for space.

"Those who came before us made certain that this country rode the first waves of the industrial revolutions, the first waves of modern invention, and the first wave of nuclear power, and this generation does not intend to founder in the backwash of the coming age of space. We mean to be a part of it—we mean to lead it. For the eyes of the world now look into space, to the moon and to the planets beyond."

A restless audience member turned to his right and addressed a stranger held rapt by the president's words. "Funny how this president can ignore problems here on Earth."

"How do you mean?" responded the indignant listener.

"I mean about Cuba. We interfere with a country that's the size of a state and this man talks about the rights of all mankind. Talk about a hypocrite."

The listener was about to respond angrily when someone from behind interjected and addressed the president's accuser.

"Hey, I know you. You're the one spouting off about 'hands off Cuba' on the street corner."

"Not just the street corner, sir. I've been interviewed on the radio and TV. I'm Lee Harvey Oswald," the man said as he turned around to shake hands.

Here was a man who loved to attract attention to himself, thought the person beside him. Meanwhile, the listener from behind struck a glancing punch off Oswald's shoulder that was intended for the face. Oddly enough, security seemed to be on top of the situation and separated the two before a major scene ensued. Oblivious to the slight altercation in the midst of the huge crowd, the president continued.

"There is no strife, no prejudice, no national conflict in outer space as yet. Its hazards are hostile to us all. Its conquest deserves the best of all mankind, and its opportunity for peaceful cooperation may never come again. But why, some say, the moon? Why choose this as our goal? And they may well ask why climb the highest mountain. Why, 35 years ago, fly the Atlantic? Why does Rice play Texas?"

The audience laughed and the sound broke the president's rhythm, but he quickly recovered.

"We choose to go to the moon. We choose to go to the moon in this decade and do the other things, not because they are easy, but because they are hard, because that goal will serve to organize and measure the best of our energies and skills, because that challenge is one that we are willing to accept, one we are unwilling to postpone, and one which we intend to win, and the others, too. It is for these reasons that I regard the decision last year to shift our efforts in space from low to high gear as among the most important decisions that will be made during my incumbency in the office of the presidency."

Kennedy noticed the great many who fanned themselves in an effort to stay cool. He joked that he was doing all the work and that the reentry temperatures experienced by the Saturn rocket would almost be as hot as today. He hoped his listeners would stay cool a moment longer while he finished up.

"Many years ago the great British explorer George Mallory, who was to die on Mount Everest, was asked why did he want to climb it. He said, 'Because it is there.' Well, space is there, and we're going to climb it, and the moon and the planets are there, and new hopes for knowledge and peace are there. And, therefore, as we set sail we ask God's blessing on the most hazardous and dangerous and greatest adventure on which man has ever embarked."

CHAPTER 5

October 19, 1962

President Kennedy's Executive Committee, EXCOMM, debated the viable options available to them on Cuba from a military as well as political perspective. Four days earlier a U-2 reconnaissance aircraft discovered several Soviet SS-4 nuclear missiles in Cuba. The joint chiefs of staff adopted an aggressive viewpoint in suing for an immediate air strike if not invasion, but Kennedy was mindful of a possible reprisal against West Berlin, an island of democracy surrounded by East German repression. Beyond West Berlin's being a strategic asset, he had a promise to the people of Berlin to keep. The heated discussion went back and forth in considering a blockade of Cuba, an invasion of the island nation, or just disregarding the missiles. Everyone agreed, however, that overlooking the missiles was not an option since it would leave South America open to what they coined as "nuclear blackmail." It became apparent to all that no perfect solution would be found.

"You're in a pretty bad fix, Mr. President."

General LeMay's voice was unmistakable in Jack's ear as Jack continued to mop the corridor floor in his guise as a White House janitor. The microsentinels transmitted voices from the Oval Office directly into his brain.

"What did you say?" prompted Kennedy.

"You're in a pretty bad fix."

"Well, I think you're in this with me."

"Yes, sir," LeMay responded in a sheepish tone.

Proconsul al-Rahiim proposed a meeting with Jack on the National Mall. The long strip of park that extended from the Lincoln Memorial to the Capital was well trafficked by walkers. Nonetheless, the two men had complete confidence in their security.

At the Mall, Jack spotted al-Rahiim walking toward him. The proconsul seemed a lot less gray in person than in his holographic image. Of course, in person, the light doesn't shine through someone to wash out any colors.

They were still thirty yards apart when Jack saw a heedless bicyclist speeding down a sidewalk behind al-Rahiim. Not having time to call out, Jack contented himself with watching the collision unfold. At the last second, al-Rahiim turned around to note the bicyclist passing through him. None the worse for the incident, he continued on his way. The men met and shook hands.

"Well, looks like secure conversation wasn't the only benefit of phase-shifting for the meeting," said Jack.

"Oh, I'm certain the bicyclist would have noticed me otherwise."

Both men looked after the young man on the bike who was already at the Washington Monument.

"What a great advantage, this phase-shifting," ruminated al-Rahiim. "I sometimes wish it were legal back home so I could check up on my daughters."

"I can't imagine that they'd be anything but sensible."

Al-Rahiim grunted at the ignorance of the younger man. "Do you have teenagers?"

"No. Still a few years away from that part of fatherhood."

"When you get there, you'll find that 'sensible' and 'teenager' are mutually exclusive terms. Have you ever seen someone about to make a stupid mistake, but you knew that you couldn't talk him out of it? Couldn't stop him from doing something dangerous? That's what parenting teenagers is all about." Al-Rahiim gazed at the ground and shook his head.

Jack found the man's dilemma amusing but didn't let on. Then the proconsul returned to the moment at hand. "Be that as it may, let's get down to business. We have reports that another Earth in an adjacent reality just went to nuclear war. It started in

Cuba between the United States and Soviet Union." He began to walk one of the pedestrian paths.

"Was that supposed to happen?" Jack was horrified.

"Yes. Near as we can tell from the probability models."

But back to their own situation. "Okay, so what does that mean to us?"

"With all the data we've been collecting and inputting into the models, nuclear war cannot be allowed to happen here if we are to maintain a safe spatial distance between universes. The bad news is that anyone who is tampering would simply have to provoke either side of this touchy standoff on Cuba."

The cleaner shook his head. "Hard to fathom that anyone would want to bring down that much destruction across several realities."

"Jack, there are people who simply refuse to believe in the parallel realities. And that's in spite of the fact that they themselves have traveled to them. Flies in the face of what they believe existence to be." Al-Rahiim smiled. "Stubborn lot. Have you ever tried to reason with someone who rejects rationality in favor of superstitious dogma?"

"Does that mean you think the old Religionists have something to do with this?" Jack had heard that suggested.

"Yes, I do. Haven't they made it plain that they won't believe in anything that disputes their claim to the one true reality, created by their one true god? Parallel universes aren't even real to them. Destroying these other false realities, as they call them, would be wholly consistent with their philosophy."

"And they won't believe that they would be destroyed too?"

"They believe that they would not only be saved but also rewarded in their version of a hereafter."

Al-Rahiim looked around and took in all the people on the mall before continuing. "You know we look at the people here with their quaint beliefs as being less mature as a civilization than we are. But even in our so-called advanced society, we'll always have pockets of those who hang on to superstitions."

Al-Rahiim pursed his lips and shook his head as he considered the misguided of both societies. He changed the subject. "I notice you're spending a fair amount of time on Cape Cod."

"Part of my research."

"Is that so? Are you researching to see what draws you there?"

Jack just smiled, having been found out. "It's so relaxing. It feels as if part of me belongs there."

"Which part is that? Never mind—don't answer me. Just be sure you steer clear of Mrs. Kennedy." Al-Rahiim delivered a penetrating look. "Keep me posted on this crisis and let's hope we don't have to make a drastic intervention."

Monday, October 22, 1962

The members of EXCOMM gathered to watch the president address the nation by television. Several days of contentious debate had led to the plan of action that Kennedy was to outline. In midspeech, Dean Rusk entered the room and stood beside Robert Kennedy.

"What did I miss?" he asked the president's brother.

"He just called Gromyko a liar."

They both smiled as they listened to the rest of the speech.

"Acting therefore in the defense of our own security and of the entire Western Hemisphere. And under the authority entrusted to me by the Constitution as endorsed by the resolution of the Congress, I've directed the following initial steps be taken immediately.

"To halt this offensive buildup, a strict quarantine on all offensive military equipment under shipment to Cuba is being initiated. All ships of any kind bound for Cuba from whatever nation or port will, if found to contain cargoes of offensive weapons, be turned back.

"It shall be the policy of this nation to regard any nuclear missile launched from Cuba against any nation in the Western Hemisphere as an attack by the Soviet Union on the United States requiring a full retaliatory response upon the Soviet Union."

"That ought to get their attention," commented MacNamara.

Several hundred British citizens launched a protest outside the American Embassy in London. BBC journalists reported that the crowd was upset over the perceived bullying by the United States of a smaller sovereign nation. The U.S. ambassador called Washington to report the incident.

Dean Rusk hung up the phone and cursed. Leaving his office, he met LBJ in the corridor.

"Damn British are making a spectacle of themselves," blurted out Rusk as he dashed past the vice president.

Kennedy, in response to Rusk's agitation, pulled a letter out of his drawer from a noted British intellectual, Bertrand Russell, and handed it to his secretary of state. Dean Rusk read the note and focused on the key words: "desperate," "mass murder," and "madness." Russell subscribed to the *Tribune*'s view that Kennedy had provoked the crisis to bolster his party's candidates in the upcoming election.

"I can't say as I'm surprised by this, Dean," Kennedy told Rusk. "We could have expected something like this in Europe. Our best course of action is to continue to pressure the Russians and negotiate. We'll just have to weather the slings and arrows as best we can."

Somewhat mollified, Rusk returned to his office.

Friday, October 26, 1962

EXCOMM pored over the latest communiqué from Moscow. The mood in the meeting room was giddy. Khrushchev appeared to have adopted a less confrontational attitude. His letter indicated a willingness to remove the missiles in exchange for a pledge not to invade Cuba.

"I guess adding POL (petroleum, oil, and lubricants) to the quarantine list did the trick," kidded Walt Rostow, chair of the State Department Policy Planning Council.

"If your idea ended this crisis like that, then I'd like to offer you a job in my department," returned Bobby Kennedy. "Maybe you could bring down Hoffa by taking away his Vaseline."

The group laughed, but some tension remained. The missiles were still in Cuba. A careful response to Khrushchev's offer had to be formulated.

In the basement, an incongruous looking janitor, Jack, sat back with his sunglasses on in spite of the dark room. He appeared to be in a trance but was actually monitoring the proceedings in the Oval Office in real time on the inside of his lenses.

"So the crisis is defused?" asked al-Rahiim.

"It would appear so," said Jack to the holographic transmission.

"Well, unless a would-be tamperer missed a golden opportunity, I'm starting to think that we never had any tampering. Our predictive sciences aren't infallible."

"Shall I wrap it up here?" questioned Jack.

"You sound disappointed," said al-Rahiim.

"Well, it did seem to be my one chance at adventure." Jack smiled.

"Adventure may yet be yours, although I sincerely hope not. We're running some numbers again based on new inputs from agents in nearby realities. Until we have more confidence in our models, I'd like you to stick around. This world's politics are forever volatile. Let me know about anything significant."

With that final order, the image of al-Rahiim dissolved, and Jack prepared for a relaxing evening. He went to the phone and dialed a number on the primitive device. A woman answered. Jack pictured the buxom blond on the other end of the line.

"Hi, Marilyn," he said but then caught himself. "I meant, hi, Debbie. You remind me of a prettier version of the actress," he smoothly corrected.

Debbie giggled.

Saturday, October 27, 1962

Intelligence confirmed that a U-2 spy plane had accidentally flown into Russia. Coincidentally, another spy plane was shot down over Cuba. The president declined to order an attack on the surface-to-air missile site but yielded to his staff by agreeing to strike if any additional planes were attacked. The tension was further heightened when the CIA reported five of the Cuban medium-range ballistic missile sites were now fully operational.

The feeling of relief from the day before dissipated in the face of these new developments. The timing worried the president, and his instincts were confirmed when EXCOMM received a second letter from Khrushchev. This time, he demanded that the U.S.

remove its missiles from Turkey in addition to a public promise not to invade Cuba.

"I think we're looking at an insupportable position on this," said Kennedy. "To the rest of the world we'd look like trigger-happy Americans if we declined such a reasonable trade."

"At least we have that as a bargaining chip," Bobby Kennedy responded.

"I suppose we can be glad that we didn't remove the obsolete weapons last year," added Secretary McNamara.

"Bobby, how's your relationship with Ambassador Dobrynin these days," asked the president.

"I'd characterize it as friendly."

"Can you read him fairly well?"

"What do you have in mind?"

"I want to put the Turkish missiles on the table but don't want that to become public. I'd like to see if you can maneuver him on that point."

The Kennedy brothers exchanged a look. "You're worried about our allies' reactions if we bargain with the missiles in Turkey?" Bobby guessed.

"Yes! Particularly De Gaulle. He'd be the first to announce that we sold them out."

With a plan in place, and Bobby scheduled to meet with the Russian ambassador, President Kennedy dismissed EXCOMM but met privately with Secretary of State Dean Rusk.

"Dean, what's the state of our provisional government plans, post nuclear war?"

Secretary Rusk blanched at the casual way the president referred to the aftermath of a nuclear exchange. Unbeknownst to either man, so did Jack, the janitor who continued to monitor Kennedy's progress on this crisis.

"We've been doing dry runs since the 16th, Mr. President." Rusk then tentatively added: "Do you think it will come to that?"

"I think it would be foolish not to be prepared for the worst. I hope not, but I've placed our nuclear strategic forces on high alert."

With that, Jack raced out of the building and headed to his apartment to consult al-Rahiim. Kennedy's posture didn't jibe with the latest predictions made available to Jack. The proconsul wouldn't be happy at this sudden turn of events.

Al-Rahiim took the news surprisingly well. It almost seemed as if he was expecting it.

"I thought you'd be more upset," said Jack.

"Oh, I'm upset all right. It's just that this news is consistent with other events that fall outside our most recent calculations."

"What else has happened?"

"Remember what we were talking about the other day? The old Religionists. Right now, there's a meeting of the Catholic Church hierarchy. You may have read about it in the papers. It's called the Second Vatican Council. Their agenda is to aggressively unite all Christians.

"The Americans have also mounted an unexpectedly robust challenge in the space race. A couple of weeks ago, Wally Schirra completed six orbits of the Earth.

"The Cold War, Vietnam. There're other things too. A confluence of events suggests a level of conflict that our models say is 82 percent improbable. Khrushchev is taking an atypical risk. The crisis may put this universe dangerously close to another like it. Somebody must be tampering."

Nikita Khrushchev consulted in private in his office with his latest confidant, Ilya Petrovich. The men sat in cushioned, brown leather chairs by a small table with a lamp. Each man held a glass in his hand, and a half-consumed bottle of Vodka sat on the table between them. The two had formed a bond in their plans to address missiles, like those in Turkey, aimed at the Soviet Union.

"I think you're being too soft on the Americans, Nikita. You've created this advantage. Don't squander it."

"You think I should demand more?"

"Why not?"

"Ilya, I think it's possible that I may have misread Kennedy. He's showing more backbone than I would've thought." Khrushchev's peasant face showed grave concern, and he set down his empty glass.

"It's all a bluff in my opinion. They can't risk losing face to the world by invading Cuba."

"Perhaps, but I think Kennedy is out to prove something," Khrushchev disagreed. "He's not going to be cowed like he was last year in Vienna. Don't forget the Bay of Pigs disaster was still a fresh wound at that time. He may have gotten over his embarrassment since then."

"So now you think he won't back down no matter what. I still say let's test him."

"And risk nuclear war? I'd hate to fail that test." Khrushchev sighed.

"I'm betting he backs down before it comes to that. Why don't you take another step? Nothing too provocative, just something to test his resolve. Then we can see if he can be pushed further." Petrovich poured them each another vodka.

CHAPTER 6

On Sunday, October 28, 1962, the CIA early morning intelligence update indicated that Russian and Cuban technicians had never ceased working on the missiles in spite of the blockade and the ongoing negotiations. All of the medium-range ballistic missile sites were now functional. Several missiles were being prepared for launch.

Al-Rahiim boarded a plane in Omaha bound for Washington. He didn't think he'd be returning so soon, but the apparent tampering had to be countered. He scheduled a meeting for his staff at 5 a.m. on the 29th to discuss the crisis, including news from his agent in Cuba that Castro was planning to use mobile tactical nuclear weapons in the event of an American invasion. Kennedy and EXCOMM were, at the same time, unaware that these weapons existed in Cuba.

At just after 3:30 a.m., al-Rahiim consulted his watch/computer to confirm a troubling instinct. The device indicated that his plane was well off course, as al-Rahiim suspected.

"Stewardess," he called as she passed by.

She stopped, and her demeanor suggested stress.

"Have we been diverted to another airport?"

The question seemed to alarm her, and she looked around to see if the other passengers had heard. She appeared relieved to find that those within earshot were asleep.

"Unfortunately, our flight is subject to a slight delay. The captain made a course correction due to some stormy weather ahead."

Al-Rahiim could tell that she was lying. Reaching into the breast pocket of his jacket, he pulled out a card that identified him as United States Military Intelligence on assignment to NORAD, North American Air Defense.

"What's really going on, ma'am?" he asked in hushed tones.

She looked around again, leaned in closer and fought back tears as she informed him that the plane had been hijacked. They were on their way to Cuba.

Jack was awakened by an alarm coming from his sunglasses. Groggily, he turned on the light and put them on. An image of the praetor appeared. Jack anticipated the worst judging by her expression.

"Jack, we have some bad news. Al-Rahiim's plane went down in the Gulf of Mexico."

"The Gulf? What the hell was he doing there? I thought he was coming to Washington."

"He was. Before the plane went down, he contacted us and reported that the aircraft had been hijacked. It was on its way to Cuba."

"That seems awfully coincidental."

"Someone, tamperers perhaps, anticipated our countermeasures and took this action. Or at least that's our working hypothesis right now."

"What can I do?"

"Al-Rahiim already put a plan in motion just before we lost communication. Stand by for possible contact from another agent."

"I mean, what can I do to help al-Rahiim."

"We've launched a search-and-rescue effort. You just stay there in case you're needed. The priority for all of us now is to disarm this crisis, stop any tampering, and track down whomever is responsible. Once we identify them, then, cleaner, your unique skills will be called upon."

Monday, October 29, 1962

A Coast Guard cutter searched for debris from the missing plane. The Gulf was relatively calm under cloudy skies, and the search proceeded as well as could be expected. Officials held out little hope that anyone had survived the crash, but the mandate was to search even in the face of such long odds. Navy Intelligence was particularly insistent that secrets not be lost to the Communists, especially now.

Captain Duncan worried about the morale of the crew. The timing of this operation couldn't have been more unwelcome considering how it delayed the crew's plans for safeguarding their families. Truth be told, even Duncan was somewhat unnerved to be this close to the source of a possible missile attack on their homes. The closer they got, the more tense they became over what was happening a couple of hundred miles southeast of their position.

Thankfully, a crewman broke the tension by spotting a field of flotsam off the port side of the cutter. He reported it to the captain, who ordered the helm to steer in that direction. Once they confirmed that it was debris from the downed plane, they start collecting the pieces.

A warm breeze ruffled the shirt of the crewman who'd spotted the field. He sifted through the water with a net for the less massive material from the wreckage when a sporadic flashing caught his eye. About ten feet from the hull he spied a pair of sunglasses. Strange that sunglasses would flash like that, he thought as he reached with the net to retrieve them. Before he could get to them, however, the crewman was startled to find that the flashes were actually some sort of picture that appeared in midair.

As he stared, the man realized the image was of a man from the chest up. The transparent projection was like busts he'd seen of famous people but for one exception. The image moved. The man seemed animated. His eyebrows twitched, and his mouth moved as if he was talking yet the crewman heard nothing. The crewman froze with the net extended, his mind trying to make some sense of what he was seeing.

"What's the matter, ensign?" asked Officer Hill.

The ensign turned to see the tall black man who had been assigned to the search by Navy Intelligence.

"Something funny, sir. Just beyond my net."

"Why don't you reel it in, son."

With the spell broken by the interruption, the Coast Guard ensign netted the glasses and presented them to the intelligence officer.

"They're in pretty bad shape. No wonder the signal was sporadic."

"Signal, sir?" said a confused ensign.

Barney Hill didn't reply, but instead touched his fingers to an odd-looking cuff on his sleeve. The ensign sensed that Hill expected something to happen. Unnerved by the intelligence man's indifference to him, he started to back away. After a few steps, something compelled him to look upward. Hovering in the sky directly above the boat was a metallic disk with a diameter at least three times that of their vessel. The gleaming metal of the disk contrasted sharply with the gray skies above.

For an instant, the disk looked as if it was falling, and the ensign crouched down reflexively. Eventually, he realized the disk wasn't falling and he straightened up in time to see a shaft of light lance down from the flying object and engulf Officer Hill. Still holding the sunglasses, Hill disappeared.

Several more shafts lanced down from the disk, illuminating certain pieces of the collected plane wreckage. They also disappeared. Then at unimaginable speed, the hovering craft ascended with a thunderous concussion as the air was split asunder and then slammed together after the craft's passage. In mere seconds, the disk became a small point in the far distant sky.

All the crew members were on deck now and they watched in awed silence, allowing the phenomena to be seared into their life's experiences. Abruptly, the silence was again broken when a high-pitched tuning fork sounded painfully, inducing them to cover their ears.

A few minutes later, the crew went about their duties as if nothing had happened. They proceeded on their search assignment seeming to have no memory of the extraordinary events that had occurred. All evidence was erased from the minds of the men.

Or was it? On the bridge the captain answered a hail from Captain Lee Packwood on a sister boat.

"Duncan, are you all right?"

"Sure, why wouldn't we be?"

"Didn't you see anything strange?"

"Now you've got me worried. What's this all about?"

"A few moments ago we had some weird radar blips that appeared to come from the air space at your location."

"Really," said the captain as he exchanged looks with the helmsman who just shook his head. "What kind of blips?" he then asked, no doubt hoping not to hear the word "missiles."

"I'm not talking missiles, Duncan," said Packwood as if reading his mind. "This was more like planes except I've never seen a blip move that fast. Seemed to be doing at least Mach 20."

"No, Lee, can't say as we can confirm that visually. Are you sure your equipment is working correctly?"

"Who knows? Possibly not. No plane or even missile could've moved that fast. Must have been a ghost reflection."

"We've been pretty busy with the search. But I'll keep an eye out for any UFOs, okay?" The captain grinned.

"Smart ass. That'll teach me for showing concern. Packwood out!"

Duncan signed off with a smile. He'd needed even a small diversion from this assignment.

Rick and Jack sat silent, both staring at the floor in Rick's apartment. Rick looked off into the distance while exhaling smoke through his nose. Eventually something occurred to Jack and he chuckled causing Rick to look up.

"I just remembered when I first met al-Rahiim," said Jack. "He was full of bluster and I was a little intimidated. It was the reputation he had, you know. But then he tripped over an edge of the carpet as he came around his desk to greet me. I couldn't help but laugh even though al-Rahiim glared. It was a nervous laugh until I saw him break up too. From then on we had a pretty straightforward relationship. Oh, he was gruff all right, but I knew when he was serious and when it was for show."

"I know he thought well of you, Jack," said Rick. "I met him years ago in the service. We were both assigned to the Earth where the Mongols ruled all but Africa and the Americas. A primitive place to be assigned, but we did derive some pleasure in North America where the moral code was open to one's own interpretation. You probably never knew that side of him."

"I can't imagine that he had other sides, never mind one where he acted like a typical young man." Jack chuckled yet again.

"I could tell you stories that would curl your hair." Rick looked down at the floor once more to hide the moisture that was collecting in his eyes. "Our daughters were friends. I suppose I'll have to tell Dee that her uncle Usama has passed away. I'll miss him," added Rick with a quaver in his voice.

Jack realized that in spite of his close relationship with al-Rahiim, he'd never called the man Usama. It was a line of respect Jack never entertained crossing. He would miss the old man, too.

Al-Rahiim woke up with a start. The last thing he remembered was floating in the water as he watched the plane sink. No one could've survived. And he realized he wouldn't have either if it wasn't for his ability to phase-shift during the impact with the water. But now where was he? Had he been rescued? His sunglasses, wherever they were this moment, hadn't looked like they'd been in any condition to broadcast an SOS after the crash.

Eventually, he realized he was standing on the deck of a vessel looking down at the water. Funny that he hadn't registered that fact till now. His thinking was sluggish. Trying to take a step, al-Rahiim realized he couldn't, just as he couldn't raise his hand. Some sort of paralysis, yet he wasn't alarmed. Finally, he sensed other presences around him, but they were outside the range of his peripheral vision. All he could do was stare at the sea, which had a calming effect on him. The regular undulations were hypnotic as the waves rose and fell reflecting the sunlight that was breaking through the clouds.

As he stared, however, something began to happen. The level of the sea dropped as if some terrestrial giant had pulled a plug. Ever so slowly, the surface of the water began to recede. Only moments later al-Rahiim realized that the sea wasn't dropping—the

ship was rising. The ascent was so smooth and absent of any iner-
tial force that his senses had been fooled. He started to hyperventi-
late. Then, when he was on the verge of panic, a small hand like
that of a child reached up and touched his forehead. That contact
immediately calmed the proconsul, and he speculated on the size
of the individual who had touched him. His eyes closed, however,
as he seemed to drift off to sleep.

EXCOMM learned that Radio Moscow had released the text of a
Khrushchev letter announcing the Soviet Union accepted the proposed solution to the missile crisis. The statement didn't mention
the Turkish missiles, just as Bobby Kennedy had stipulated to
Russian Ambassador Dobrynin. Not wishing to be provocative in
the face of such capitulation, President Kennedy suspended U-2
air surveillance over Cuba. He also prohibited any military action
against ships approaching the quarantine line. Certain of the joint
chiefs, however, pushed him to reconsider air strikes due to the
possibility of Soviet deception. In no uncertain terms, Kennedy
clarified his position on letting a peaceful solution play out.

The president talked with his advisors in regard to verifying
the removal of missiles from Cuban soil. Kennedy's desire to include the U.N. in the process had been countered by threats from
an angry Castro. Castro, feeling marginalized after being left out of
Khrushchev's decision, warned that he wouldn't allow U.N. inspection of the dismantling process.

"The question is how do we maintain satisfactory intelligence
about Cuba since we can't rely on the U.N. to do it," said the
president.

"I think we should at least keep the surveillance and quarantine options in effect until U.N. machinery can effectively replace
them," stated Rusk. "Because if we give up on that point, we may
be subject to a massive trick here."

Several separate group discussions broke out within
EXCOMM about whether U-2 flights would actually be capable of
revealing camouflaged attempts by the Soviets to hide their missiles. Some argued that U Thant, the secretary-general of the
United Nations needed to survey the situation. At that point, Kennedy regained control of the group.

"Only continued aerial photography can prove whether the missile sites are actually being dismantled. U Thant doesn't know what the hell to look for, any more than I would. We just have to watch, and if the Soviets continue this conventional buildup in Cuba, then we'll draw conclusions at that time. I think we'll just have to stay on it."

Wrapping up the meeting, Kennedy called in his secretary, Evelyn Lincoln. As she entered, he pondered the current state of fashion that tolerated the popular yet unattractive horn-rimmed glasses that she wore.

"Evelyn, lets have some commemorative calendars made for the month of October, with the dates of the crisis highlighted."

Ever the proficient secretary, Evelyn anticipated his next instruction. "Gifts for each member of EXCOMM?"

Kennedy smiled and nodded his head as she left the room.

November 21, 1962

Just over a month after the crisis began, JFK terminated the quarantine when Khrushchev agreed following several weeks of tense negotiations at the U.N. to withdraw Soviet IL-28 nuclear bombers from Cuba. Once again at Rick's, Jack and Rick discussed the status of their assignments.

"The crisis seems to be averted for sure this time," stated Jack. "Damned if I know how it happened though."

"At least we'll have a happy Thanksgiving," Rick told him in a lighthearted fashion.

Jack didn't share the mood, however, and Rick tried to clarify the situation. "Didn't the praetor say that al-Rahiim put something into motion before his plane ditched?"

"Yes, she did. But she also said that I'd be contacted when my skills were required."

"Your skills as a cleaner, you mean."

"Yes. No one ever contacted me," answered Jack curtly as if to avoid more questions. By now he was reasonably sure that Rick was unaware of his "last resort" assignment.

"Perhaps that means there was no tamperer."

"Or that they haven't found one yet."

"Not a comforting thought." Rick drank from a soda he'd left unfinished on the table.

"This whole assignment has been unsettling. I expected to be home long ago. Every time I think we're onto something, it seems to evaporate. We're dealing with a very shadowy conspiracy here. It's not like any I've ever heard of." Jack felt frustrated and unsure of his position now. If he wasn't going to be used, then he didn't know why he was being kept on.

"I must confess that it is puzzling," Rick agreed. "And I've seen my share of corrections. Up to now I thought that no tamperer could avoid detection by the computer models. Especially for this long. Usually, the more the natural course is changed, the more accurate our fix on the changer becomes."

Rick looked off into space before continuing. "You know what else puzzles me?"

Jack looked in his direction.

"We never found al-Rahiim's communicator, the glasses."

"They're sturdy but not indestructible." Jack shrugged.

"True, but it was working well enough to send a sporadic signal according to my sources. Why then was it never picked up? It could have answered a lot of our questions."

Jack became curious now. "Maybe it was picked up."

"You mean the locals?"

"I mean a rogue agent or agents who know what to look for. And how to suppress the homing beam."

"That's not easy to do. It would take a fairly resourceful organization to operate the equipment to do that."

"An organization that would be the equal of our own elite intelligence service, the Varangian Guards," mused Jack.

"The Guards? They've been above reproach for centuries. Ever since their charter to the Byzantine emperor."

Jack thought for a moment before expanding on his thought. "If they are involved, it would explain why it's been difficult to zero in on the tampering. Our models best detect small unsophisticated groups. A well-heeled organization like the Guards, who know the science, would be quite different. They'd understand how to cover their tracks."

Jack stopped a moment and then went on. "And, if you'll recall, their history was built on the protection of a religion. Christendom as they called it." Jack gave Rick a meaningful look for emphasis.

"C'mon. That's old news. People with their education and training don't take that stuff seriously now. I can assure you that they're not working with the Religionists if that's what you're implying."

"Would you bet our existence on that?"

That statement hung in the air. Both men felt a palpable sense of anxiety.

Jack chose a setting that always brought him peace of mind, the sea. Nantucket Sound was a lonely place this time of year, but boating there met his need for quiet reflection. After the tragedy of losing al-Rahiim, he longed for a respite to contemplate the people and environments that were at once familiar and comfortable. His sexual escapades were diverting, but they did wear thin relative to the companionship of his wife and three children. The oldest, Kathleen, was named after her deceased Aunt Kick. Jack recalled how difficult the birth had been and shuddered at the prospect of losing his sister's namesake. In this reality, he was sure that local medical science would have lost her.

Jack's sister Kick had died in a plane crash while still a newlywed. He remembered her as someone full of life but who never got the chance to realize the promise of it. Perhaps his daughter Kathleen could fulfill that legacy. She certainly reminded him of his sister. Parents weren't supposed to have favorites, but he wished he could hold his eldest now to affirm life once again.

A screeching gull caused him to look up. The steel-gray sky made the white bird stand out in sharp relief. It brought Jack back to the present as he felt the chill sea breeze on his tousled mane. The boat gently rocked from side to side while the billowing sail pulled it through the water. A white wake trailed behind him in a V-shape and the craft hurtled forward. The ability to daydream while still piloting the sailboat spoke of the comfort that he felt on the water, not to mention his expertise.

The small wooden craft was nothing like the computer-controlled fiberglass sailboat he enjoyed back home, but the need to manually control the sails and the rudder made him feel more of a master of the elemental forces. It was empowering to achieve travel with nothing more than wind and sail.

His thoughts now in order with the help of this wintry sail meant that it was time to take stock of his sailing position. Martha's Vineyard was clearly visible. Jack realized he had been on the water far longer than he'd expected. Coming about smoothly, Jack headed back to the mainland.

Olaf of the Varangian Guard met with Rick. The two friends embraced and then walked through Boston Common while they reminisced. Their breath steamed out, punctuating each point. Rick confided in Olaf of his suspicions concerning the Guard. Olaf let out a guffaw as if at a private joke and clapped his leather gloved hands together.

"What's so funny?" asked Rick as he lit his first cigarette of the day.

"Nothing. It's just that we in the Guard had the same kinds of conversations about you."

"Me?"

"Not you personally. The Agency."

"So you've been puzzled by the so-called tampering, too?"

"Oh yes. We've gone back and forth several times. Is there tampering or is it a statistical aberration? We use the same models as you. They've never been so erratic."

"I wonder if we've finally encountered a situation where the math breaks down?"

"Possibly. Chaotitians are working on that now. Hopefully, they'll refine the science so the models make more sense."

"Well, I'm relieved to hear that the Guard aren't tamperers. But there goes my theory of a well-backed group defying detection."

Both men became pensive before Olaf changed the subject. "Sorry to hear about al-Rahiim. I know you guys were close."

"I try to console myself by reciting that we all know the risks before going into the service. I'm afraid it's not much help."

"My contacts tell me that al-Rahiim brought a cleaner over."

"Your contacts are good."

Olaf ignored the compliment. "I'm assuming the cleaner is still unaware of his purpose?"

"He's unaware of his real purpose. Policy hasn't changed on that."

"I'm sure it hasn't. Who would sign up, otherwise."

CHAPTER 7

The praetor summoned Jack to her office in Washington. It was the first time he'd met her in person, and he discovered, to his surprise, that he was attracted to her. She wasn't young, but she was well kept and unconsciously moved with a suggestive air. At least he thought it was unconscious. Her direct manner, however, focused his attention.

"Jack, I want to let you in on a highly confidential practice. Only top management knows about this. I'm going to waive the need for a higher security clearance for you since this mission requires you know something that may disturb you."

Whoa, thought Jack. *Where is all this going?* Without further delay, the praetor walked over to a wall on one side of the office suite. She purposefully touched several patterns on the contemporary wall covering. The way she did it gave Jack the distinct impression that she was manipulating the keypad of a safe. Confirming his thought, the whole wall slid aside to reveal a device that could only have been a massive computer with lighted vertical and horizontal bars randomly illuminated on a dark glass panel waist to chest high. A counter extended once the wall withdrew completely, and Jack saw lighted controls on it. Below the counter was a brushed-aluminum plain cabinet face. Jack knew the machine was on and strangely enough sensed that it knew he was there.

"Hello, Jack," said the machine.

Jack stared, having recognized the voice of al-Rahiim. He looked to the praetor who obviously expected him to answer.

"Proconsul?" asked Jack tentatively.

"Yes, Jack. It's me."

At that point the praetor spoke up. "It has been standard practice of the service to periodically copy the psyches of top executives. This copy of the proconsul was made just prior to his ill-fated plane trip."

Jack was shocked. "Why tell me this now?"

"Because this version of al-Rahiim insisted on speaking with you."

"That's right, Jack," confirmed the computer.

Jack had heard of the technology to download personalities, but he still found it eerie to be talking with someone he thought dead. Ultimately, however, he composed himself and conversed with the machine.

"What can I do for you, proconsul?"

"You can remember your training."

That sounded like al-Rahiim, thought Jack. "My training, sir?"

"Jack, I know you felt you had little choice in your selection for this, but I've come to know you as well as any lifer in my employ. And I've come to appreciate that your commitment is as great as any of theirs."

That didn't sound like al-Rahiim.

"You're an expensive asset, Jack, and I want you to remember that, as you execute this crucial assignment. Make sure you bring all your training and instincts to bear."

"Is this a pep talk, coach?"

"Remember what I told you at the National Mall about my daughters? About teenagers in general? Use your adult judgment. Rational and 'cleaner' don't have to be mutually exclusive terms."

Jack furrowed his brow in confusion and looked at the praetor. She had nothing to offer in clearing up al-Rahiim's meaning. It struck Jack, though, that she was concentrating mightily on what the computer model of al-Rahiim was saying. Her finger hovered over a lighted control, and Jack suspected it would cut off al-Rahiim, if he said something that she didn't approve of.

"I'm not sure I understand, proconsul?"

"Just be ready to adapt as the situation changes."

"Yes, sir," Jack assured him, even without picking up on his meaning.

"Good luck, and be careful in the Sound. Don't want you daydreaming and running aground on the Vineyard. Especially this time of year."

Jack jerked his head up at that comment. How could this personality simulation, recorded before al-Rahiim was lost, know of his most recent sail? Was it a lucky guess? The praetor looked at him suspiciously, and that, too, made Jack raise his guard.

"I'll be careful. Thank you, sir," said Jack as he composed himself.

The next thing he knew the praetor had whisked him into another office.

"Well what was your impression of your former boss?"

"He seemed a bit detached."

"Not a bad word," said the praetor, and she smiled. "Downloading the complete person into a computer always results in some loss. There's still nothing like the human brain to contain every nuance of our life experience."

"I suppose so," agreed Jack. "Do you know what he was trying to get across?"

"All I know is that he was insistent on speaking to you."

"Funny that he didn't have a clearer message. Maybe we should try it again."

As he took a step back toward her office, the praetor jumped up and caught his arm.

"It's no use, Jack. We've heard the same message from him a couple of dozen times now. We were hoping that it would have been different if we had you in the room. Why don't you go home while we continue to work on this. We'll call you in again if there's some progress."

Jack conceded the point and left the building.

Outside, he replayed al-Rahiim's words over and over in his mind. Jack was sure they held a hidden meaning. A meaning that the proconsul apparently wanted to hide from the praetor. And what about that current reference to his sailboat ride? The proconsul could only have known that if he was still alive. Was it possible? And if so, was the praetor playing some game with Jack? Or did she even know he was alive?

Jack returned to his apartment, got out pen and paper, and jotted down everything before he forgot. Al-Rahiim's daughters. What had his boss told Jack at the Mall about his daughters? He couldn't talk them out of doing something dangerous. That was it. Did that mean Jack was doing something dangerous? What could it be? With his head spinning, Jack decided he needed a diversion. He opted for a most pleasurable one. One that involved a sexual encounter.

CHAPTER 8

The dozen men known to themselves as the Shadow Group sat down at the large meeting table. As usual, they started the proceedings with a prayer. The practice differentiated them from most of the population in their reality—Jack and al-Rahiim's reality. Prayer wasn't the only thing that separated them, however. Their abiding distrust of the science of parallel realities stood in stark contrast to the consensus that all their world's scientists trusted. The Shadow Group not only denied the importance of recognizing parallel universes, they actually dedicated themselves to their destruction. In that way, they'd preserve the one true existence from whence all good things come. The idea that the destruction of other realities would hurt their own was dismissed as propaganda from the intellectual elite. These elite were only interested in preserving reasons to maintain funding for their studies. Keeping the spirit of exploration alive for visiting other realities was a boondoggle to them.

The prayer ended with an "amen" by the group.

"How could we have been so wrong?" asked Bart.

"There was never any guarantee that this plan would work," answered Simon.

"We had to move subtly or our hand would've showed," added Tom.

"Maybe we can't afford to be that subtle anymore," said Bart.

Bart noted the expression on Tom's face. "What's the matter, Thomas," asked Bart using Tom's full name for effect.

"I'm just dubious about the risk-reward ratio. What if we're caught? Is the price we'll pay worth what we're trying to gain? We've lived alongside these other realities for a long time."

Bart exhaled and noted the indignation on Peter's face. "Peter, do you want to answer that?"

"Blasphemer!" cried Peter, staring at Thomas. "How dare you try to denigrate the will of those who give voice to the one true existence. May quantum chance rain disaster on your house."

All eyes turned to Thomas. James, Andrew, John, Phillip, Matthew, Thaddeus, Judas as well as all who'd spoken before turned malevolent stares at their meek colleague. Thomas was somewhat surprised that he alone had doubts, but the reaction of the group disabused him of the notion that he had won over any sympathizers.

"Please forgive me," he pleaded, and he dropped to his knees. "I pray for strength in carrying out this holy mission. And hope never to anger this august body again."

The sign of compliance placated his colleagues. Bart actually helped Thomas back into his chair. "May we each pray for strength when our will to do the holy bidding deserts us. I hope you will all join me in embracing our colleague after his painful petition."

All nodded to Tom in a reassuring way including Peter whose gesture seemed to be the least heartfelt.

"Getting back to the business at hand," said Andrew. "Kennedy surprised us by his reasoned approach. Who would've thought, after he was so unknowingly cooperative in our scheme to embolden Khrushchev, that he would rally in the end."

"Everything seemed to be following our model," agreed Bart. "Kennedy's missteps at the Bay of Pigs and his poor performance at the Vienna meeting with Khrushchev seemed to assure our victory. Yet this reality veered no closer to the next one. No Big Bang to wipe out this existence.

Bart became thoughtful. "All right. What have we learned from this?"

"Kennedy was too rational an actor for our purposes," summarized Thaddeus. "We'll have to work to elevate someone on this world's stage who can be counted on to react with passion, blind conviction instead of thoughtful reason."

The rest of them conceded to this logic by nodding their heads.

"Here are some promising developments," continued Thaddeus. "I've detected the seeds of a movement that may aid us in this matter. An influential journalist has just made a very telling statement that I think you'll find interesting. His name is William Buckley and he said 'I'd rather live in a society governed by the first 2,000 names in the Boston phone directory than in one governed by the 2,000 members of the Harvard faculty.' Sounds reasonable doesn't it? Sounds like it empowers the common man. He's a Republican though, a very eloquent Republican who can use language to seduce the not-so-moneyed masses. With the right platform he and his kind could dupe the citizens into voting against their own interests."

"Sounds sort of anti-intellectual to me. Do you really think people would reject the superior-minded candidate in an election?"

"I do, Bart. I think it's possible that a mob or hive mentality would take pride in rejecting know-it-alls and would tend to pick their leaders that way."

"Hard to imagine what that leader or president would look like. Anyway, are we all agreed at least that we should still effect a course change with this United States?" asked Bart.

"It still projects to be the major player on the world stage for several centuries more," chimed in Andrew. "I think it goes without saying that this is the place to concentrate."

"If everyone is agreed, let's move on to planning our next step," summarized Bart. "And let's at least try to continue to confuse the Agency even if we have to be less subtle. Now what's the next event candidate that we're targeting for change?"

PART III

The King is Dead

CHAPTER 9

March 1963

A delivery truck drove down West Neely Street in Dallas and stopped at number 214. The driver got out with a long, thin package from Klein's Sporting Goods. He hopped up the two steps and rang the bell. An attractive woman answered the door wearing the headpiece of a portable hairdryer with the tube hanging down her back.

"Package for A. Heidel," said Jack.

"He's not home right now," the woman told him in a thick Russian accent.

"Are you his wife?"

"Da. I'm Marina."

"Okay, could you sign here please?"

She signed for the package, and as she did, Jack examined the living space behind her. Unbeknownst to Marina, an invisible device, a microsentinel, entered her apartment.

That night, in a Dallas club, several groups of men roared their approval at the stage show. One such group was made up of workers from a local package delivery service.

"Hey, Jack, get me another beer while you're up?"

"Sure thing," answered Jack as he made his way to the bar.

The microsentinels would've fed the entertainment into Jack's visual cortex, yet he couldn't take his eyes off the stage. The dancer, Darlene, gyrated to a primal rhythm while she deftly, tantalizingly removed items of clothing. She worked the crowd into a lather with her well-studied movements. She had the type of full-figured body that Jack admired. Her scant costume enhanced the swell of her breasts and the curve of her posterior as she swung back and forth in hypnotic fashion.

Returning to the table, Jack placed the beers down in front of his friends from the package delivery service. "So did I miss anything?"

"Just a couple of bare tits," said one of his companions.

The revelry lasted well past midnight. The shows wound down then, and some of the girls, now dressed, walked through the room as they prepared to leave. Darlene, however, sat beside

Jack and struck up a conversation after he lit her cigarette. About a half-hour later, a group of policemen who were obviously friends of the owner left. Now the owner was eager to leave, too, and spied Jack sitting with Darlene. Jack Ruby became red faced and walked over to confront Jack.

"Hey, asshole," shouted Ruby before getting close to the talking couple.

Jack, with his back toward Ruby, ignored him. Darlene, however, used to Ruby's manic outbursts started to get up in fear. Ruby clenched his fist and was about to punch Jack in the side of the head when Jack finally turned around. Ruby froze under Jack's stare. The blood left his face, which turned from red to white. Getting up, Jack placed the palm of his hand on Ruby's chest and slowly, yet forcefully, pushed the club owner into a chair. Taking an amazed Darlene by the hand, he exited the club.

CHAPTER 10

Early Summer 1963

Another invisible tour from Jack's universe wended its way through a Boston neighborhood. They stopped long enough within a living room to get a view of a popular television show, *77 Sunset Strip*. The program was displayed on a small black-and-white screen set in a bulky cabinet. Most of the tourists hadn't seen one in operation. They were fascinated by the primitive device as well as the hold it seemed to have over viewers in spite of its faults. After the typical questions, the guide got an atypical one from an overly observant little girl.

"Why do you need a gun? Is there any danger here?"

The tour guide thought he'd taken the gun out of the storage compartment unseen, but the little girl must have been playing around the buses before departure. All the adult passengers now looked at him with renewed attention and concern. *Have to be cool,* he thought.

"A gun?" he repeated with a confused look. "Oh, wait. I know what you mean."

He pulled a gun-shaped device out of his jacket pocket. "This is just a scanner for your ticket badges."

To demonstrate, he approached a woman in the first row and scanned her badge. It registered with a ping, and the woman's ID picture appeared on the plasma display above the driver's head.

"You all had this done back at the tourist center, but in case of confusion we're equipped to process tickets on the bus as needed."

Everyone seemed to relax at that. The guide noted the little girl still had a question but shrank back in the wake of such a forceful contention. She was astute. Probably would make a good agent, he thought. For now, however, this guide, slash agent, felt good at disabusing the public of any possible danger. It was over two years since his Langley-detected possible tampering with the Kennedy Presidency. If people realized how imminent a universal catastrophe could be, the panic could bring one on by itself.

The cable bus moved through a dense area of tree branches in spite of being in the city. It passed through the solid matter with nary a breeze to mark its passage. Eventually, the bus cleared the foliage and descended downhill before entering another house.

"That was Ronan Park in the neighborhood called Dorchester," said the guide. "We're now entering an apartment house known as a three-decker. Does anyone remember, from the beginning of the tour, what the significance of this address is?"

The people looked out to note they were at the intersection of Adams Street and Hecla. As usual, no one volunteered a response even though the tour guide could tell that a few knew the answer.

"No one remembers? I'll give you a reminder. We were talking about probability calculations based on events occurring in adjacent universes."

This time a smart-looking teenage boy spoke up. "A boy lives here who will someday sense the existence of parallel universes."

"Very good. Now can anyone tell me his name."

One of the adults who was getting annoyed with the quizzing shouted it out in a gruff tone. "Michael!"

A six-year-old boy woke from a half-sleep. He lay in a single bed against the wall of a small bedroom. Across the nightstand, against the other wall, was another single bed. His parents used it as a guest bed when his mother's aunt visited. He heard someone call his name and in his half-wakeful state looked over expecting to see his grand aunt. No one was there, and now fully awake he remembered there were no house guests. Puzzled, he stared at the empty bed before scanning the rest of the room. No one appeared, and he heard no other noise. Total silence filled the apartment. His parents and sister were still asleep. He wasn't scared since it was early morning and the sun was up, but he wondered if he had heard a ghost.

June 26, 1963

Apparently the bonhomie that de Gaulle initially offered to the American president didn't mitigate the French leader's true ambitions. This had become plain to all in the administration over the course of the last several months. Kennedy now understood the reservations Roosevelt and Churchill had in dealing with the self-appointed leader of France at the time of the war. De Gaulle's long standing goal remained to create a third world power constructed of states along the Rhine, Alps, and Pyrenees. Like Charlemagne before him, he excluded the Brits from his vision. In his mind the English were far too cozy with the Americans. They figured in the Anglo-American alliance that represented one unified world power, as the Soviet Union represented the other. The French leader's bloc of select European countries would serve as arbiter between these two forces.

Kennedy staked out his somewhat contrary position in favor of the Multilateral Force or MLF. It promised a stable and wholly united Europe as opposed to de Gaulle's handpicked states. In his efforts to preserve the MLF, Kennedy had recently employed the most secret and delicate diplomacy in dealing with Great Britain, which wanted an independent defense strategy. The Brits pressured their American allies for weapon systems solely devoted to the defense of the United Kingdom and not of the MLF.

De Gaulle overtly tried to scuttle the MLF concept and any collective relationship it would have with the United States. Unfortunately for him, anti-American sentiment was waning, due in large part to the charms and popular positions of President Kennedy. Pressing this advantage, Kennedy visited America's European allies in a grand tour of the continent.

He stood in front of the Schöneberg Rathaus City Hall in Berlin, his voice ringing out over the adoring crowd. His words were serious, but in the midst of them he couldn't help turning to the translator to thank him for translating his attempted German. This elicited laughter before he continued in a more serious tone.

"There are many people in the world who really don't understand—or say they don't—what is the great issue between the free world and the Communist world.

"Let them come to Berlin!

"There are some who say that Communism is the wave of the future.

"Let them come to Berlin!

"And there are some who say in Europe and elsewhere we can work with the Communists.

"Let them come to Berlin!

"And there are even a few who say that it is true that Communism is an evil system, but it permits us to make economic progress.

"*Lass sie nach Berlin kommen!* Let them come to Berlin!"

Invisibly hovering above the crowd, a tour tram containing a lucky group of tourists from an unguessed-at reality reveled in their good fortune to be here at this moment. The tour guide, knowing the president's schedule, had timed the tour well.

"Freedom," Kennedy continued, "has many difficulties and democracy is not perfect. But we never had to put up a wall to keep our people in."

How easy would it be to take out this paragon of virtue, thought the guide with morbid fascination. A shot from this invisible perch would leave the locals mystified. How would it feel to deal death yet be totally untouchable by them? Tingling sensations ran up and down the guide's back as he imagined the rush, the power. But he caught his thoughts before any outward signs appeared. Looking back to the interior of the bus, he noted all eyes fixed on the president. His sociopathic fantasy remained hidden.

"All free men, wherever they may live, are citizens of Berlin, and therefore, as a free man, I take pride in the words, *'Ich bin ein Berliner.'*"

The crowd erupted in near hysterical adulation.

CHAPTER 11

The inside of his sunglasses displayed the route to his destination. Its microprocessors accomplished the task with a fraction of its full capabilities. Dealey Plaza would be uncrowded today, several weeks ahead of Kennedy's arrival.

Dallas was abuzz with news of the president's visit. Security staked out the route amid an apprehensive atmosphere. The Texas city wasn't thought to be a friendly environment for the president. Local papers had been known to call for his impeachment citing a softness on Communism. A railroad worker inspected the yard behind the fence at Dealey Plaza. From above the knoll, he carefully observed the route the president would take. Satisfied that he had a good vantage point, he removed a camera-like device from his pocket, set it atop the fence, and trained it on the route.

The next day an observant street cleaner noticed the same man but this time wearing the uniform of a city sewer worker. He had a manhole cover opened with a worker's cage surrounding it to warn drivers. Orange cones surrounded it as well, and so did a sewer system truck parked on the side of the road. Yet again the man removed a camera-like device from his pocket, set it up at the drain under the sidewalk, and trained it on the exact same location that the fence camera still watched.

In the FBI offices in Dallas, Agent Carstairs greeted the visitor just led into his office.

"Hello, Mr. Gonzalez. I appreciate your coming in."

Gonzalez timidly shook the agent's hand and seated himself in the chair in front of the desk. Carstairs went around to his own seat.

"Sounds like you noticed a possible security breach for the president's visit?"

The venetian blinds were open, revealing a pleasant November day in Texas. The sun actually blinded the guest as he leaned in, so he spoke with his back pressed against the seat. Carstairs noticed the discomfort but did nothing to alleviate it.

"Yes, I think so."

"You think so? You seemed fairly certain an hour ago, sir."

"That's before I was treated like a criminal by your staff."

"Oh?"

"I'm just a citizen doing my duty in reporting something I thought would be of concern."

"You'll have to forgive my staff. They do get a bit overzealous when it comes to the wellbeing of the president. Please tell me what you saw."

"I'll tell you exactly what I told your people, and then I want to go home."

"They'll be no one stopping you if that's your wish."

Gonzalez seemed to relax.

"Well two days ago, I was cleaning the street..." He took out a pack of Marlboros. "Do you mind if I smoke?"

Carstairs pushed an ashtray across the desk in response.

"Two days ago I was cleaning up... I work for the city you know. I saw a man in the train yard who I'd never seen before."

"So?"

"I know most of the people who work there by sight, and I know I'd never seen him before. He put something up on the fence. It looked like a camera. I thought it was odd that a railroad guy would do that. But I didn't think too much of it and went back to work.

The next day, though, I saw the same man again. And this time he wore a sewer worker outfit. He had another camera. At least I thought it was a camera. I'd never seen one like it, but he placed it under the curb at the street drain. That's a funny place to put a camera I thought.

"I guess by this time I was staring because when I looked up he was watching me. The look he gave me made my blood run cold. I know he was up to no good."

Gonzalez paused and Carstairs realized he was done with his story. "What did the man look like?"

"He was tall, light skinned..."

"Anything else? Color hair? Color eyes?"

"He wore a construction helmet, and I wasn't close enough to notice his eyes."

"Okay, then how tall? How much did he weigh? Any tattoos?"

"I think he was over six feet. Maybe weighed two hundred pounds, something like that."

"I don't suppose you saw a name tag?"

"Jack. Yes, Jack was the name on the shirt."

"Good. How about a last name?"

Gonzalez just shrugged his shoulders.

"How about what he drove. There must have been a truck or a van."

After a few more moments of fruitless questioning, Carstairs dismissed Gonzalez with a handshake.

On his lunch hour Carstairs sauntered around Dealey Plaza. He couldn't get the Gonzalez report out of his head. For some reason it reminded him of his time on the *USS Farragut* during the war. Back then he must have sounded a lot like Gonzalez when he struggled to describe a crewman after the sailor was injured in a torpedo attack. Lieutenant Carstairs, at the time, knew the sailor, had worked with him from time to time, but could never come up with a mental image when asked to describe him. It was very odd and very troubling to encounter this phenomena again considering what the city was preparing for.

Admittedly, the agent wasn't even certain that the president's route took him to Dealey Plaza, but something alarmed him about the purposeful man Gonzalez noticed, yet who defied description. Considering the other details from the account, Gonzales appeared to be an observant individual. Why then the vagueness of his recollection of this man?

The agent went up to the wooden fence on the grassy knoll and walked along it. Not quite sure of what he was looking for, he remained vigilant for anything unusual. Walking back down the slope then, he crossed Elm Street and walked along the grass as he located the street drains on the knoll side of Elm. What was that, he thought, as he spotted something unusual. Retracing his steps, he noticed a thing that shimmered only when he observed it a specific angle. At a different time of day with a different position of the sun, he might never have seen it.

Carstairs crossed the street again. Careful to avoid any traffic, he kneeled down on the street so he could see into the storm drain vertically cut into the curb. Nothing was there, yet something shimmered when he saw it from across the street. Turning his head and body so he could put his arm in, he felt around with his hand. Finally, he felt something about the size of a pack of cigarettes. It was fixed in place, frustrating his efforts to remove it. Withdrawing his hand, he bent down, looked in but saw nothing. This time he nearly lay flat on the street so he could look in and feel all at the same time. His hand found the object, yet his eyes didn't. Oblivious to his position he stared for several seconds. Then he saw it. It was like using one's will to make a two-dimensional object on paper appear concave or convex.

As he got up he noticed a small group had gathered around. Some had looks of concern.

"It's okay, folks," said Carstairs, and he flashed his FBI card. "Just doing a little investigation."

He stepped up on the sidewalk as the group dispersed except for one person. Carstairs recognized the uniform of a city worker. Now he recalled seeing one such worker by the Triple Underpass when he'd first arrived. The man with a name tag that said Jack approached him, and it was only then that the circumstances of Gonzales' story hit home. Somehow, due to body language or posture, Carstairs was certain this was the same man Gonzalez had seen the other day. He started to address the man.

Fifteen minutes later Carstairs was back in his office catching up on some report forms. His friend Derrick poked his head in.

"I thought you were going out for lunch," he said.

"Changed my mind at the last minute. Paperwork you know."

"Yeah, I've got my own pile. By the way, Ferguson is looking for you. He's not happy you took his parking space."

Carstairs looked up. "No I didn't. I parked in my own space."

"Well then your car must've driven there by itself."

Carstairs got up and looked out the window. His car wasn't where he thought it was.

"Must be senility. I guess I'll move it, but I could've sworn I parked in my own spot this morning."

"Remind me not to let you valet-park my car," said Derrick grinning as he dashed off.

Carstairs went downstairs to move his car. At the curb he took out his keys, but before getting in, he felt the hood of the car. It was warm. The car had been driven recently. Why would anyone move his car to another space?

"One space isn't enough for you now?"

He turned around to find Ferguson staring at him.

"Something's wrong here, Ferguson. I parked in my own space this morning."

"Yeah and then you parked in my space at noon."

"Can't be. I never left the building."

"Are you pulling my leg, Carstairs? I saw you drive into the space from my window a little while ago."

Carstairs started to open his mouth to argue but thought the better of it. Instead, he just got into the car and moved it back to his space. *I've never had blackouts,* he thought, but then recalled a similar incident in the war. He'd been assigned to the destroyer *U.S.S. Farragut* when he found himself on the bridge with no recollection of how he'd gotten there. The ship's doctor questioned him about it later in connection with a strange crewman. The same crewman he'd been talking with prior to his blackout. The same crewman who'd been injured in a torpedo attack.

As he headed back up to his office, he ran into the floor secretary, Maggie.

"Finish your tour of Dealey?" she asked.

"What?"

"Did you find what you were looking for at Dealey?" she repeated.

"I was going to Dealey, wasn't I?" he remembered and walked away leaving her to comment under her breath on his manners.

He remembered wanting to go but had no recollection of being there or why he'd wanted to go. He did, however, remember a

Mr. Gonzalez who had inspired his curiosity in the first place. In his office he opened a drawer and took out a file labeled *Gonzalez*. The notes were ambiguous. Vague suspicions on the interviewee's part concerning men working around Dealey. Carstairs jotted down Gonzalez's home address and decided to visit.

He drove to the neighborhood and looked for the street address. Eventually, he found the house with a lot of cars parked nearby. A fair amount of foot traffic went in and out of the front door. Carstairs got a sick feeling in his stomach. Finally finding a spot to park, he walked up to the front porch. On it two women were embracing tearfully.

"Mrs. Gonzalez?" he asked the woman who noticed his approach.

"Yes?" she said as she disengaged from the other woman.

"Is your husband available?"

Mrs. Gonzalez broke down sobbing and ran into the house. The other woman, however, confirmed his suspicion. "Mr. Gonzalez died this afternoon in a traffic accident."

November 22, 1963

The president and Jacqueline arrived at Love Field in Dallas at 11:40. They stepped off the plane onto the mobile stairs amid cheers from an enthusiastic crowd. The sun shone brightly from blue skies as the president and first lady descended onto the runway. Kennedy waved and shook hands with as many as he could reach when he got close to the barriers. The people's reaction seemed to dispel his aides concerns about a hostile city. Police officers worked to keep the straining crowd from breaking down the waist-high barriers.

At another, distant, vantage point, Jack, the cleaner, observed the spectacle with clinical interest. Making sure no one was watching, he trailed a cord from a device hidden in his pocket and plugged it into a mating receptor in his sunglasses. Instantly, the real-time image of Dealey Plaza appeared on the inside of his lenses. The devices he'd strategically placed on the fence and at the drain transmitted images so clear that one would almost believe he was on the spot. Jack noted stragglers starting to congregate around the president's route. Some had staked out places on the lawn across the street. It would be about an hour before the object of their curiosity arrived.

With his glasses and mental projection, Jack manipulated the transmitters to scan the plaza. Even the School Book Depository Building could be placed in the field of vision. Satisfied that the angles were covered, he conducted a diagnostic of the devices' main function. The firing solutions seemed set. At this point in his mission it was critical that the non-passive capabilities didn't fail. Timing was key. If the computer predictions were off by a fraction of a second, he knew their discharge could be noticed by onlookers. Still, the risk must be taken.

The execution of his mission had to be flawless. What had al-Rahiim told him? He'd said many things, though "remember your training" was foremost among them. But then something nagged at Jack about the other things that the computer model of al-Rahiim had said. It said "be ready to adapt as the situation changes." And the reference to al-Rahiim's daughters implied that Jack was about to make a mistake he couldn't be talked out of. Were these the ramblings of a machine ill-suited to contain the psyche of the proconsul? Jack decided they had to be and then proceeded with his preparation.

The president's motorcade rolled slowly down Main Street. People crowded both sides of the street to get a glimpse of the young leader. They cheered wildly for the popular president and Kennedy acknowledged them with smiles and waves.

Jack drove a faster route to the Plaza but could see the parade in his mind's eye due to the microsentinels that shadowed the president. The agent was calm. Very little else remained to be done, and he trusted his preparations. Still, he couldn't get al-Rahiim's words out of his head. The teenager analogy in particular stayed with him. Now, all of a sudden, al-Rahiim's exact words at the Mall came back to him. "Have you ever seen someone about to make a stupid mistake, but you knew that you couldn't talk him out of it?" A stupid mistake. Was someone, maybe even al-Rahiim, observing him as he was about to make a foolish mistake?

At 12:25 the motorcade approached Dealey Plaza. Jack arrived well in advance and was securely in place to complete his mission. He momentarily allowed himself the luxury of looking forward to finally going home. Just a few more steps to execute, he thought, but then doubts intruded, and they were more insistent than ever. This time it wasn't al-Rahiim's words but something the praetor had said to him.

At 12:30 the president's motorcade turned right from Main onto Houston Street. Moments later, it took a sharp left turn onto Elm Street passing the Schoolbook Depository Building. An on-looker, Abraham Zapruder, took advantage of a perch on the pergola near the grassy knoll to film the president.

The limousines inched onward. Kennedy and Texas Governor Connelly beamed at the crowd. The amateur filmmaker on the pergola trained his lens at the limousine. Jack took it all in, including the proximity of the president to the devices he'd set, as well as to the upper floors of the closest building, the Schoolbook Depository. He noted the position of the trees and the Stemmons Freeway sign as possible obstructions. Even the Secret Service men jogging alongside the vehicle had to be accounted for.

And then the shots came just as the computer models had predicted. Everything seemed to slow as the cleaner's mental processes operated outside the dimension of time. A bullet tore down and through the president's neck. Mrs. Kennedy appeared to notice the president clutching at his throat and unhurriedly leaned over to find out what was wrong with him. A while later, Jackie nearly got hit by a second bullet that passed through her husband's skull.

Jack witnessed a crimson cloud slowly emanating from the wound on the president's head. Mrs. Kennedy, in a panic, tried to climb onto the back of the limousine, no doubt in an effort to escape. A Secret Service man pushed her back as the car sped up.

Coincidentally, flashes of light and gas betrayed Jack's devices, as they too went off to add to the violence of the moment. Jack's stomach constricted before he realized that the local onlookers probably wouldn't notice them the way he could. Still in crisis mode, though, Jack observed the reactions of a few people who flinched as his devices discharged. They were perceived after all. There was always that risk and the Agency could only hope that the locals would supply their own rationale. Perhaps they would think it was another gunman.

Now, in the midst of this carnage, Jack finally recalled the praetor's exact words. "Downloading the complete person into a computer always results in some loss. There's still nothing like the human brain to contain every nuance of our life experience." He finally understood, but too late! Jack's conscious mind was being crowded out as the president's replaced it. He had been told that the devices would upload Kennedy's psyche somewhere, but what they were actually doing was transferring it to a receptacle particularly suited to contain it: Jack's brain.

He'd also been led to believe that as a last resort he would physically replace the president. That so-called real purpose was also kept secret from the public in his own reality, in favor of the more ominous disinformation about cleaners—hit men for the Agency. A fiction that the Agency wielded as another misdirection.

Jack lost control of his mind and body with al-Rahiim's warning ringing in his head. Very soon he would lose the capacity for thought, and with it all that he held familiar and dear. He had made a stupid mistake. He'd trusted the Agency.

What remained of Jack's mind impelled him to leave the scene awkwardly. The clarity of perception that he'd enjoyed just a few moments before dissipated to be replaced by noisy confusion. Vaguely, he observed people running and screaming. Some dropped to the ground trying to protect themselves. Others were too stunned to do anything. The crowd ebbed and flowed in several directions at once not knowing what to do, but as Jack ran he noted that some others ran after him with purpose. Even through the pain of what was happening to him, he knew his pursuers were with his own agency. Blackness closed in on his vision just as he felt arms saving him from a fall. Then all went black and he slept, slipping into unconsciousness for perhaps the last time as Jack Fitzgerald.

A few hours later, with the president already pronounced dead, the business of government fell to his vice president. Air Force One carried the body of the fallen leader as well as his successor and widow and several necessary government officials. Jackie Kennedy's clothes bore the stains of her husband's blood as she stood beside Vice President Johnson. She was remarkably composed as Sarah Hughes, a federal judge, swore in Johnson as president.

President Kennedy awoke with a start. He remembered a searing pain in his throat but felt for the wound and found nothing there. Had it been a dream? With that guess, he recognized his surroundings as his bedroom in his home at Hyannis. With all the numerous residences of the Kennedy family, this was probably the one he was most familiar with. *I was in Dallas,* he remembered. *What am I doing here?*

Determined to investigate, he got out of bed gingerly expecting the typical pain that emanated from his back whenever he moved this way. It never came. Its absence was remarkable, and it made him take note as he tested it again. Still no pain. He tested it again and again and couldn't replicate the sensation he'd become so familiar with. He felt for the scars from all the back operations. Not finding them with one hand, he felt with both hands. There was no trace of any surgery. Given their absence and his befuddled mind, he assumed he was still asleep and having a very realistic dream. He recalled a similar frame of mind when he'd been stranded on Plum Pudding Island in the Pacific after his patrol torpedo boat was sunk. Sleep, in that crisis, was an escape.

Standing now, he walked to the bathroom, bent over the sink, and splashed water on his face. He straightened then and looked at himself in the mirror for the first time since seeming to awaken. It startled him. The president was naturally a young looking man, but he was surprised at how strikingly youthful his features appeared in the mirror. He ran his hand over his face, testing the reality. It seemed as if he was in a fog although physically he felt fine. Actually he felt better than that. Perhaps better then he ever remembered feeling. The intestinal distress that he'd become used to since childhood was notably absent, just like his back pain.

Registering the stubble on his chin, he started to shave his dream face. He went through the motions mechanically. What a strange hallucination, he thought. For a moment he considered the possibility that he was dead, but then another thought intruded. The president sensed that he wasn't alone, yet he knew no one else was in the room. Ultimately, he realized that the other presence wasn't in the room, but within the confines of his own mind. Somehow the realization didn't startle him. There was an odd familiarity about it.

The president continued to shave absentmindedly. Presently, he cut himself, and in undreamlike fashion, it hurt. Blood welled up from a long gash and the red stood out starkly from the shaving cream. As he observed it, however, it stopped. Wiping away the foam, he actually saw a scab form and then disappear as new skin replaced it. With each unnatural revelation, the president started to doubt his sanity. Still, mechanically, he finished his shave, got dressed, and went outside. But for the ocean, the neighborhood was quiet. It was an eerie quiet though as if something was wrong. It was the same kind of quiet he'd perceived in the country after Pearl Harbor.

The *Victura* floated invitingly at the end of the dock. *Perhaps a sail would help clear my head,* he thought. But when he started down the path to the dock, several men appeared and blocked his way. They had been there all along, but the president had ignored them as if they were unimportant. Now the other person in the president's mind informed him that they were colleagues in an agency from a different reality. Subconsciously, things seemed to make sense, but as new information fed into his conscious mind, JFK wasn't comforted.

His attitude turned hostile to these men. He was going to take that boat ride, at whatever cost. He began to run, and either they had orders not to physically stop him, or with him in operation at 100 percent adrenaline, they simply weren't able to. Once on the boat, he cast off.

CHAPTER 12

The praetor sat in Rick Gerard's living room considering Rick's statement. She rolled the lack of information around in her mind to test its believability.

"So you have no idea where Jack could've gone?"

"He's a very good sailor, Madame Praetor. If he's gone renegade, who knows where he could've piloted that boat. Is it unusual for a cleaner to take off like that?"

"This is the first time."

"So we're in virgin territory here."

"We're in extremely dangerous territory here. Someone with his knowledge could bring down a calamity ten times worse than the one we were trying to prevent."

"What happened? Why didn't he come in?"

"My guess is that al-Rahiim prevented the process from completing."

"But al-Rahiim is dead."

"Is he? I wonder. Jack talked with the computer simulation just before the assassination. I was there, and I was suspicious that the real al-Rahiim was sending signals somehow through the computer. Maybe they were prerecorded but I can't shake my suspicion that al-Rahiim is alive and gone renegade."

Rick was flabbergasted. If he wasn't in the midst of trying to quit smoking he would've reached for a cigarette out of habit. He had achieved closure over his dead friend, but was it premature?

Al-Rahiim was allowed to move freely around the ship. His captors had somewhat taken him into their confidence since he'd helped them warn Jack by sending a message through the computer holding the al-Rahiim psyche. Of course that wouldn't have been possible without their assistance in remotely linking to that computer.

The tactic had been only partially successful, however, since Jack had still downloaded JFK. At least Kennedy wasn't in the hands of the Agency. The news that elicited the most relief, though, was that the assassination had happened as it was supposed to. At least realities wouldn't collide over interference in that event. Up to now, al-Rahiim and his handler, Metluna, had wondered if indeed a third force would try to influence the end of Kennedy's life. The proconsul had explained his suspicions concerning the Religionist party in his reality to the aliens.

Now, al-Rahiim entered the bridge and addressed Metluna, who was standing by an instrument console. "Any luck finding Jack yet?"

Metluna looked up at al-Rahiim with those probing eyes. The size of them still unnerved the proconsul even after several weeks on the ship. As usual, the mode of their communication was silent but the intent flowed into al-Rahiim's thoughts.

"We're having difficulty. Apparently the process that was interrupted during the assassination seems to have created an amalgam personality. The man we're looking for is neither your agent nor JFK. It seems both personalities are working together as one. Ever had this happen before?"

"No, but in theory there was always that possibility. From our studies, JFK was very open-minded. He once said that he wouldn't make a good politician because he could too easily see the other guy's point. Our Jack is the same type of person but with a different history. I could imagine that they would be an exceptional case."

"Now JFK has access to the biological and nanobotic improvements in your Jack. I'm worried that he might get drunk on their power and effect some changes."

"JFK isn't a warmonger if that's what you're worried about."

"I didn't mean he would become aggressive in that way. I'm just considering the possibility of a new, improved JFK changing the course of history in this universe."

"In other words doing something to cause the distance between realities to shrink."

"That's right. Now we're in the same business you were in. Having to tamper to prevent your tampering from causing a collision of realities. Even if he just told somebody who he is or something about the other realities—any slight slip of information could be enough to cause a Big Bang. It's too delicate and dangerous a game to play." Metluna seemed to have a way to prevent the others on the bridge from overhearing their mental conversation. Around them, the quiet crew activity went on as usual.

"We were foolish to breach the barriers of realities," agreed the proconsul. "I see that now. Even our observance changed the natural progression of other realities."

"All we can do is hope to effect a subtle fix that won't disturb the time lines. Then we'll have to agree to stop the universe-hopping."

Al-Rahiim nodded his head in agreement.

PART IV

Bifurcated President

CHAPTER 13

The amalgam personality called Jack, confident that he was alone and undetected due to his nanoshields, watched his own funeral. Not an extraordinary thing since it was televised, except that he watched it on his holographic projector by virtue of some nano-probes that he'd left in Washington. Every now and then, he commanded the image to show the television news special as well as his closed circuit transmission. Jack frequently wiped his cheeks as tears involuntarily streamed down his face not out of self-pity but out of guilt over leaving his young family. His young son saluted the funeral procession at Jackie's direction. JFK simultaneously smiled and cried.

Abruptly, the door opened. He had been careless in leaving it ajar to catch a breeze, and now he was found out. However, the agency was too high tech to catch him in this low-tech goof— but Father Herlihy stood confounded at what he saw.

"I'm sorry I should've..."

His voice trailed off as he struggled to make sense of the holographic image.

"What was that?" asked the priest as Jack fumbled to switch off the device quickly.

Father Herlihy was hoping for a plausible explanation but an episode of the *Twilight Zone* came to his mind in the long while before Jack could manufacture an answer.

"Are you from the future?" the priest asked in a half-serious way but then observed Jack for any telltale reaction.

An internal conflict raged momentarily within Jack's mind while he considered telling the priest the truth. Two disparate personalities debated how loyal they now had to be to the praetor. Eventually, an angry president's indifferent side won out. Jack allowed his body language to confirm to Herlihy that he'd been found out.

"No," Jack said as he exhaled. "No, I'm not from the future, but I'm not from your world either. The explanation of all this comes from well outside of your concept of reality."

The priest, so intent on what he'd heard, dared not breathe for fear of missing any detail. "Are you a Martian?"

This time Jack smiled. "I'm not an alien either. I'm human just like you but from another universe, another reality."

"Excuse me?"

Jack got up and walked around the room as he thought of ways to explain. "I'm from a parallel universe. One that's very close to yours on the spatial plane. We're very similar, our universes, yours and mine. They contain virtually all the same quantum manifestations right down to the people. The only significant difference is history. We progressed faster. Achieved peace more quickly so our technology advanced unhindered. At least that's the theory. Anyway, we're able to visit other realities like yours."

The look on the priest's face suggested that wasn't enough of an explanation.

"All right. In my reality, the existence of parallel universes was discovered about two hundred years ago. Eighty years ago we discovered how to travel to them. Yours is one that we have studied greatly."

"But how, why?"

"Gravity is the key. It's the only force that isn't confined to one universe. It spreads across all realities. Manipulating it is the way we get from one universe to another. It's the weakest of the four universal forces only because it permeates all universes. The electromagnetic and atomic forces don't. That's why they're stronger. They're concentrated on only one plane of existence, one universe or reality if you like and don't travel between them. Anyway, we ride self-generated gravity waves to the closest universes where we discover conditions similar to ours. Farther ones tend to be inhospitable."

The priest appeared totally perplexed, and Jack sensed Herlihy wasn't looking for a technical answer to his question. Still, Jack continued in the hope of distracting the man from asking why again.

"For instance, in one alternate universe, dinosaurs never became extinct and mammals never came to dominate the Earth. That's an extreme example, but there must be countless billions of realities representing every possibility that ever was. I have no doubt that physicists and mathematicians have guessed at this phe-

phenomena here. Your universe is so similar to ours that someday you'll learn to breach the barriers between realities as we have."

Herlihy became a little less tense and flopped down in a chair but obviously still had trouble with what he was hearing.

"All this abstract stuff isn't what I'm used to. If I can't see and feel it, I can't wrap my mind around it."

Jack raised an eyebrow. "Now that surprises me, Father."

"Why do you say that?"

"From where I'm sitting I see a man who has devoted his life to an unseen controller of the universe, a god. Can there be any more abstract thinking than that?"

"It's something we call faith," stated the perturbed priest.

"You have faith that a two-thousand-year-old story is the literal truth about existence?"

"In general, yes."

That interchange hung in the air between them. JFK recalled questioning a Catholic priest when he was a young man, after returning from Jerusalem, about why we should believe Christ any more than Mohammed. It was a young man's exercise in critical thinking, but the shocked priest then warned JFK's father, Joe Kennedy, about raising an atheist. At present, Jack and Father Herlihy each seemed to consider what the debate revealed about the other.

The priest finally broke the silence. "Of course we realize that the writers of the Bible were fallible men, subject to their own interpretations. But the basic tenets are that God created the universe and man. He put man on the earth and tests him for admittance to heaven."

"An interesting experiment he has set up then. Why did he make man vulnerable to..." Jack thought the better of continuing the debate. The only inevitable outcome would be to strain a relationship he enjoyed.

Herlihy seemed unwilling to continue the argument as well. He was still curious, however. "Why are you so advanced in the sciences?"

"Hard to say for sure, but my guess is that we had a less volatile sociopolitical climate."

"Come again with that?"

"History, I mean. For instance our Roman Empire never fell—it just faded away as I've heard people say. It actually continued to grow beyond where yours stopped. With the use of the steam engine, it encompassed the Mongol Empire and nearly the whole of Africa. Eventually it dissolved to leave most of the states that both of us are familiar with like France and Germany. When that happened, though, it was more like the peaceful dissolution of your late British Empire. In other words, with less war we had time to explore and discover where you did not."

"Why are you here?"

Jack had hoped the priest would forget the *why* question after his answer to the *how* questions.

"I told you. We study adjacent universes."

"No. I mean why are you here, personally? Are you studying religion? Is that why you've been hanging around the church?"

Jack stared at the priest, but somehow Herlihy understood the action to be part of the answer to his question. As Jack continued to stare the priest took in the features of the strange visitor's face. The features never changed, but Herlihy had the impression he was seeing them for the first time. Little by little, his mind pieced together his host's face until at last he had a clear perception of it. He recognized it only now, and the realization made him jerk back in his chair.

"Mr. President," he exclaimed. "I thought you died in the..."

The words trailed off as Jack raised a hand signifying silence.

"I'm not your president, not the JFK you know."

"I don't understand."

"I'm from a reality that's close enough to yours so that we have people in common. There are several versions of you and me across countless local universes. You could say that I'm the JFK from my universe, and because of that I was chosen as an agent to visit yours. I observe and if necessary clean up the situation. Stop any interference, in other words, from rogue agents," said Jack, spouting the fiction the Agency had led him to believe.

The priest tried to digest this by replaying Jack's explanation over in his head. During this reflection, Jack had the courtesy not to interrupt Herlihy's thoughts. Finally, the priest spoke up with a disturbing revelation. "You were disguised until this moment. Do you intend to replace the president?"

"Not a disguise. Just a sort of mind trick. And no, I won't be replacing him. Apparently, that was never the plan. I'm guessing that our most recent models show that President Kennedy's death preserves the safety of the local universes."

"Does that mean you had him killed?"

"It means events in this reality unfolded without interference from other universes."

"So you're saying that if he'd lived, if someone saved him, several realities would be in danger?"

Jack resigned himself to sitting down and explaining the nature of reality, the dangers when inter-reality travelers tampered with other universes and his civilization's goal to protect existence for all.

"And these parallel universes can be thought of as sheets of paper that may bend and oscillate. And touch each other—but with calamitous consequences," explained Jack.

The priest was intrigued. "Okay, so this has been the case for billions of years and now you're saying there's some danger. These sheets—I mean these universes can touch."

"If they touch, gravity will concentrate into a single point, a singularity, and it'll be the Big Bang in reverse. A catastrophic contraction of two universes will send shock waves throughout the other parallel realities. That was the cause of the Big Bang fourteen billion years ago. Two parallel universes touched, collapsing all the galaxies in both realities into a single point that eventually exploded, creating all you now know."

Astonished, the priest said, "So I owe my existence to the destruction of two universes? Possibly two universes full of people and cultures?"

"That's about right."

"But how could God allow this?"

Jack smiled.

"Oh, yes. I forgot," remembered the priest. "Your people don't take the Bible literally." Father Herlihy paused and then continued. "Can your people prevent this from happening now?"

"Maybe. It's complicated. It's all about managing probabilities."

"But why do you think it could happen again?" He furrowed his brow.

"Because we suspect someone is tampering with the normal progression of this universe. Our first suspicion came when Kennedy didn't order air cover for the Cuban invasion at the Bay of Pigs."

"Now I'm confused. Why would his actions affect the separation of realities?"

"Because, my spiritual friend, space-time and thought are intertwined. As sentient beings we think, take action, and seed the quantum field with new possibilities. When our actions are influenced by someone outside our universe it causes history to unfold differently. And when that happens, the timeline invariably becomes too similar to an adjacent reality. It reduces the spatial distance that would've separated them. We suspect you're on a path that isn't dissimilar enough from an adjacent universe. You're in danger of touching, to put it simply."

"And touching means another Big Bang."

"Yes. It would be the end of everything you know. And it would send catastrophic ripples through the other universes including mine until equilibrium is regained."

Jack let that remain in the air for a while until he was satisfied the priest had absorbed it. One can't alter the view of another's reality so radically and not expect the person to need time to digest the new view.

After an appropriate pause, Jack continued on. "Sometimes I wish we'd never learned how to travel to other universes. It would have spared you the destructive tampering of our twisted rogue agents."

At this the priest looked up with a surprised expression. "Rogue agents? Why would anyone with your knowledge of the potential disaster dare tamper?"

"Funny you should mention that. Would you believe there are people who, out of mythic traditions, refuse to believe that there are other worlds, other people in them?" Jack scowled.

"Why the grimace?" asked the priest as he noted Jack's expression. "I'm not going to like the answer, am I?"

"Probably not. The people I refer to are called Religionists."

"You mean religious people are the ones who are risking existence? That doesn't seem to make sense. Not with any religion I'm aware of." Again, his expression reflected a sense of surprise.

"Perhaps not, but I think you'll admit that there are those even in Christendom who would sooner kill than have anyone deny the existence of a god or their perception of reality. I read about your Crusades. But in any case, I think these people simply don't believe the science. Instead, they choose to place their faith in dusty old texts that supposedly define reality."

Both men quietly contemplated that for a few moments.

"Are you sure the tamperers are from your world? Maybe they're from another reality," suggested Herlihy.

"I wish that were the case. Clear-cut good guys and bad guys. No, I'm afraid we're the only ones who can shift from one reality to the another. The enemy is among us."

"But you said there were countless realities. Are you sure there aren't others that have the same technology."

"We can detect anyone opening a portal anywhere on this Earth."

"What if they arrive off the Earth and get here with some sort of space ship?"

Jack not only had no answer for that, he'd never even heard anyone consider the possibility.

CHAPTER 14

The frozen ground crunched beneath Hill's booted feet. Or at least this was the physical essence of Hill as interpreted and then constituted by the captors of Betty and Barney Hill. The man didn't so much hear the crunching as feel it through his heavy outfit. Trudging for hours taxed even *his* reserves, a man who had broken all kinds of endurance records during training. Fatigue forced him to stop by the shore of a calm sea where he allowed himself a respite to appreciate the beauty of the reflective surface.

Sinking to one knee, Hill put down a gloved hand to steady himself. The surface felt like roughened ice scattered over with tiny glass beads. *How long,* he wondered, *have I been walking? And, more importantly, how much further do I have to go?* After a while, he forced himself to his feet. Even here, the weight of his backpack was prohibitive. He had to remind himself that it meant life, or else he'd be tempted to discard it.

Checking his wrist band indicated he should follow the shoreline. If only he'd had a chance to pack the instruments that would estimate distance from the signal strength. The Others, however, had made short work of that waystation and Hill realized he owed his escape only to his training. Someday, perhaps, effective countermeasures would be invented for them. No use worrying about that today though. Life was ahead of him, and only death lay behind. He had to go forward and hope his equipment lasted the trip.

Twenty hours ago he'd taken great bounding leaps. Now it was all he could do to shuffle forward. The sound of his own breathing seemed to thunder around his helmet with his efforts. If not for the lighter gravity he would have been done for a long time ago.

Saturn reflected off the liquid methane sea. Noticing it, he looked up at what had been described as the most beautiful planet in the system. Even through the orange haze of Titan's atmosphere, it was an awesome sight. The rings reminded him of old vinyl records with their grooves and gaps.

Suddenly, the vibrating wrist band broke his reverie. It demanded his attention as he wrenched his eyes away from the planet. The band indicated he had reached his destination, and as if on cue Hill felt the ground rumble.

Jeremiah Sawyer gazed out through the university's telescope. He felt privileged to have scored time at the observatory but was fully prepared for an uneventful evening. Boredom was part of the price when one's passion was the heavens. Tonight, however, afforded rare views of Saturn's largest moon, and he wasn't going to miss one second of observation time no matter how little it changed. To him the planets represented the best kind of art. He could gaze at them for hours coming up with new ways of seeing the same thing over and over again.

Taking a bite of the sandwich he'd packed, he started his night's observation. About a dozen seconds into his surveillance, he stopped chewing. A plume erupted from Titan in such a fashion that he had to remind himself he wasn't watching a solar flare arcing from the sun. The ejected matter and energy not only escaped Titan's gravity but Saturn's as well. As he watched the spectacular blast unfold, it became obvious that whatever had left Saturn's moon was heading towards Earth.

Hill landed a few minutes after leaving Titan. He was concerned that his alternative faster-than-light arrival could've been detected by someone equipped to notice the spatial warp footprint. At the same time he didn't worry about the physical disturbance on Titan that marked his departure since it was unlikely someone would have been watching at that moment. Of course none of that would've been an issue had the original plan to arrive by planetary shuttle worked out. The bold incursion by the Others on Titan base had scuttled that idea. *They must have spies everywhere to have found our base,* he thought. In any case he was now on to the matter at hand.

The Potomac River reflected the night lights of Washington. Hill's choice for a beam-down point offered proximity to his target as well as a certain seclusion... or so he thought.

A woman screamed at his sudden appearance. Hill's luck betrayed him as a group had gathered along the river banks to observe the recovery of a stolen vehicle. Police, divers, and pedestrians crowded the typically obscure location. Trying to be nonchalant, he walked away unhurriedly in spite of the woman's screams. By this time the police had taken notice and gave chase. Before Hill could break into a run, however, his escape route was cut off by a squad car.

As he was being handcuffed, he thought it odd that the screams of a startled woman could exact such a reaction from local law enforcement. It didn't seem to fit with the United States he'd studied, a country that prided itself on due process. But before he knew it, he was hustled into the back of a car and ridden to the precinct jail. At least this would give him an opportunity to gather his strength, he thought.

Carlos had taken up residence in the basement jail of the precinct for yet another petty theft. He didn't fear getting caught and was almost just as happy here since it assured him of at least a free meal or two. Of course about half the time he got away with the bracelet, or the cigarettes or whatever caught his fancy. The way he figured it, he was ahead of the game.

He heard the barred door open at the end of the corridor and got up to see if he would recognize the new resident. Eventually, a tall black man came into view. The stranger was escorted by a policeman on either side of him. He didn't look like a street thug, thought Carlos. As a matter of fact, the new man was remarkable inasmuch as he showed no attitude whatsoever. If it wasn't for the handcuffs, Carlos could just as easily imagine the guy strolling down the aisle of a supermarket.

Later on he heard the guards talking about the newcomer. Apparently, they had also been impressed with the man's cool demeanor.

"Startled a woman at the site of the dredging over on the river," said one cop to another.

"And?"

"That's all. Whatever he did started her to scream loud enough to get our attention."

"So you arrested him?" the guard asked in an accusing tone.

"What's with the third degree? It was a white woman. You know the policy."

Carlos saw from the look on the other cop's face that he did, indeed, know the policy, but had trouble accepting it. He accommodated it, though, just as he must have on numerous other occasions.

That night Carlos was awakened by a loud commotion in the cell block. Groggily sitting up, he noticed a couple of guards racing past his cell. Now fully awake, he heard screaming. He recognized the voice and it curdled his blood since he knew the owner to be someone who feared nothing on this town's mean streets. Carlos had no way of knowing, however, that his blockmate experienced something well beyond anything from the street or even from this world.

Suddenly, one guard flew by his cell, seemingly having been thrown airborne by some force. Gunshots rang out now as the other guard backed past his cell while firing at something beyond Carlos's range of vision. A look of confusion as well as horror defined the guard's face, and he continued to shoot at something he seemed to have trouble aiming at. Carlos had the impression of bones snapping even though he couldn't hear it over the sound of the gun.

The screams stopped abruptly. Fear and dread the likes of which Carlos had never before known prompted him to flatten himself against the cell wall. He tried not to breathe as the shadow of the guards' antagonist appeared on the floor outside his cell. As the shadow slowly advanced, the petty thief bargained with God that he would go straight should he survive the night.

Finally, the tall black man whom Carlos had seen earlier appeared. He looked exactly the same, but now that identical non-threatening individual seemed to exude a frightening aura. After what seemed an eternity, the man casually passed Carlos's cell. Even when he'd gone Carlos held his breath several more seconds for fear of revealing his presence. What the hell had happened here?

Portsmouth, New Hampshire in early spring presented a bare, forbidding landscape to the two men from Washington. With no leaves on the trees, the gnarled branches reminded them of the lifelessness of the place. They pulled their collars tighter to keep out the pervasive cold as they walked up to the address from their notes. Ascending a couple of porch steps, they rang the doorbell of the residence. A middle-aged woman answered the door.

"Are you Mrs. Hill?" asked the shorter of the two.

"Yes, can I help you?"

"We're from the FBI. I'm Agent Monroe and this is Agent Philby," said Monroe as both showed their IDs.

"Is this about the UFO incident again after all this time?"

The agents exchanged glances. "No, ma'am. We'd like to talk with your husband, Barney."

"He's not here right now."

"When do you expect him?"

"I'm not sure. Maybe not for another couple of hours. What do you want to talk with him about?"

"Do you know where your husband was yesterday at about 2:30 p.m.?"

"He was at work of course."

"The post office?"

"Yes. What's this all about? Is Barney in some kind of trouble?"

At that moment Barney Hill pulled into the driveway. It was obvious that he'd been fishing, judging by his outfit and tackle box. His rod and reel were secured to the roof of the car. He got out of the vehicle while casting a suspicious look at the visitors. Betty's agitation was plain for him to see.

"What's going on here?"

"Barney, these men are asking questions about where you were yesterday."

"Mr. Hill, I'm agent Monroe and this is agent Philby from the FBI," Monroe said as they flashed their badges again. "We just have some routine questions for you."

Seeing no gain in antagonizing them, Barney ushered them into the house. After all were seated, Barney started the conversation. "Does this have something to do with the call my boss got yesterday?"

Betty Hill directed a meaningful look at Barney. It conveyed the 'why didn't you tell me?' question.

"I didn't want to worry you, Betty. It seemed like it had been cleared up."

Monroe answered Barney's question. "We're following up on that call, Mr. Hill. Did you know that we found your fingerprints on the dead bodies of a couple of guards at a D.C. jail. Witnesses described the attacker as looking an awful lot like you."

"Yet I was nowhere near Washington."

"We realize that. That's why we're here. Can you explain this?"

"Well, I don't have a twin if that's what you're asking."

"Is there anyone that you know of who would want to frame you for any reason?"

The agents continued to fish for a plausible explanation for the implausible. After a little over an hour, they concluded that they weren't getting anywhere. Consequently, Monroe and Philby politely excused themselves and departed, leaving the Hills to wonder why they were singled out for alien abductions and look-alike killers.

CHAPTER 15

At the Treasury building, George of the Secret Service visited his colleague's office. The man behind the desk looked up in surprise.

"I thought you were in the field this week?"

"My schedule has been changed, Tom. They thought it best if I have some down time."

"Now that you mention it you look like hell. Got the flu?"

"I wish it was as simple as a bug. At least I could sleep then."

Tom lost the will to be funny now that he registered his friend's state of mind. "What's going on?"

"I saw the president."

"Okay, you saw the president. And?"

"I mean I saw Kennedy."

Tom couldn't help but let out a guffaw but then he noticed that George wasn't kidding. "What do you mean you saw Kennedy? The last time any of us saw him he had a gaping hole in his head."

"I know that," said George in a short-tempered way. "But I saw the president alive and walking around."

"No wonder they gave you down time."

George went on to tell his story in spite of Tom's attitude. He seemed to have a need to get it off his chest.

"Last week we had motorcade duty for LBJ. I was jogging alongside the president's car, scanning the crowd as usual. That's when I saw him."

Tom played along. "That's when you saw Kennedy?"

"Yeah. I looked right at him. He was looking at Johnson's car. Now that I think of it, it was more like he looked through the car. And he didn't look happy."

"What are you saying? You mean like he thought Johnson had him shot?"

"If he's really alive, I'm sure he would've heard that rumor. Anyway, it must've been about ten seconds before I had to look away for a turn. When I looked back I couldn't find him in the crowd."

"Maybe it was somebody who looked a lot like him."

"That's what I thought at first, but then I saw him again. Another public appearance by Johnson. A different day and a different crowd, but this time as I watched him he noticed me. We made eye contact. When that happened, his features became less familiar and I got the distinct impression that..."

"Go on," said Tom.

"You'll think this is nuts, but I got the impression that my mind was being manipulated. Somehow I started to lose my focus. I started to struggle to remember what I had seen. If it wasn't for the loud blast of a car's horn that broke the spell, I doubt I would've remembered any of it."

In Havana, Jack sat overlooking a large plaza where Castro was conducting a rally. Attendance was mandatory. As he watched, Jack recalled the words of LBJ that he'd picked up with his microsentinels. Once he'd heard them, he was satisfied that his vice president was innocent of any conspiracy resulting in his assassination. Johnson had lamented to Bobby that Kennedy went after Castro, but that Castro had gotten him first. An enraged Jack didn't stop to vet LBJ's theory. He simply accepted the speculation as confirmation of his own suspicion.

The scope's crosshairs centered on the dictator's face. An excellent vantage point. Jack had chosen a building with enough floors to provide a clear line of sight high above the plaza. Quickly, he assembled his rifle. Satisfied that it was in good working order, he took careful aim out the window. It would be an easier shot than the one that had killed him, he mused. His target was stationary and Jack's breathing was controlled despite the maddening histrionics of the speechmaker. He timed his heartbeat.

The shot would come between beats to avoid the slightest interference with his steady aim. After all these preparations, he squeezed the trigger to a point just before firing. Vengeance was at hand. He was ready. And then he wasn't. Like so many times before, rational thought stayed his hand and overpowered his blind desires. Jack chose not to become an assassin.

CHAPTER 16

JFK and Barney Hill walked purposely toward one another. Once they met, both men unloaded deadly arsenals of martial blows. Each hit would have felled an ox, but these were more than human opponents with more than human resistance. For what seemed like minutes, neither combatant could claim an advantage. The flurry of blows and counterblows rained on in lightning-like fashion. Eventually, however, Jack's genetic constitution coupled with his nanobotic technology started to prove too much for the other. The other's parries became less effective. Jack connected with more debilitating strikes. The other flagged under the onslaught, his facial expression revealing his beaten demeanor.

Just as Jack started to sense victory, his adversary disappeared. Escaped, thought Jack, using his teleportation technology. He was wrong, though. It wasn't escape. Jack felt a fist in his back. Unprepared Jack had the wind knocked out of him. He turned around but knew Hill had materialized behind him to deliver the blow. By the time he turned, however, the other had jumped again to strike Jack on the side of the face. The tide of battle had turned.

Making frequent dimensional jumps, the Hill clone connected with kicks and punches while Jack wore down. Time to change tactics, he thought. Using his microsentinels, he detected the other's presence in enough time to parry the blows. This went on for a while before Jack recognized a telltale shimmer before each of his opponent's appearances. Now the advantage was Jack's again. Before his adversary could fully materialize, Jack directed a blow at him. Without the mechanical eyes in the back of his head, Jack wouldn't have been able to engineer a comeback. Such being the case, his opponent disappeared again, this time quitting the fight for good.

Al-Rahiim shouted at his hosts. The normally subdued ship rang with the passion of his anger. "What the hell were you trying to do?"

Metluna assumed an expression on his alien face that Usama now recognized as puzzlement.

"I thought we had a consensus on this," said Metluna.

"Consensus? A consensus to kill my agent? I never remembered agreeing to that. I thought we were simply trying to stop him from observing and potentially changing the natural course of this reality?"

"How did you think we were going to accomplish that?"

"By bringing him here, damn it. He could live out his days here as I've agreed to do."

Usama tried to read the facial expression on Metluna's alien countenance again. *Have I been naive?* he thought. *Am I alive only because I'm useful at the moment?*

The moonlight cast a shadow on a very unusual three-way conversation taking place behind the Lincoln Memorial. If anyone from the surrounding traffic had keen enough night vision, he would have noted that one of the participants could be seen through. Of course discretion accounted for the late hour and the obscure meeting place. The other two participants were no less remarkable inasmuch as they occupied the very same body. The holographic image of Proconsul al-Rahiim spoke first.

"Glad you got my message, Jack. I don't have full liberty with my hosts and had to send it off in secret. "

"You son of a bitch. I had a feeling you were alive when I spoke with the computer in the praetor's office. You were sending me a message somehow, weren't you?" accused Jack Fitzgerald.

"Trying to, anyway."

"We all thought you died in a plane crash. What happened to you?"

"I was in a crash. And then I was rescued. But not by any of our people."

"Who? The Religionists?"

"No. Someone else. A different people. An alien people."

Jack recalled the words of Father Herlihy. The priest had guessed correctly that others were visiting Earth, too, and they were arriving undetected by the Agency's surveillance technology.

"But I'll get into more of that later," promised al-Rahiim. "First I want to fill you in on your real mission. The one that was kept from you. You've no doubt guessed at a lot of it but you should know the whole truth."

"Why couldn't I have been informed earlier? Why did I have to risk my identity in this horrific project?" Jack practically yelled.

"Why do you ask me a question you already know the answer to?"

"Damn right I know the answer. We were pawns, weren't we? Receptacles. A whole population to choose from for your VIP collection."Jack paused for a moment to shake his head. "All these people, unlucky enough to have famous counterparts in other realities, had their lives stripped from them? Einstein, Gandhi, Roosevelt? What could possible justify this?"

Al-Rahiim had an answer prepared. "At first, when we were new to these incursions, we asked for and got volunteers. Willing participants to be receptacles. We owe a lot of our scientific and social development to these great minds from other realities. As time went on, however, all of the volunteers descended into insanity and death. We're still not sure why, but we did eventually find a simple way to preserve the transplanted minds. It involved preconditioning and withholding the true missions from the receptacles. You were conditioned, Jack."

"Conditioned and lied to!"

"Yes, conditioned and lied to."

"Am I going to go insane?" asked Jack softly.

"I don't know. You're an unusual case. You've been conditioned, but you figured out the receptacle plan in mid-download. You are angrier than I've ever known you to be, but for good cause I suppose. If it helps, I'm now dedicated to terminating the program."

That statement seemed to mollify Jack. Or at least Jack had exhausted his anger. JFK, on the other hand, had been silent through the exchange between his altar ego and Proconsul al-Rahiim. He had become comfortable with the bizarre idea of personality downloads and parallel realities by tapping the knowledge of his alter ego, Jack, and he was taking in all of these newest revelations.

"Obviously, you're taking a risk by meeting with us," said Jack. "I appreciate that. What did you want to tell us?"

"First, I wanted to establish contact with you. I've come to be wary of my alien benefactors and we may need to counteract them at some time."

"Oh yes. I wanted to get back to them. But why choose me to help you?"

"Who else? I can't go to the Agency. They suspect I'm alive and are suspicious of my new agenda. Besides, I've known both of you to be reasonable men. You will support the common good."

"Does that mean you think your new friends are hostile to the common good?"

"Maybe. Although they've impressed me with their position on our activities. They say that what our Agency is doing in observing other realities is just as dangerous as tampering with them." Al-Rahiim had learned a great deal from the aliens' explanations.

"You know I always wondered about that. The Uncertainty Principle, isn't it? When observing an experiment changes the result?"

"We're not talking sub-atomic particles here, but yes, that's the idea. I've reviewed their records and have seen enough precedent to believe them. Apparently they went through a similar phase of proactive monitoring as we're in now."

"What happened to make you suspicious of them then?"

"For one, they just tried to kill you."

"The black man was one of them?"

"Not exactly. They aren't like us physically. The man who attacked you was an individual engineered from the DNA blueprint of an abductee. That man's name was Barney Hill. His doppelganger is a hit man for them." Al-Rahiim was quite relieved that Jack hadn't died.

"I wondered where that teleportation technology came from. We don't have anything like that. Why did they want me dead?"

"Killing you was their simple solution. Eliminate someone directly interacting with the locals. To their way of thinking, interaction is far worse than just observing. And it requires a drastic response. So be careful. I don't know what their plans will be after that failed attempt. I don't even know what their plans are concerning me. After all, I'm interacting with their reality." Al-Rahiim hoped to stay one step ahead of his captors.

"Thanks for the news."

"There's more."

"I was hoping so. You've yet to tell me about these aliens."

"I'll get to that. And believe me it'll be worth the wait. But we have higher priorities."

"For instance?"

"The Religionists are involved, as I thought. They tried to instigate a war between East and West during the so-called Cuban Missile Crisis. They didn't account for JFK's reasoned approach though."

"I'm complimented," said JFK. "Did they have anything to do with my assassination?"

"No. That was a natural event in this universe, Mr. President." The proconsul was a bit awed at talking with such a historically significant figure.

"Who was responsible?" pressed Kennedy.

"It was Oswald alone, sir. A misguided man presented a chance opportunity to gain notoriety. I'm sorry, Mr. President."

"Is that all?" asked Jack.

"I wish it was. The Religionists are still hell bent on destroying this reality. And they believe their best chance lies in starting a nuclear war. That would bring this reality into a collision course with an adjacent one.

"My hosts seem to be trying to prevent that, but they too are opposed by a splinter group like our Religionists. All I know about them is that they're called the Others, and they tried to prevent your assassin from arriving on Earth."

"They sound like nice people."

"Maybe I'll try to sort it all out with the help of my host's technology. Jack, hold out your hand."

Jack did so warily. The image of the proconsul removed something from an inside pocket of his jacket and depressed what must have been a button with his thumb. Almost immediately a thin object the size of his palm materialized in Jack's hand.

"That will allow you to personally phase-shift like our tour buses," advised al-Rahiim. "But unlike our technology, it will enable you to adjust how much of a shift you want. It's a continuous scale. Remember that if the Agency's phase-shifted agents catch up with you. They can only phase three degrees."

Jack examined the compact device in his hand. The apparent control was a dial in the middle of the dark-blue front that seemed painted on. He was about to ask how to use it but then somehow the operation seemed obvious to him. Impressive, he thought. The Agency needed machinery about the size of a steamer trunk to do the same thing.

"So your hosts agree with us. That there is a danger if realities collide?" asked Jack.

"They strongly believe so. At least as far as that's concerned we're on the same page as they."

"All right, now tell me. Who are they?"

"My rescuers are a people alien to us in looks and origins. They are not from any Earth."

"An alien people? From where?"

"Mars."

"Mars? Are you joking? There's no life on Mars."

"There's no life on Mars in any reality we've explored. Apparently they're from yet another parallel universe. One where conditions allowed that planet to spawn intelligent life."

Jack looked skeptical.

"Given your experience, is it that hard for you to imagine such a possibility? What's more, they, the Martians and their archaeologists, unearthed artifacts of an unimaginably more ancient civilization on Mars. One that may have had some interaction with intelligent life on both worlds. At least in their universe, anyway. Some of the Martians speculate that those ancients may still be monitoring us. But since the artifacts are billions of years old, no one seriously believes it."

Jack finally spoke. "We never really had a handle on any of this, did we? Sounds like we were fooling ourselves to think we were policing existence. It's bigger than any of us could even conceive, much less manage."

"I still believe we were effective even if only in a small way. And the Martians may yet prove to be our allies."

"Sure. If the Others don't thwart them like the Religionists thwart us."

"I know it sounds daunting, Jack. But you just became aware of these other players. You'll get used to the idea as I have. There still seem to be just two opposing sides. One that tries to preserve the different realities' natural evolution, and another that tries to change them for misguided or destructive purposes."

Jack took a deep breath. "How can we be sure of that now? Didn't you say a mysterious ancient race may still be around. If so, what's their purpose? How are they affecting us? I just wonder if we're doing the right thing."

Al-Rahiim didn't disagree completely. "You may have a valid point, but until we have solid evidence to disprove our beliefs, we'll just have to proceed based on the information we have. It's all we can do. Trust in our science and continue to protect parallel realities from interference by adjacent ones. Even the Martians with their superior science believe in that. They're even more meticulous than we are at eliminating interference."

"Yes. I gathered so. They tried to kill me."

That did worry al-Rahiim. "Yes, well, I'll try to talk to them out of that. Try to use some diplomacy. I think I'm reading them right, though, when I sense that they have little appetite for another bold incursion. It would leave too big a footprint on this universe for their tastes."

"I hope you're right."

"Leave it to me. If I can't dissuade them, I'll let you know. I have to sign off now, but I'll be in touch."

Al-Rahiim vanished abruptly, leaving Jack/JFK alone with their thoughts.

The addition of the Martians and their adversaries, the Others, as well as a mysterious ancient race made life seem a lot more complicated. In spite of the implications, however, Jack was fascinated by this new revelation. History in a reality with intelligence on Earth and Mars must've been fantastic. How would each race have reacted to the discovery of the other? What did that mysterious ancient race feel when they observed such a meeting?

CHAPTER 17

Alternate Mars

The minds of an entire race followed the progress of its probe into the young solar system. So vast were these minds that they could split their concentration in nearly limitless divisions and monitor their various works across space-time. Now, they perceived a revolving disk of debris surrounding a newly ignited sun. The accretion process had already begun, with perhaps four, possibly five, rocky worlds to be formed.

The probe valued nothing more greatly than sentient life, and this system held promise due to the size of its sun, the amount of material available, and the likely orbits of still forming planets. The development of intelligence would take time, however, as the ongoing, violent creation of these worlds so far left too hostile an environment for organic existence. Another billion or more years would be needed.

The probe completed its survey and prepared to leave, but not before depositing a presence that was also a catalyst for life. The system was now seeded with life's chemistry. Only time and the mechanism of random chance were required to produce a biological structure capable of spawning some form of self-aware being with intelligence. Once that being sprang from the primordial slime, the catalyst would protect it from competitors.

A creature remarkably similar to a bush baby climbed down from his home in the forest canopy. It foraged at night to avoid the jungle predators. Its large eyes, keenly adapted to night living, spied several of its favorite food insects. The little animal scurried at once to the manufactured hills that teemed with the activity of industrious insects. Feasting on the unlucky colony, the bush baby constantly scanned his surroundings. Even the unearthly darkness was no guarantee of safety.

With slowly awakening intelligence, his kind had started to master the rudiments of a language. Armed with this important tool, they communicated experiences to enlighten and warn. This bush baby had been impressed by crude accounts of a new breed of predator, carnivores that were becoming more and more adept at night hunting. Indeed, with the sun more than 140 million miles away, most of the creatures on the planet had to operate in faint light.

Happily chomping away on his insect dinner, the little creature's ears pricked up to the sound of danger. A stealthy pad nearly indistinguishable from the rest of the noises of the forest aroused his attention. He felt the approach more than he heard it, as the ground transmitted the vibration. Stopping his chewing, he trained all his senses on the leafy fastness surrounding him.

There, in the anemic twilight, stood a creature of nightmare. The most frightening jungle carnivores would be no more than prey to this monster. Its scimitar teeth were nearly as long as the bush baby's body. Even in daylight, this killing machine would blend into the forest with its green-and-brown striped camouflage. A jungle cat, about a dozen feet high at the shoulder, stalked the night. The little forager had never seen this kind of animal out this late, but the long-lasting drought had stressed the wildlife, forcing them into unusual behavior patterns.

The bush baby remained still. The safety of the trees was nearby, but the giant cat could nearly reach the top of some of them on its hind legs. The small forager knew it wouldn't have time to climb out of range before the monster was upon him. It also knew that the cat knew he was there but not exactly where.

The feline started to emit the low growl typical of its kind. It was trying to provoke a reaction, get its prey to give away its position. When that didn't happen, it stepped into the clearing. By now, the insects crawled on the bush baby, stinging it, yet it dared not move.

The big cat sniffed the air and edged ever closer. Its eyes were huge but not disproportionately so. If the two small moons had been full, it would've been able to see its prey, but the moonlight seldom lit the jungle floor.

With the cat nearly on top of it, the little forager resigned itself to making a risky dash for safety. If it could reach a tree and keep the trunk between it and the monster, it might have a chance. Just as it was about to bolt, the cat yelped, turned its head, and licked at its hind quarters furiously. The insects had found a tender spot as they climbed the giant invader's legs. In that instant, the bush baby dashed for the nearest tree.

When the cat turned back, the night forager was already climbing the trunk. With two mighty bounds, the cat was at the tree but fate intervened another time in the bush baby's favor. Looking into the monster's eyes, the semi-intelligent forager noticed a reddish flare. The predator's eyes reflected a cosmic calamity.

Four light minutes nearer to the sun, the third planet was hit by an equally large planetary mass that liquefied most of both bodies. Even though the molten rock lit the heavens in the solar neighborhood, the phenomena would not have been visible on the night side of Mars had it not reflected off an artificial satellite, the ancient catalyst. The catalyst left behind by the solar probe a billion years earlier sported a highly polished surface that naturally reflected energy.

The predator was temporarily blinded as the bush baby climbed to safer territory. It had been saved, but more than that its increasingly intelligent descendants would be spared from future competition for the solar system. Intelligent life would never arise on the third planet.

One-hundred-million years later, the whole of the fourth planet resembled the insect hill that the bush baby had feasted on. This time, however, it was his intelligent, large-eyed descendants who engaged in the industrious activity. And the bulk of that activity concerned itself with providing water for the thirsty billions. Most of the world forest had disappeared in favor of a more diverse, although drier, landscape. There were small oceans but the majority of the civilization's watery resources were funneled from the poles in sophisticated canal systems. The populace went about their business confident that their otherwise dry world would provide enough water, given the government's infrastructure.

Unconcerned with this vital resource, two scientists occupied a lab in the capital city of their world. The object of their scrutiny lay on the table in front of them, the alien relic commonly known as the Artifact. It had fascinated not only their generation but several previous generations. What ancient technology had spawned this device? Since its original discovery, the question had resounded throughout antiquity.

The Artifact had proven to be a sophisticated computer and sentient being, all at once. It had long since ceased functioning, but it revealed that it had witnessed the birth of the inner planets. Only recently was Martian science able to plumb its memory. The secrets the Artifact disclosed were unbelievable, but each scientific advance confirmed this account of cosmic history. A controversial interpretation held that Martian primacy in the solar system was due to the actions of this sentinel. Purportedly, this device had prevented the rise of intelligent life on the third planet. Life that would have aggressively competed with the Martian race for resources and control.

"This probe, or whatever it is, doesn't seem to have been aware of alternate universes," said Mr. Lek.

"Yes," responded Mr. Bix. "Odd that such an obviously sophisticated society didn't discover what we have."

"That's not what I was thinking about."

"Oh?"

"I was considering the infinite possibilities that make up the other realities. There must've been one in which sentient life arose on both Mars and Earth."

"You're right. I wonder how we would've fared with another intelligent species right next door."

"If you believe the theory that the probe exterminated life on Earth, then you have to wonder what it was afraid of, either for itself or us."

Lucius climbed the marble steps of the government building. A portentous wind rippled through his clothing carrying the chill of autumn. He didn't notice. He was preoccupied with how he would start his conversation with the senator. The senator, a long-time friend, would not be pleased with what was about to drop in his lap.

"Hello, Lucius," said the senator with a hug and a handshake.

"Hello, Senator," replied Lucius.

"Hello, Senator? Not hello, Marc? Surely this isn't an official visit."

"Well, to be honest, Senator, I'm here on formal business. And I don't think you're going to like what I have to say."

"You know, I felt something was wrong when you came in. Guess we've spent too much time together. Sit down. Tell me what's bothering you."

"I'll just get right to the point. I think you'll have to reopen last year's committee investigations." Lucius said this as carefully as possible.

"Lucius, this had better not be a joke. You know I never wanted to be dragged into that charade. I was very happy to leave it far behind me."

"I wish I were joking, Senator, but there's been another incident, this time involving an unimpeachable witness. A government witness who has already rallied support for further investigations."

The senator put his face in his hands. "As if we don't have enough problems. I didn't think people were that gullible in this day and age. Well, what is it this time? Crazed religious zealots given rides on unidentified flying objects?"

"No. No zealots. It was me."

At That Moment in Orbit

A wedge-shaped craft, the center of frenzied activity, received and launched shuttles continuously. Mr. Kue peered out the large viewing window and experienced momentary blindness when the sun reflected off one of the shuttles angling to return. It caught him daydreaming. He mentally chastised himself for being mesmerized by the blue planet below. So blue, he thought. Blue with the precious compound that his planet so desperately needed. Unlike the homeworld, even the clouds that swirled below him were laden with water, not dust. A planet rich in the substance of life, yet now, one that might be off-limits.

"Your eminence?" asked a junior associate to get his attention.

"Yes?" replied Mr. Kue without turning around.

"You asked for some information?"

"Yes, please report."

"The natives of this world know of our planet. Some have even guessed that it may harbor life. But so far they haven't associated our visits with our homeworld, their neighbor. At least for now we're safe. But in spite of all of their many languages, word of our presence is spreading quickly as you predicted. Worst of all, one of their more aggressive nation states in the West is investigating our covert appearances."

Mr. Kue turned to face his junior. "I must learn how this happened. Is Mr. Lyx back on board?"

"He is, your eminence."

"Good. Send him in please."

The officer left the room and was soon replaced by Mr. Lyx.

"The council expects our report, Mr. Lyx. Why weren't we able to keep this planet ignorant of us?" asked Mr. Kue.

"First, your eminence, I want you to know that I accept punishment without malice. I'll try to do a better job serving those, now like myself, who will be left behind on the home world."

Mr. Kue waved the comment aside. "I'm not convinced that there was anything you could have done better. And even though honor demands it, I do appreciate your sacrifice of a place in the evacuation."

"Thank you, your eminence."

Mr. Kue wanted to make a rational evaluation of the situation. "You may yet find life possible on our dry world while we perish in the unknown voids between the stars. It's a calculated risk. One that I doubt your generation appreciates. The scheme to move as many offworld as we can is an adventure that may not deliver us to safety. Even if we make it to another world with water, it may be inhabited by a race at least as aggressive as the one on this world."

"That doesn't seem likely," objected his subordinate. "Even in our most distant barbarous past, I've never heard of anything that rivals the savagery of this race."

Mr. Kue turned toward Lyx and peered into his incandescent eyes. "Please tell me what happened. How did they find out about us?"

"Well, we were setting up the mass driver at the landlocked body of water. The storage tanker was in low orbit, and we were almost prepared to start the process when one of their military units rounded the point of the beach."

"You had scanned the area previously?"

"Of course. But apparently some element in the landscape hid them from our instruments."

Mr. Kue nodded in understanding. "This planet is rich in materials and ores. I'm not surprised that something blocked your sensors. Tell me about the man. The one called Lucius."

"He was the only one who didn't flee. Somehow our illusions didn't dissuade him. He approached us, brazenly. At this point we were unaware that he had the ability to see through our facades."

"Another reason to worry. If he's the first of many to evolve this special trait, that's one less defense we have against them."

"Anyway, we were able to use the mind beam to subdue him and take him on board our shuttle."

"Why did you do that?" Mr. Kue grimaced.

"We wanted to examine him. See if we could discover how he was able to defeat our illusions. But I'm afraid this was our error. Before we had him through the entrance, he also defeated the mind beam. I don't think he consciously tried to defeat it. It was the reflexive response of a sub-mind that's still evolving in his race. At that point, we tried to subdue him physically. But he, being bred to this world's gravity, overpowered us all and easily broke away. He escaped, having seen us and our craft. And since we were in mental contact with him, he probably has knowledge of our operation."

"I see. And you're sure this was an official of the aggressive state?"

"Yes. He's already spreading the word to certain of his people. Very unlikely that they'll dismiss it or cover it up. Especially with how much he knows. And who he is."

Mr. Kue groaned. "Based on what you've told me, then, I don't see any alternative but to recommend to the council that we quit this world immediately. Even for water we can't risk provoking them. And they're so easily provoked. Let's hope for our racial survival that they have short memories. "

"Wouldn't we have any hope of reasoning with them?"

"Perhaps in the future. Maybe by the time they develop the ability to come to our world, they'll have matured as a race. Our specialists predict that that will be in your great grandchildren's time. If you survive till then, you may be able to come to terms with them. If not, you castaways will envy us even if we lie in interstellar tombs." Mr. Kue truly saw the future as grim.

"Maybe we could fight. Our technology is superior."

"It's not in our makeup. We didn't evolve in the kind of competitive environment that they did. It's given them a huge capacity for savagery. They would eventually overcome any advantage we might hold now. Sometimes I wonder if our people would be better off with that kind of mentality. No, we'll have to bet on the stars for our survival. Stars with planets in the habitable zone with liquid water. Hopefully, they won't be able to follow us out of this system too soon."

Almost Simultaneously on Earth

On the beach, the Martians stood as still as statues, totally surprised by the interruption of their clean-up process. Once again, a band of humans approached. Eventually, sensing the humans' intent, the Martians tried their natural defenses. Some of the humans faltered, obviously affected by the illusion. The leader, however, immune, exerted greater control over his subordinates. The humans kept advancing. Within arm's reach, the docile Martians succumbed to the savagery of humanity, and in the process lost their lives, their instruments, and perhaps the survival of their race.

In a tavern frequented by senators and government officials, two men furtively moved into the back room.

"Marc, are you sure this room is secure?"

"Not only has it been secure since I became senator, but since my father did before me. There'll be no leaks. Now tell me, Lucius, has our crisis passed?"

"It seems to have. But I just can't help feeling that it was too easy. We can only hope they won't be back someday in force and with more resolve. So I don't think it's a good idea to let down our guard. I know you don't agree, but I still think we should mobilize the public. Enlist their help for the future."

"Lucius, I'm not disagreeing that someday that may become necessary but right now we're at war," countered Marc. "And our more earthly enemies, much to our shame, did a lot of damage with their surprise attack. We need our people focused on the rebuilding effort in the here and now. So let's not divert state funds to disappearing demons when our future is at stake."

"Okay, you've made your point but I'm going to take you up on your suggestion to keep a record of all this. Agreed?" Lucius felt uneasy enough not to let the matter simply drop.

"Agreed, but bury it somewhere till the time comes when we may need it."

"I suppose I can live with that."

Still Later

The speaker droned on for what seemed like a lot longer than his allotted hour. His monotone filled the auditorium like static from poorly tuned in radio stations. The audience of approximately 80 internationally recognized astronomers squirmed in their seats. Some of the more distracted in the group contemplated the high arched ceiling.

"Is this day ever going to end?" whispered John to his colleague seated next to him.

"Look, you wanted a couple of free meals, didn't you? Well this is the price," replied Jennifer. "But cheer up. Things are about to get better... or at least a little more bizarre."

"You mean the next speaker? It's about time. This is the guy with the theory that you lured me here for, right?"

"Uh, huh."

"So, what's he going to talk about?"

"I told you before. You'll have to hear it for yourself to believe it. So stop trying to pry it out of me."

"Okay but this better be good."

The current speaker finished up, and Dr. Reed Cotter climbed the steps to the stage then confidently approached the podium. He signaled to someone in the back, whereupon the movie screen behind him displayed a picture of Mars.

"Good morning, ladies and gentlemen. I'm sure you'll all recognize this picture as one taken from *Viking 2* while still approaching Mars."

A bored murmur of consent rose from the audience.

"I know we're all ready to go, but I think you'll find this next bit worthwhile. If you'll please indulge me for a moment, I'd like to review the prevailing consensus about the natural history of Mars. One: Mars is currently a lifeless world. Most certainly absent of any sentient life whatever is said about microbes that might have lived there in the past. Two: Mars holds no liquid water, at least on the surface. Three: whatever our predecessors imagined about the planet, we now know that its surface more closely resembles our moon's rather than Earth's. Four: and this is important, our present knowledge suggests that there was once liquid water on Mars. Some have estimated as recently as 300 million years ago."

He paused for effect. "Have any of you ever read Percival Lowell's observations of Mars?"

Some people tentatively nodded.

"Just to get everybody on the same page, Percival Lowell created quite a sensation back in the 1890s. He had some interesting theories on the purpose of the so-called canals. In his published opinion, he stated that the canals were obviously the work of intelligent beings. And the reason they were constructed was to channel water from the poles to fertilize an otherwise dying world. The last desperate act of people—Martians—prolonging their existence on a world with vanishing supplies of this necessary component of life. Certainly these were self-delusions. Well, ladies and gentlemen, I have evidence to prove that he nearly had it right."

"Now do we have your attention?" whispered Jennifer to an open-mouthed John.

"Shhh, I'm listening!" he answered.

"Sure, Mars is now a world absent of any intelligent life, probably due to lack of water. But there was water there. And it was there a lot more recently than 300 million years or even 3,000 years ago. How do I know this, you ask? Would you be surprised if I told you that this information didn't come from direct observation of the planet? Or for that matter even from an astronomer?"

He paused to enjoy the expressions on his audience's faces.

"A friend of mine in the archaeology department, one Professor Remington, introduced me to two men whom he met on a dig in Italy. These two men have provided me with this information about Mars in their log recordings. Recordings, I should say, that have been secreted away from the rest of us for a very long time. You see these men kept records on their efforts to prevent a sentient race of Martians from raiding our water supply. They didn't realize who it was at the time. But the materials they confiscated in battle have the same trace elements and, yes, even the microbe evidence that was found recently in some Martian meteorites. The names of the two men are Lucius Catalus and Marcus Augusta. Both high officials of the Republic of Rome around the time when Hannibal's army crossed the Alps. That, ladies and gentleman, was about 2,200 years ago."

PART V

Time Marches On

CHAPTER 18

January 1968

The temperature was remarkably comfortable on this day in the Indochinese jungle. Jack, continuing his tour of the war zone, harkened back to his PT boat days while island hopping in the Pacific theater. Oddly enough, he found it to be a pleasant memory despite the constant tension then of imminent engagement with the Japanese.

The path started to get narrower as he proceeded. Obviously, this section was less well traveled. Taking out his machete, he hacked his way through thickening jungle growth. The sunlight became diffused as it struggled to penetrate the leafy canopy. Even the ever-present green turned dark, then almost gray with the severely filtered light. Every now and then, water would rain down as Jack disturbed an elevated frond cupping the liquid. He also noted that his microsentinals turned into equal parts bug repellent and sentinel. Frequently, he would perceive a miniature aerial dogfight between his hovering defenses and an aggressive insect.

Up ahead, Jack spied what he looked for. A crudely concealed pit hid the entrance of a manmade tunnel. The tunnels were a favorite hideaway for the Viet Cong. Lifting the camouflage, Jack entered and replaced the concealment.

The crude tunnel was poorly lit by torches at regular intervals. The president's newfound enhancements compensated for the sporadic illumination and provided him a clear picture of his surroundings. Further up, he heard voices, tense voices that told Jack a serious operation was being discussed. From his days as a roving senator, he recognized the Indochinese dialect.

The tunnel opened out into a room with walls just as crude as the rest of the underground complex. Three men stood gathered around a table pouring over several maps. Jack remembered enough of his military training to identify the documents as plans of attack. It confirmed his fears that the Viet Cong intended to use the Tet celebrations as a cover for their operation.

Having come to a consensus, the group started to disband. One of the men turned away from the table and walked to the tunnel entrance where Kennedy stood. The startled president froze as the man passed through him. *This phase-shifting takes some getting used to,* he thought. His alter ego chastised him for not sharing control of his mind since if JFK had, he wouldn't have been startled.

Later that month, across several population centers of South Vietnam, 84,000 men stormed the unprepared country. The news inflamed the American public who recently had taken General Westmoreland at his word that the U.S. was winning the war. Political pressure to seek an end of American involvement strengthened.

In Saigon, Kennedy listened to the military radio broadcasts. The Tet Offensive had failed. Westmoreland was no fool, he conceded. The Viet Cong had gambled with almost all of its fighting force, and had lost, and now they were vulnerable. It was a great opportunity as the general said. The U.S. knew exactly where the enemy was, but would the public see it through?

June 1968

Jack blended into the crowd at the Embassy Ballroom of the Ambassador Hotel in Los Angeles. Robert Kennedy, a leading candidate in the Democratic primaries, delivered an upbeat and ultimately serious speech. Buoyed by his imminent California primary victory, he looked tired yet pleased. Jack was proud of his brother Bobby and decided he would approach him and reveal himself when the timing was right.

Concluding his speech with a victory sign, Bobby announced, "Now on to Chicago, and let's win there!"

The place erupted. "We want Bobby! We want Bobby!"

Grinning, Bobby made his way through a kitchen door that represented a shortcut to the press waiting in the Colonial Room. Jack opted not to follow his brother, but his microsentinels followed the crowd that surrounded the candidate. That distinguished crowd included football star Rosy Grier, decathlon champ Rafer Johnson, and writer George Plimpton.

As Senator Robert Kennedy slowly made his way forward, he noted the approach of one of the many hotel personnel. He prepared to shake the hand of yet another admirer, but the small, swarthy young man leveled a gun in Kennedy's direction and opened fire. Time seemed to slow down as the small caliber weapon flashed. Some of the crowd froze while observing the unreal calamity engulfing their political hero. Robert Kennedy fell sideways while others in the crowd dropped to the ground in an instinct of self-protection. Speechwriter Paul Schrader collapsed when one of the bullets hit him in the forehead.

Too late, the maitre d', Uecker, caught the shooter's gun arm and forced it down onto a steam table. Even then a third and a fourth shot fired into the crowd. Rosy Grier and Rafer Johnson among others struggled to neutralize the shooter. It took the better part of a minute, or seemingly an eternity, to wrest the gun from the assassin's fingers.

Shooting victims Senator Kennedy and his speechwriter sprawled on the floor in obvious pain. A seven-year-old was also caught in the kneecap. William Weisel, ABC-TV director, clutched at his stomach where he was shot. Another's hip had been shattered, and an artist lay unconscious, bleeding from the head.

Juan Romero, a busboy, fell to the floor beside his favorite candidate and pleaded, "Come on, Mr. Kennedy, you can make it."

He pressed a pair of rosary beads into the senator's upward palm. Bending over to hear the candidate, Juan made out the words, "Is everybody all right?"

Doctor Stanley Abo moved between Kennedy and his weeping wife, Ethel. He found a hole below and behind the right ear. Prodding the wound, he opened the coagulation to allow the free passage of blood, whereupon the senator's breathing became more regular. "You're doing good, sir," the doctor encouraged.

Jesse Unruh of the California State Assembly held the assassin in an armlock. The huge man released the gunman into the custody of two newly arrived police officers who couldn't hide their shock upon arriving at the scene. The policemen ushered their prisoner to the squad car parked outside the hotel, running the gauntlet of angry citizens shouting threats and invectives at their captive.

An ambulance hurried the injured Kennedy to Central Receiving Hospital a few minutes away. Ethel accompanied her husband in the vehicle along with some of his trusted advisors. The doctors at the hospital assessed the need for a neurosurgeon. Unfortunately, with no one of that specialization on site they rushed him to Good Samaritan Hospital.

At Good Samaritan, doctors discovered two more wounds on Senator Kennedy's side. Press secretary Frank Mankiewicz, in front of the hospital, reported to the press that Kennedy was about to undergo an operation.

"What's the senator's condition?" asked a reporter.

"Critical," replied Mankiewicz in a very serious tone.

Surgeons operated for three hours to remove a blood clot that had formed behind the brain, and as many fragments of metal and bone as they could. After the procedure, Kennedy could breathe by himself but had suffered an impairment of blood to the mid-brain. Now in critical care, he was under around-the-clock supervision. The next 12 to 36 hours would be crucial. At noon, an EEG test revealed Kennedy's brain waves to be below normal. Five hours later doctors called his condition extremely critical.

A dark, chilly night did not dissuade crowds from collecting outside. The outdoor conditions reflected the mood. A devoted public kept vigil till long after midnight. Their attention was trained on the hospital and a jury-rigged press center that occupied an auditorium across the street. At two in the morning on June 6th, almost 26 hours after the senator was shot, the crowd spied Press Secretary Mankiewicz leaving the hospital. His body language revealed nothing other than a listlessness. In the makeshift press room, he took his place as the crowd hushed.

Jack witnessed the announcement the same as the crowd even though he knew what was coming. His cheeks were streaked with tears while he stood in the street outside the hospital. Unlike others, however, he didn't provide or seek comfort from the surrounding people. At least he didn't appear to. Any observer would have said the man was in a trance.

"My brother Bobby died when he was twelve," said Jack to the president. "Being here in this reality was a gift to me, to see him as a man. The way I view it, you enjoyed thirty more years with a brother I never knew as an adult."

The president was silent in his own mind. He didn't respond to his alter ego but radiated an emotional pain that took hold of both personalities. Jack worried that JFK's state of mind would adversely affect the body that they both shared. The medical science of his world recognized the mind's effect on the body, a truism still denied in this reality. Jack feared the potential physical manifestations of the president's mindset if sustained. He could utilize the nanobots in his system to force the release of endorphins, but didn't know if the president would permit it.

"Why didn't they download my brother?" interrupted the president.

Jack knew that JFK understood the answer but seemed to want to vent.

"Well, for one thing, we didn't have a suitable receptacle. As I said, my brother Bobby died at twelve-years old. Drowned."

"I thought events paralleled those of our reality. How could he have drowned?"

"You don't know how many times I asked myself the same question as I relived the experience over and over again. And that was well before I knew anything about other universes. Or other Bobbys. For the longest time I was guilt ridden. I blamed myself because I couldn't maneuver our damn boat to him in time."

That seemed to impress the president enough to shake him out of his depression. "Yet now you have the same love of sailing that I do. How do you manage it?"

"Just channeled the emotional pain into something positive. I was determined that no one else would drown due to my poor seamanship."

The president could've expected that answer. He himself had done the same thing with personal tragedies most of his life.

"Is this interference?" asked the president in a newly angry tone. "Did someone want my brother dead?"

"It's possible, I suppose. I'm not sure if we'll ever know. Al-Rahiim couldn't even answer that now."

Both men were interrupted in their thoughts by an external voice.

"You okay, sir?" asked a policeman from his squad car.

The two conversationalists looked around them to note that the crowd had dispersed. It must have looked strange to the beat cop to see someone standing in the middle of the sidewalk oblivious to all.

"Yes, officer, thank you. I was just lost in thought."

"Can I drive you home?"

"No, I think I'd rather walk. It's been a trying night, and I could use the air."

The policeman looked as if he was deciding whether to press the issue or apply a sobriety test. The tone and appearance of Jack, however, didn't indicate a drunk or a dope addict. He would let it go.

"Okay. Be careful then," the officer said and drove on down the street at a leisurely pace.

Jack started to walk, knowing that the officer would watch in his rearview mirror for as long as he could.

Senator Kennedy's assassin, Sirhan Sirhan, occupied the news broadcasts for the next several days. By this time, JFK was numb to the endless speculation and conspiracy theories. With renewed vigor he planned and worked toward a personal goal that he decided to keep from everyone including al-Rahiim, if possible. He enjoyed his freedom even though he accepted the proconsul's direction more often than not. Life, such as it was, proceeded smoothly until October.

Sitting at a table at a cafe on the Cape, Jack sipped his coffee while in his own personal world. He engaged in an internal conversation when the voices of two middle-aged women jolted him.

"Can you believe it?" said the dark haired one.

"I never liked her," replied the woman with the scarf on her head. The garment didn't conceal her curlers very well.

"What are you talking about? You always said she was the best thing for the president."

"I mean I haven't liked her since the assassination. She's only out for herself. I just didn't know that before."

"Well if you're right she's really hit the big time. There'll be no wanting from now on for our Jackie."

"Except for maybe a husband of a decent age. Is all that money really worth marrying that ugly old Greek?"

"Let me see the picture again?"

A newspaper passed between the two. The caption read "Jackie marries Aristotle Onassis."

Jack sent his microsentinels over to view the picture of his widow broadly smiling as she walked with the bespectacled Greek tycoon. He nearly spit out his coffee.

"Easy, Mr. President," cautioned Jack. "It makes sense that she would remarry."

JFK fell silent, keeping his own council in the part of his brain that was sealed off from Jack. Even so, there was no hiding his anger from his other personality. They left the cafe and Jack noted that JFK's stride was more forceful than normal, as the president commandeered the body. He wasn't going to any specific location, but the way his feet pounded the pavement made his mood evident in spite of his self-control.

Abruptly, his attention diverted to a mental picture broadcast to his mind's eye by the microsentinels. Jack recognized the pattern of surveillance that he himself was trained to practice. He had been discovered by the Agency. Agents nonchalantly circled and attempted to tighten the trap. Jack casually continued his walk and didn't let on that he knew they were there. I got careless, he thought. Of course they'd lay a trap here. They know my preferences. The praetor has, no doubt, been notified and is mostly likely directing the operation to subdue and capture me.

Swiftly, Jack ducked into an alley between two shops but then waited. Jack knew that the other end would be covered by agents so he saw no use in trying to escape that way. Momentarily, two large muscular men ran into the alley from the same entryway. They practically skidded to a stop, surprised to see their quarry casually waiting for them.

Time to use the phase-shifter that al-Rahiim gave me, thought Jack.

The proconsul's words rang prophetic since he'd predicted the device would be handy if Jack encountered agents. They could phase-shift too, but only three degrees off the plane of existence. Jack's device allowed him infinite adjustment to shift as much or as little as he liked in order to avoid the agents. In the instant that Jack reached into his pocket for it, JFK launched their shared body into their pursuers. Caught off guard, Jack allowed the president the use of his abilities.

The president utilized the genetically and biomechanically enhanced body to great effect. He kicked the nearest man in the mid-section doubling him over. The speed of his attack caught by surprise the second man, who succumbed to a powerfully thrown punch to the face that staggered him.

Meanwhile, the doubled-over agent recovered enough to tackle Jack. With unnatural quickness, though, Jack sufficiently avoided the charge to remain on his feet despite being precariously balanced. As the tackler glanced off him, Jack gave the man additional impetus to send him face first into the wall. The agent's head jerked up from the impact.

All of a sudden, a thunderous concussion caught Jack's jaw as the previously staggered assailant connected with a roundhouse punch. Jack's head spun from the impact, but it would take more than that to hurt him, due to his enhanced constitution. The only standing attacker, however, pinned Jack's arms with a full nelson and waited for his partner to recover so they could finish the job.

The man on the ground slowly rose and wiped away the blood that oozed from his nose. Looking at the supposedly helpless Jack, he moved to him, no doubt anticipating delivering a pounding. Jack, however, kicked the man in the face, knocking him unconscious. With the same foot, he kicked backward landing the hard heel of his shoe squarely on his captor's shin. The man let out a groan and released his hold. Jack spun around and relished the moment as he lined up the man's face with a vicious haymaker. An instant later, both agents lay unconscious at his feet.

"Did you enjoy that?" Jack asked the president.

"God damn right I did, as President Truman used to say. I needed to blow off some steam considering the way this year has been going for me. This came in very handy."

"Well I hope you've had enough because other agents are running our way. Can we use the phase-shifter now?"

The president took it out of his pocket and dialed up a domain out of the reach of the Agency.

Later in the year, Jack's old nemesis, Nixon, won the presidency. He campaigned on the promise to end the Vietnam War and in TV ads decried the opposition party for its penchant for starting wars. *Are you tired of Democratic wars?* the commercial asked, suggesting a tendency of the Republicans to favor peace over the warlike Democrats.

"This has been a hell of a year," thought JFK to his co-personality. "A cut-and-run policy effectively worked for Nixon as a slogan."

"I think you're handling it remarkably well," said Jack. "Regarding the bigger picture though, we haven't detected any interference. It seems that all events are proceeding normally for this universe. Nixon was supposed to be elected. Even al-Rahiim seems pleased."

"Forgive me for dwelling on some of my own personal sorrows. It's difficult to see one's life work go down the tubes."

"Meaning that the Republicans are in office?"

"Yes, but mostly the ending of my brother's political ambitions. He would have made a fine president. And I can't forget that my kids are being raised by someone else. Not someone I approve of either. What kind of life lessons are they being taught?"

Jack changed the subject. "Nixon won on the promise of ending the war in Southeast Asia. Wasn't that something you wanted?"

"If it's done smartly and with minimal damage to our international position. I fear that the news has simply steeled the Viet Cong. They'll dig in, knowing that they just have to wait for our departure. And if that's the case, it'll be a big embarrassment. Tough to deal meaningfully with the international community after that." JFK had lost none of his political instincts despite being dead and sharing a body with a man from another universe.

"Do you think Nixon will be so easy to predict?" asked Jack.

"I hope that I'm wrong about him."

March 1969

In the region where Cambodia, Laos, and South Vietnam met, peasants tended their terraced rice patties on a crystal clear day. Their pointed hats bobbed up and down while they worked. A slight breeze rustled the clothes hanging to dry near their huts and houses. All was quiet but for the sounds of birds that occasionally settled and splashed in flooded patches left by the wooden irrigation system. This far from the population centers, the people were totally oblivious of the war around them. They regarded the changing regimes with total indifference since it had no impact on their daily lives. They worked hard but were happy. Generations worked the fields in ways that had hardly varied over the course of centuries. The life provided food, activity, and fresh air and water. Villagers enjoyed each other's company, and their modest expectations meant few wants. Contentment reigned undisturbed.

But now, one of the older women stopped her chores and looked up. A sound had disturbed her, a far-off sound from the sky. Eventually, the droning grew loud enough for all to stop and examine the sky. Something was coming.

Planes came into view, many planes. They frightened the woman. From her perch on the side of a hill, she saw things dropping from them as they neared. Her vision took in the sight as if it were in slow motion, but when the bombs hit, things speeded up. The bombs rained down close enough to the village to hit their fields. People started running in all directions. The woman just stood there and wondered if she were dreaming.

At the U.S. Military Control Center in South Vietnam, members of all branches of the service monitored the progress of Operation Menu.

"Target Lunch has been destroyed with no casualties, sir," said an eager lieutenant.

The general to whom he directed the statement just grunted. *Of course there are no casualties,* he thought. *The enemy are only farmers. This is what we get when a president dictates strategy. Nixon thinks he can have it both ways. Withdraw the troops but bomb the enemy into submission before we leave. Damn fool!*

In another part of the country, Major Colin Powell observed the war from the ground. He knew the situation better than most and was under no illusions. The war was being lost. Maddeningly, the war was being lost in spite of their visiting huge losses on the Viet Cong during the Tet Offensive. A competent military backed by intelligent policy makers could have won the conflict handily. Not naive to politics, however, Powell knew the American public had lost its appetite for further war plans. *In the future, these wars will be fought smarter,* Powell vowed. *What we need is a doctrine to avoid the mistakes we've made here.*

Jack conversed with al-Rahiim. As usual the proconsul appeared to him as a semi-transparent figure.

"Can't seem to get you off the water," observed the proconsul.

"Our species belong to the sea," responded Jack. "It refreshes us."

"Some more than others. This boat is a bit more ramshackle than you're used to, isn't it?"

"It's what I salvaged from a fishing village after one of our bombing runs. I'll return it when I'm done," Jack promised with a laugh.

Al-Rahiim noted Jack's use of the word 'our' and wondered if the president's personality was subsuming Jack's.

"I've observed your visual logs," continued the proconsul. "There is definitely interference with the Cold War, but I'm still trying to determine if the Vietnam War is being manipulated."

"I can't see why the Religionists would bother with it," observed Jack. "We seem to be doing a fine job of needlessly prolonging this conflict by ourselves. The VC were beaten after the Tet Offensive was thrown back, yet we didn't pursue our advantage. Although even if we had, I'm not sure the war could've been salvaged. We had lost the battle for the moral high ground long before this."

Jack looked out to sea and seemed far away. "You know why?" he continued.

"Tell me."

"Because we allowed the unlawful assassination of Diem, leader of this sovereign country, and our ally in this war."

"All right, I'll play devil's advocate with you," said the proconsul. "President Diem became an embarrassment over his treatment of the Buddhists. How could we allow him to continue to slaughter them?"

"We could've stopped his abuse of the Buddhists in other ways. Brought political or economic pressure to bear."

"Do you think we would have been any better off if he were still in power? He wasn't exactly rallying support."

"We sure as hell didn't gain the people's confidence after his execution. By encouraging the coup in '63 we stripped the government of all legitimacy. I didn't learn my lesson with the Bay of Pigs. I trusted the wrong people. Butchers, as it turned out."

Both men became silent but for different reasons. A breeze blew Jack's already tousled hair, though al-Rahiim was unaffected since his presence was just a projection. Almost to himself, Jack muttered a regret. "I still can't believe I allowed that to get out of hand. No wonder the south is collapsing."

Now the proconsul lost patience with the president's dominant personality. "Jack, we didn't allow anything. That was not our doing. Did you forget this isn't our reality? Not our war."

"Whether it is or isn't, we own it now."

"Nixon got elected on the promise to disown it. I believe he's sincere in his desire to end this war."

"He's still trying to win it though. Drawing down our forces while at the same time stepping up the bombing? Who's he trying to fool?"

"Well, in any case, I can't see this conflict escalating into a third world war." Al-Rahiim tried to turn around the conversation.

"I agree but we shouldn't take anything for granted."

"We'll continue to monitor it. Hopefully we can avoid having you intervene again like you had to during the Tet Offensive."

July 1969

Jack relaxed in his city apartment while watching a news special on his color television. The front windows overlooked a fairly empty Boston Common. Considering the clear summer day, the park was unusually quiet even in view of the warm, humid conditions. Typically, people didn't stay indoors on hot summer afternoons. In spite of the humidity, Jack remained comfortable by virtue of an air conditioner. Rare, even for the well-to-do, the device kept Jack cool, leaving him undistracted as he concentrated on the broadcast.

Jack's fortunes had risen dramatically since he'd entered this reality. Some savvy business deals that he attributed to the president, but which were guided by his own knowledge of the progression of technology, made living here a much more comfortable proposition. Jack had come a long way since he'd first moved into a Dorchester apartment.

Jack absentmindedly accepted a tall, cool iced tea from Niles Babineaux, a business associate whom he had come to trust more and more. At the same time, Jack riveted his attention on the scene playing out on the TV screen.

Walter Cronkite conversed with various experts in trying to communicate the wonder of technology to the television audience. The prelude took hours as each of the networks scrambled to cover and make sense of the greatest event in human history. Cronkite seemed giddy while the time ticked down to the lunar landing.

One of Jack's other guests, Jean, watched but not with the same introspection. She was a bundle of nervous energy who constantly asked questions.

The rest of his guests were quiet as if they didn't want Jack to regret his invitation to watch his color TV with him. They'd all piled into the living room, and for the most part, watched in silence. For a brief moment Jack allowed himself to appreciate their friendship. They were the closest thing he had to family these days and in some ways were even closer.

He especially looked forward to having time alone with Eva after the group left. What a stunning profile, he thought. She reminded him of Inga Arvad, a reporter with the *Times-Herald* whom he'd dated early on in the war. A Nordic beauty who was twice married, she'd taught him things about sex but also about relationships. Jack often wondered what life would have been like with Inga Binga, as he'd liked calling her.

Eventually, the Lunar Module or LEM, as it was known by

the astronauts, separated from the command module and started its descent. Television sets around the world allowed for an inspection of the mottled lunar surface at a distance never imagined. Eventually the features became clearer, and viewers could make out smaller details like boulders and small craters. As the LEM continued its descent, the surface appeared to rush by, causing most of the billion watchers to hold their breaths. Jack, too, wondered if all was well.

Soon, however, the background slowed and came into ever better focus as the distance between moon and spacecraft decreased. Finally, the motion stopped amid a slight puff of sand. Jack tried to listen to the transmission between mission control and the LEM as his guests erupted in applause and cheers.

"We copy you down, Eagle," reported Houston.

"Houston, Tranquility base here. The Eagle has landed."

"Roger, Tranquility. We copy you on the ground. We've got a bunch of guys about to turn blue. We're breathing again. Thanks a lot."

Jack wiped an involuntary tear from his cheek. He knew that he was a lucky man to see, after his own death, the realization of one of his most important goals.

Neil Armstrong descended the LEM's ladder. "I'm at the foot of the ladder," reported the astronaut. "The LEM foot pads are only depressed in the surface about one or two inches. Although the surface appears to be very, very fine grained, as you get close to it. It's almost like a powder. It's very fine.

"I'm going to step off the LEM now. That's one small step for man, one giant leap for mankind."

The president recalled the words that had launched the nation on this magnificent journey. It filled him with pride at this historic moment. He mouthed the words from memory: *I believe that this nation should commit itself to achieving the goal, before this decade is out, of landing a man on the moon and returning him safely to the Earth.*

Buzz Aldrin now walked on the surface of the moon. If Neil Armstrong's first statement was rehearsed, Buzz had a more impromptu comment. "Magnificent desolation," he noted. It was a description he delivered in respectful awe.

Some time later, both astronauts were out on the surface collecting samples for scientific analysis back home. Neil listened to the sound of his own breathing as if it were a far-off thing. Intent on finding the most interesting rocks, he concentrated on what appeared to be ancient ejecta from a crater. It reminded him of when he was at Southern Cal earning his Master's. He and a group of like-minded students would hop in a car after finals and head for the beach with the appropriate spirit for relaxation. They'd sit on the sand sipping their beverages while ogling the female student bodies and laying their plans for later. The surf would roar as they laughed the afternoon away, temporarily at least, without a care in the world.

Neil recognized that he had a smile on his face as he looked up to see if an ocean lapped at these ancient sands. No ocean, and he felt kind of silly when he spied Buzz a couple of hundred yards away, partially obscured by a crater rim. He wiped the smile from his face before realizing that Buzz wouldn't be able to see it anyway, due to the reflective surface of his faceplate. Somewhat embarrassed, he continued to scan for specimens, and he turned around to face the LEM again.

He consciously noted the breath catching in his throat when he saw Buzz close to the lunar lander, intent on his own collections. As quickly as he could, Neil turned around again to see who or what he'd mistaken for Buzz on the other side of the crater. Now, all of a sudden, he registered the red color of the stranger's space suit. There were other differences, too, which his mind had refused to acknowledge when he'd first seen the apparition.

Suddenly, just like that, it was gone—disappeared behind some convenient lunar landscape. Russians, he thought, but then dismissed the idea, given the intelligence he himself had reviewed on the Soviet space program. Plus, if they were here, they certainly wouldn't keep it a secret.

Neil looked skyward and noted the stars as sharp points of light that no view from Earth could approximate. Without an atmosphere, the moon supplied no distortion here, no filtering of the alien light. This naked landscape blanched under the onslaught. Neil stood defenseless to the whims of the cosmos. What unknown effects acted on man out here? Would the ravages of this undefended existence affect the human mind, his mind? He looked back toward the place he had seen the interloper. There was no sign. Forgetting his samples, he trudged back to the LEM. Inside, he addressed his fellow astronaut.

"Good specimen hunting, Buzz?"

"I would say so. Although by now I think I've seen every type of rock that this area can supply. How about you? Anything interesting in the crater's ejecta?"

Neil considered for a moment before deciding to broach the subject of his experience. "Interesting may not describe what I saw."

Now he had Buzz's attention. "I saw another astronaut."

"Another astronaut?" said Buzz coolly.

"You saw no one I take it."

"Just you, Neil."

"You don't seem to be too surprised. Are you sure you didn't see anything?"

"Very sure, but I don't doubt that you saw something."

"You're not humoring me, are you?" Neil wondered at Buzz's calm response.

"Remember the Gemini 7 mission with Jim Lovell?"

"Yes. December 1965, right?"

"That's right. Jim and Frank Borman piloted the capsule and they had a sighting."

Lovell: BOGEY AT 10 O'CLOCK HIGH.

Capcom: This is Houston. Say again, 7.

Lovell: SAID WE HAVE A BOGEY AT 10 O'CLOCK HIGH.

Capcom: Gemini 7, is that the booster or is that an actual sighting?

Lovell: WE HAVE SEVERAL...ACTUAL SIGHTINGS.

Capcom: ...Estimated distance or size?

Lovell: WE ALSO HAVE THE BOOSTER IN SIGHT...

"I remember something about that now. It was all hushed up pretty quickly though." Neil felt a quiver run through his body, head to toe.

"Wouldn't do to have the country's best and brightest appear to crack up in front of the press. But they saw a UFO during their second orbit. Frank noticed it first. Cape Kennedy told them that they were seeing the final stage of their own Titan booster rocket, but Jim confirmed that he could see the booster rocket as well as something else."

"So what are you saying? That there's a big traffic jam up here?" Neil laughed nervously.

"I'm saying I'm not surprised that you saw something. It seems we're not the only ones out here. But fortunately, at least so far, whoever else is hovering around Earth orbit isn't interfering with us."

Buzz looked directly into his fellow astronaut's eyes. "If I were you, Neil, I'd just forget about it. Even if you report it, it'll be swept under the rug."

"You mean to say nobody is investigating this?"

"Nobody that NASA will tell us about anyway."

The proconsul attended a meeting of his hosts as they discussed the possible motive of the Others for allowing themselves to be seen by the various personnel of the Soviet and American space programs. The Martian council speculated that they were engaging in reckless tampering to prove some point. The council was also forced to admit, however, that no real contamination had occurred to date. They resolved to monitor, as best they could, the activities of the Others and to guard against possible contamination.

CHAPTER 19

April 29, 1975

Jack looked up at the roof of 22 Gia Long Street in Saigon. If this had happened 10 years before, it wouldn't have had the negative repercussions on U.S. foreign policy as it was having now. A helicopter perched on top of a stairwell housing on the roof. A ladder led from the roof up to the vehicle. Several people were climbing the ladder, but Jack knew that not all would be taken away. This ride had been ordered up for the highest-level CIA operatives.

Friends and allies would be abandoned. *A shameful time for the America I cherish,* thought JFK.

November 1978

Newt Gingrich savored his victory over State Senator Virginia Shapard for Georgia's sixth congressional district. The South in general, he knew, was a bad place to support the Equal Rights Amendment as his opponent had.

"Third time is the charm," gloated Newt to his friends at his celebration party.

Jack Flynt had beaten Gingrich on the new congressman's first two tries for public office in 1974 and 1976, but Newt saw a trend in those defeats as did his opponent. Flynt, the conservative Democrat, had served since 1955 and opted not to seek reelection in 1978 in spite of a chastened Republican Party after the Watergate scandal.

Flynt could see that the political winds were shifting in the region. A reliable bloc for the Democrats since the days of Lincoln, the area's true nature began to reassert itself by going Republican. The voters had switched from Lincoln's party in protest over the Emancipation Proclamation that granted freedom to slaves, and they were switching again now from the more tolerant Democratic Party in a similar protest over equal rights.

A cynical Gingrich knew how to play this to his advantage in the South, and he knew the appeal of his party to the intolerant.

While Gingrich contemplated his new job, he also considered a strategy for further down the road. His plan would call for the destruction of the Democratic Party as a serious contender on the national stage. Politics is war without blood, as he would say, and he would up the ante with harsh invective to achieve his goals. Early on, he'd decided his fortune would not be made by serving the poor and the politically voiceless. He would get ahead by serving the interests of those who could enrich him in turn. His reward would come by championing their causes.

July 1979

The blue planet endured a withering assault from the sun's heightened solar activity. The previously placid outer layers of atmosphere churned with the extra energy. A normal byproduct of such activity, heat, caused the boundary of the Earth's air envelope to expand into space. Caught in the enlarged thermosphere was a product of both man's ingenuity and penchant for designed obsolescence. Skylab still traveled through its denser environment but experienced increased aerodynamic drag. The friction of atmosphere on its exterior slowed it down and hastened the expected orbital decay. It fell toward the Earth with new urgency. The retired spacecraft was waiting to die, but its earlier-than-expected reentry prompted anxious contingent planning at NASA.

On July 11, 1979, ground controllers held their collective breath while the space station disintegrated on reentry. Hopefully, their instructions had been received by the doomed station and implemented to avoid potentially deadly consequences for any population centers. If all went well, the Earth reentry footprint would be a narrow band about four degrees wide, beginning at about 48° S 87° E and ending at about 12° S 144° E. In other words, somewhere in the Indian Ocean around Western Australia would be ground zero. This was where an unguessed-at cargo would rest after having been created in the precise environment of Skylab in orbit.

January 1981

The Shadow Group finished its traditional meeting prayer with an "amen." The mood was festive as they saw good progress in their plan to destroy the local reality.

"Let us toast President Carter, shall we? For being such a stooge for our purposes," saluted Bart.

"It was uncanny the way he mishandled the Iran hostage situation. A total misreading. I think he actually thought they'd respect his restraint," said Simon with a smile.

"You can thank our efforts for that," chimed in Thaddeus. "We've been prodding the Islamic faithful for quite a while now. They'll be instrumental here on out."

"The beauty of it is that they're so easily agitated. They've become belligerent since they can't figure why they lag in this world in spite of their faith," confirmed Simon.

"I'm amazed that with all the religions of this world they don't question themselves as to why there are so many," said Bart. "Surely they know they can't all be right."

"Judaism, Buddhism, Christianity, and all the rest are just bastard religions," stated Peter. "They have no clue as to what's real."

"Spoken like a true zealot," agreed Simon with a grin as he raised his glass.

The group followed suit with a toast.

"Okay, what are our plans for Reagan?" Bart asked Phillip.

In answer Phillip stood and turned on a view screen.

"As you know," he began. "The Cold War has separated this world into two rival factions, Communist and Capitalist. The area that each controls is roughly even, as you see on the map."

"Isn't Communist economic power an illusion?" asked Andrew.

"You're getting ahead of me. But yes, that's right. Their real production is actually far less than the statistics they publish. Capitalism has it all over them in that regard. Probably because there's no economic incentive behind the Iron Curtain. You can only get ahead by moving up in the party hierarchy. Even then, you'd be hard pressed to enjoy the bounty available in the West."

Phillip played the professor, which, in his private life, he was.

"How does this help us?" asked Peter.

"By itself, it doesn't. Worse than that, if we leave well enough alone, the Communist system will eventually collapse from within. What we need to do is provoke a conflict between East and West before the East declines and the struggle resolves itself peacefully."

"This is where Reagan comes in?" suggested Bart.

"Exactly! Like most in his political party, Reagan takes a short view. For instance, he's not overly concerned about the less well-to-do, the environment, or the national debt if we can infer from his electoral platform." Phillip nodded to himself.

"That doesn't seem like the United States that I've studied," interrupted Bart. "Are you sure you're reading this Republican Party right?"

"Most conservative Republicans truly believe the party dogma. That it promotes economic wellbeing for all. But a cynical few are only out to enrich themselves by doing the bidding of their moneyed masters." Again, Phillip seemed satisfied with himself.

"Even so, how does widening the gap between rich and poor cause a conflict between East and West?" questioned Simon.

"I was just giving examples of our candidate's philosophy. Instant wealth at the expense of the vulnerable. Some day an exaggerated gap could bring down the government I suppose, but I'm not counting on that. I calculate that Reagan will try to make his mark by escalating the Cold War in the short term. He'll be impatient, aggressive. He even talks about a winnable nuclear war with the Soviet Union. This should increase the probability of an armed confrontation. Our guidance ought to make it a certainty." Phillip's comments showed his dedication.

"Are we sure that a nuclear conflict will cause this reality to collide with another?" questioned Andrew.

"Our computer models indicate this is the most direct means," replied Phillip. "An adjacent reality has already had its nuclear war between East and West. If we can pull that off, both realities should collide."

The Soviet Union underlies all the unrest that is going on.
—Ronald Reagan

In 1980, the Honduran military was directed by its American overlords to hold elections. Thereafter, the Honduran government received $100 million of American largesse a year. Secretly, American policymakers moved their allies in the struggle with the leftist elements in El Salvador and Nicaragua into Honduran territory. These leftists were called the Contras. This group brought its own brand of retribution into play with the creation of death squads. The Contras acted as an autonomous state within a state.

In 1981, the CIA organized the Contras in Nicaragua, and they grew from 60 ex-National Guardsmen to a group that numbered in the thousands. More pressure was brought to bear on Nicaragua in the form of an economic embargo. The U.S. also pressured the IMF and World Bank to limit or halt loans to the country.

In 1982, Reagan celebrated a coup that brought General Efraín Ríos Montt to power in Guatemala. Military aid to the new regime was increased. Ríos Montt brutally escalated the counterinsurgency campaign in spite of his evangelical beliefs.

The Ríos Montt government was short-lived, however, as another coup replaced him the following year. New president Oscar Mejía Víctores took over with the apparent blessing of the U.S. administration. Rumors abounded that the CIA assisted in his ascension.

In 1983, an internal coup deposed the Socialist leader of the island nation of Granada. Even with the island out of the Communist sphere, the U.S. invaded anyway to prevent the construction of an airport that the Cubans offered to help build. Reagan rejected the claim that the airport was for tourism and moved to deny the Soviet Union a landing base. Later, the U.S. announced plans to finish the airport... to develop tourism.

In the same year, Congress passed the Boland Amendment that prohibited the CIA and the Defense Department from spending money to overthrow the government of Nicaragua. The Reagan administration nevertheless continued its efforts unabated.

The Shadow Group applauded its own subtle handiwork in provoking East-West tensions and sets out to extend the conflict into the Middle East.

"This area of the world shows lots of promise in setting off a worldwide confrontation," Andrew pointed out. "The people there are easily led by the mullahs, and the mullahs preach hate. They see it as their holy duty to seek out injustices against Muslims. Gotta love that Israeli-Palestinian conflict. Both sides oblige us by exaggerating the stories to incite their followers. Very willing participants, all. We've exploited this situation with little effort. Our hand in this won't be apparent.

"Right now we've got major operations going in Egypt, Libya, and Lebanon. Minor ones in Iran, Iraq, and Syria."

"I heard there was some blowback after Sadat was assassinated," said Bart.

"True," agreed Andrew. "The Muslim Brotherhood didn't do itself any favors with that move. Sadat was very well liked. Khomeini of Iran put them up to it. And I must admit the reaction came as a surprise to us. We're trying to radicalize the population again."

"What about Palestine?" Bart inquired.

"No need to intervene. The situation is in critical mass all the time now. Any goodwill that the Palestinians and Israelis have enjoyed between themselves is long forgotten with the recent bad blood. We just have to sit back and wait." All were happy to hear Andrew's words.

PART VI

The Birth of the New Frontier

CHAPTER 20

1988

Jack, at home in Boston, turned on the local news just in time for an interview with a newly elected state senator. The youngish looking man was middle-aged, but no one would have guessed that if it wasn't already a matter of public record. On TV, at least, viewers spotted no sign of gray on that handsome head.

"Senator Cody," yelled a reporter.

The man in front of the microphone acknowledged the questioner.

"Senator, do you credit your victory to the recent dissatisfaction with the Reagan administration's policies?"

"I think that there may have been a national reaction to Mr. Reagan's policies, but I'm not sure that filtered down to the level of state senator." Cody smiled. "I'm looking forward to my time on Beacon Hill in the state house, not the U.S. Senate. But I believe the commitment I've made to help improve the fortunes of ordinary citizens was evident to the voters. I intend to pursue that commitment with all my energy."

Another reporter yelled a question. "Are you relieved that the subject of religion never came up in the campaign?"

Jack watched the state senator-elect fleetingly regard the questioner with a disdainful look. The reaction was almost subliminal, though, before Cody mustered an answer. "I see no reason why it should have come up so I'm neither relieved nor otherwise."

Jack turned off the TV. "What did you think of Cody's performance, Niles?" he asked.

"I thought it was fine. Very poised for someone who seems to have come out of nowhere."

"You didn't notice a flash of anger at the last question?"

"Can't say that I did. Did you pick up on something?"

"I thought so. Maybe it was my imagination though." Jack knew what he had seen.

"I think Kenneth A. Cody will make a fine state senator. Perhaps will go farther than that, given his charm and looks."

"I'd like to see that," replied Jack.

Al-Rahiim noted the displeasure in his Martian colleague's thoughts. The political calculus of the United States deviated from their models, and somehow they suspected Jack.

"Any reason that you know of why your man would risk this reality?" Metluna asked al-Rahiim.

"That certainly wasn't part of his training or his beliefs to begin with. Why do you think that Jack has anything to do with this?"

"It's a process of elimination as you call it. There are only so many sources where this deviation could come from. We're not sure it's Jack, and we are looking at other theories."

"Like the Others?" suggested al-Rahiim.

"Yes. Like the Others. We believe it's possible that they could have allied themselves with your Religionists. They appear to be pursuing similar agendas to create disruptions in this reality."

"I hope this doesn't mean another assassination attempt on Jack," said al-Rahiim with a touch of anger.

"That's always an option if our models indicate he's steering this reality. For now it's still a question."

Cody dismissed his staff after his latest press conference. Unusual to have such attention paid to a state senator, he thought. A testament to the dynamic campaign he had run. Putting those thoughts aside, he resolved to make good on his campaign promises. Not only would applying himself for the benefit of the electorate be satisfying work, but he also calculated it would help further his political ambitions.

A while after everyone had left, Niles Babineaux showed up in Cody's office. The older man had become a father figure to the new state senator.

"How are you doing, Kenneth? Enjoying your new position yet?" Niles asked as he took a seat facing Cody.

"The honeymoon was short. Now it's down to the hard work of forging alliances. Or at least forming consensus if I can't leverage concessions." Cody smiled.

"No time to relax? No time for diversions?"

"I'm trying to train myself to avoid that if I get your meaning." The politician laughed.

"I've got a confession to make," Niles said blandly.

"I'm not going to like this, am I?"

"Perhaps, but we'll see. I promised a young reporter a one-on-one interview with you."

"Niles, you know how I feel about others making commitments for me. And especially now with an important vote coming at the end of the week." Cody surprised himself by snapping at Niles, a rare occurrence given that Niles had played no small part in getting the politician elected. The older man's business connections and reach in the community had paid dividends.

Cody relented. "All right. I'll see him if you promise never to do this again."

"Deal. And it's not a him, it's a her."

Before Cody could say anything else, Niles was out of his chair and inviting someone to enter the office. Cody was about to object when a woman in her late twenties entered the room. Unlike most others of her age, she was smartly dressed in a tasteful business suit that displayed personality in the understated touches of color. Not even a seam was out of place. She also carried herself with a confidence that belied her junior status. Cody attributed her comportment to her captivating good looks.

"Good evening, Senator. My name is Nicole Babineaux and I'm from the *Globe*. I'm happy you consented to be interviewed."

"Babineaux? Are you related..."

"Niles is my uncle."

Cody looked up to find that Niles had exited the room. Sly devil. He gladly entertained the lovely young woman's questions. Her voice was musical, and he was sorry when the meeting came to an end.

CHAPTER 21

1989

Gingrich succeeded Cheney as House Minority Whip. With just two years on the job, Cheney had been tapped to become President George H. W. Bush's secretary of defense. In his new role, Gingrich used his leverage to shake things up even more, often belligerently attacking the majority party. The venerable Tip O'Neill bemoaned the change of tone in Congress and blamed Gingrich for replacing polite dialogue with mercurial outbursts. All the better, thought Gingrich, if he could radicalize the dialogue of the nation to detest all things Democratic.

The Religionists didn't notice Newt's brand of divisiveness, however. They didn't take advantage of his potential to split the nation.

On November 9, 1989 at about 7 p.m., Gunter Schabowski, leader of the East Berlin Communist Party, announced that the border would be opened for private trips abroad. Consequently, massive gatherings began tearing down parts of the hated Berlin wall, a symbol of repression. Soon after, large-scale evacuation from East Berlin commenced. The genie was out of the bottle with one poorly thought-out phrase by the East German party leader. The ruling Communists dared not bring the hammer down on their people since it surely would have turned into a massacre. The public was not to be talked out of their newfound freedom whether it was misinterpreted or not.

Checkpoints opened the next day for walkers. That summer, riotous parties broke out, and on July 1, 1990, East and West reunited. Broken German families rejoiced after decades of separation. President George H. W. Bush would take credit for the work that Reagan had started.

The Shadow Group of Religionists convened in a somber mood.

"Another miscalculation!" announced Bart. "What happened to the certainty that Reagan would start a nuclear war?"

"We were right about the other predictions," said Phillip defensively. "Reagan increased the divide between rich and poor. Disaffection of the poorer classes historically brings down governments. He also ran up the national debt. The U.S. is a weakened country."

"Don't insult our intelligence, Phillip. None of that does anything to help us," ranted Peter. "We needed a war. A war that you practically guaranteed."

"I don't understand it. He started off well. Very belligerent with his rhetoric about the evil empire. Then he changed somehow. He reconciled with Gorbachev soon after the Lebanese disaster. I wonder how much the Marine barracks bombing affected him. When they were bombed in '83 he evacuated all personnel. Could he have felt remorse?"

"We need a new direction," stated Bart. "Thaddeus, you put a lot of stock in the Muslims doing our dirty work. Why don't you take over for a while. See if you can't stir them up."

"Stirring them up is the easy part," said Thaddeus with a laugh. "Getting them to adopt a coherent plan will be tougher. But I enjoy a challenge."

"I'll leave that in your capable hands. Meanwhile let's try to keep suppressing the Democratic Party. It seems the Republicans are more apt to let things rot before they interject the government."

CHAPTER 22

1990

The headlines read *Ken A. Cody Defeats Sitting Senator Kerry in Democratic Primary*. Outside of Cody's election headquarters in Boston, a well-dressed man folded the old newspaper and tucked it under his arm. The large man then proceeded to fish for change in his pocket in order to feed the parking meter. At one point, he squeezed the newspaper to prevent it from falling and managed to suppress a grimace when his arm pressed too hard against a metallic bulge under his suit jacket. Otherwise, his movements were unremarkable yet purposeful.

Jack noted all this as he watched the stranger cross the street. He was hiding something, thought Jack. Jack started to walk toward the campaign headquarters but then decided to intercept the man instead. His task was rendered that much easier when the man noticed Jack and changed direction to meet him. As Jack suspected, the man had a gun and made a silent threat with it when they met. Down an alley, out of sight of the public, the man pulled out the gun and aimed it at Jack.

"Looks like this is the end of your career," the stranger said, and he pulled the trigger.

Moments later, inside campaign headquarters, Niles, part of the Elect Cody team, noted Jack's entry.

"Something wrong, Jack?"

"Why do you ask?"

"The look on your face. Like you've just been surprised."

"I guess you could say that. I've just been mugged. Or at least an attempt was made."

"Knowing you, I'm sure you're okay. What about the assailant?"

At that moment, the sound of an approaching police siren could be heard. The squad car pulled up to the curb outside where Jack met them and directed them around the corner to the alley.

1994

Gingrich engineered the Republican Party's dramatic success in the 1994 congressional elections, and was subsequently elected speaker. Gingrich's leadership in Congress was marked by opposition to many of the policies of the Clinton administration. He presided over a House openly hostile to the president.

Phillip watched the nightly news and noted the celebrity achieved by Gingrich. He saw Gingrich as the anti-president. How could the Religionists use that to their advantage? During the broadcast, Gingrich oversaw the unveiling of a proposition with the grand title of Contract with America. What was he up to? Surely people could see through this.

Phillip got up from his chair, found his holo-communicator and dialed Bart. An image of the man who served as chairman of the Shadow Group appeared in mid-air.

"Hello, Phillip. Are you watching Newt Gingrich?"

"That's exactly why I was calling. How did you know?"

"It wasn't hard to guess. You're always one for politics, the political answer. And I happened to be watching him on the news myself."

"So you agree that we should divert some resources back to the political arena?"

"It may be worth a little effort. I'll have to think about that. In the meantime, if you put together a proposal, I'll consider it."

CHAPTER 23

Josh Malcolm was not your average teenager. He lived with his parents, brother, and sister in a cramped second floor apartment in Sacramento. In spite of, or because of, the close living conditions, it was a loving family. But that wasn't what was unusual about Josh. The overweight teen while not in school or doing homework was a high-powered consultant to the U.S. military.

When in grade school, Josh taught himself aerodynamics, coming up with ingenious ways to test his plane designs in the absence of a wind tunnel. Some of those designs had been incorporated into the fleet of U.S. military aircraft. Josh could decipher complex codes in his head and had been instrumental in translating terrorist chatter picked up by the CIA after the 1993 World Trade Center bombings in New York City. The boy had top-level security clearance and was a regular guest at the Pentagon. One would never know this by observing Josh or his living style. The typical teenager's room was filled with posters, iPods, stereo, and the expected clutter. Out of consideration for his invaluable contributions, however, the government regularly arranged passes for Josh to see his favorite band, Aerosmith.

National Security Agent Padilla dropped by the Malcolm residence to personally deliver tickets to Josh. Josh wasn't home but his mother greeted the man at the door.

"Hello, Mr. Padilla," she said and opened the door.

"Hello, Mrs. Malcolm. Josh around?"

"He's still at school. His physics teacher got him involved in a little project for tomorrow's lesson. Should be home soon, though, if you want to wait."

"Well, I just wanted to drop off these tickets, but I wouldn't mind touching base with him."

"Come on in, then."

"Are you sure it's all right?"

"Have a seat," said Mrs. Malcolm, and she showed him into their modest living room.

As the agent sat, he noticed some untidy piles of magazines and books on the coffee table. *Popular Science* was on the top and was indicative of the rest of the piles.

Beth Malcolm noticed his interest. "Those are Josh's," she offered. "I don't know where he gets his curiosity. Neither Ben nor I had much time for such things. Too busy trying to make ends meet, I suppose."

Then, she said, "Would you like something to drink? I've made up some iced tea."

"Thank you, yes. Good day for it. Unusually warm."

Josh's mother exited the room and returned with one glass in each hand. "So," she started, "has the NSA caught any aliens today?"

Agent Padilla looked over the rim of his glass as he drank his tea. "Any aliens?" he repeated.

"Anyone crossing the border illegally?"

"Oh. No that's not my detail. We leave that up to the INS."

"Well, I hope someone is paying attention to it. We're just overrun with Mexicans," she told Agent Padilla in an indignant tone.

He didn't take offense even though his father had been one of those illegal aliens. Her glib attitude actually amused him since she hadn't noticed his Spanish surname. At that moment, Josh entered the house.

"Here's Josh now," said Beth Malcolm. "I'll leave you two alone."

She went back into the kitchen as Josh unceremoniously flopped down in the chair just vacated by his mother.

"Hi, Josh"

"Hi, Mr. Padilla," replied Josh not paying much attention as he took out his laptop. Social graces weren't his strong suit, but what teenage boy can claim them?

"Looks like you've lost a little weight."

"I've been reading about the efficiencies of the cardiovascular system. It's made exercise less boring for me now that I know the biomechanics of increased performance."

"It'll help you think more clearly too."

"Uh huh," said Josh as he fiddled with his computer.

"Oh, by the way, I've got your Aerosmith tickets."

The agent puts them on the coffee table in front of Josh who visibly brightened.

"Awesome," he exclaimed, and he snatched up the tickets.

"Going with anyone special?"

"My physics lab partner is a big fan too."

Padilla wondered if the lab partner was a girl but decided not to ask in case it would embarrass the boy.

"Josh, while I'm here I wanted to find out if you've detected any new spatial anomalies."

With the help of his tutors from the school for the gifted, Josh had constructed a sophisticated sensor that acted like radar. This device, however, worked with spatial densities as opposed to light. It wasn't much more than a curiosity since it had no practical purpose; yet it was designated Top Secret to all but a few in the government.

"None for quite a while now. Space seems quiet."

"Would you do me a favor, Josh? Would you let me know if you pick up on anything unusual?"

In spite of his apparent indifference Josh picks up on the agent's meaning. "Are you expecting anything weird?"

"My brother works at Kitt Peak Observatory near Tucson. I'd be doing him a huge favor if I could tell him which part of the sky to aim his telescope."

Josh saw through the lie. "Sure. I know how it is to have to help a brother."

"I bet you've shared your gifts with parents and sister too," said Padilla. "I noticed the new Nissan Quest out front."

"I've got to use this money for something."

Padilla smiled and shouted good-bye to Mrs. Malcolm in the kitchen. She came out wiping her hands on her apron and saw him out the door. Josh went to his room. Closing the door, he took out a device that had no equal in Earth technology. After a few adjustments he addressed a small holographic image of someone he called Mr. Al.

"Yes, Josh," said the image.

"You were right, Mr. Al. I was just quizzed by an NSA agent about recent spatial anomalies."

"Hmm," mused the image. "What did you tell him?"

"Exactly what we agreed I'd tell him. That there haven't been any since the last time I reported one to the National Security Agency."

"Did he seem satisfied with that?"

"I'm not sure. This agent has been to my house before. He never struck me as the trusting type."

"Okay, Josh. Well done. Hopefully we can stay one step ahead of them."

"Or our existence goes kablooey?"

"I'm afraid so. Sorry to have to dump all this on you. I hope you're getting to enjoy your young life in spite of all this." Mr. Al seemed entirely sincere.

"Yeah. It's been a hoot," replied the sarcastic teenager.

"Keep that sense of humor," said Mr. Al. "It'll make things a little less stressful. Al-Rahiim signing off."

The image dissolved into the air, and Josh returned to his studies.

Agent Padilla, on his way back to the office, dialed his cell phone and connected with an otherworldly recipient. Metluna of the Martian League answered the phone.

"What did you find out, Agent Padilla?"

"The boy says he hasn't picked up any new spatial anomalies."

"So, either he's lying or their device can't detect our incursions."

"If he's lying, it means that he could be working with the Others. Pretending not to know when we send more agents but warning them when it happens."

"We haven't had any serious blowback yet. Odds are, they can't detect us. You should continue to monitor him just in case. Neutralize him if we have good cause to become suspicious."

"Okay. My biggest worry though is crossing paths with the real Agent Padilla."

"We've perfected our traffic models since Barney Hill's clone attracted attention to himself. We'll be able to give you plenty of notice if you're in danger of that."

"I hope so. Padilla out."

CHAPTER 24

July 1999

To al-Rahiim, Jack appeared visibly agitated. He sat with his head in his hands while moisture dripped to the floor between his fingers. The proconsul almost wished that he hadn't revealed the latest timeline model information to him. When Jack looked up again, al-Rahiim saw an expression on the former agent's face that the proconsul knew too well from their prior dealings. It was stubborn resolution. And if Jack had the presence of mind to look at the holographic image of al-Rahiim, he would've noted dire concern on the proconsul's face. As it was, Jack didn't care too much about anything at the moment other than some unspoken plan he'd formulated.

"You're not planning any interference, are you, Jack?"

Jack wheeled around to stare at the proconsul as if surprised to hear the question. "What do you think? What would you do if you were in my place?"

"I'd consider what was best for several realities. For existence itself."

"My son is going to die, according to you. I can't let that happen." He got up to leave the room.

"Wait, Jack. You're not thinking this through. How are you going to do it without contamination? You don't want to leave a trail leading to you." The proconsul genuinely worried about his former subordinate.

"I don't care about that. All I know is I've got to do something."

"Well, goddamn it. Let me at least help. I can't let you go off and jeopardize everything."

Jack wasn't exactly sure what the proconsul meant by 'everything,' but he calmed down long enough to formulate a plan with al-Rahiim's help. And with that, Jack withdrew from the room, leaving al-Rahiim to ponder whether or not to reveal similar information in the future. He had to admit to himself, however, that he would react the same way if one of his own children were in danger.

On July 17th, the national media reported that John F. Kennedy Junior's plane never arrived at its destination, the airport at Martha's Vineyard. The nationwide vigil ended when it was confirmed that on July 16, JFK, Jr. was killed along with his wife, Lauren Bessette, and his sister-in-law when the small aircraft he was piloting crashed into the Atlantic Ocean. He was 38 years old.

JFK, Jr.'s two passengers had hitched their ill-fated ride on his small passenger plane, a Piper Saratoga II HP, leaving from the Essex County Airport in New Jersey to attend a Kennedy cousin's wedding in Hyannis, Massachusetts on Cape Cod. Lauren was to have been dropped off en route at Martha's Vineyard. The wedding of cousin Rory Kennedy was postponed due to the tragedy.

Al-Rahiim appeared to Jack again. This time he wanted to receive news of JFK's son as opposed to announcing any.

"You're looking better than the last time we met," said al-Rahiim.

"Well, I'm feeling a lot better about my son's prospects."

"What happened? I read the obituary in the paper."

"JFK, Jr. is dead to the world," his father announced.

"You mean he's dead to this world, don't you?"

"Of course," said Jack as he got up to leave. "Looks like there are two amalgam personalities now. Me in this universe. And Jack, Jr. in our home universe."

"How did he take it?"

This caused Jack to stop in his tracks. He fully expected a lecture, but the concern in al-Rahiim's voice seemed genuine, and he did want to talk about it.

"He was confused," said JFK/Jack.

"No surprise there."

"No, I suppose not."

"Well, what happened?"

"I stowed away on the plane," admitted Jack. "No one knew I was there. I was phased."

"You used the device I gave you?" asked al-Rahiim.

"It works perfectly. And it's portable, unlike our clunky phasing device. Anyway, the flight started out fine. I actually dared to hope that you were wrong, but then the trouble began. It was a murky night and I couldn't make out the horizon. Apparently, neither could John, although he never let on to his passengers."

"Did they sense any problem?"

"Eventually, it became obvious. The plane started to list as we say in boating. But when a plane lists, it turns. John had trouble fixing the horizon. He couldn't seem to get it level. I think he started to panic. Lauren's sister began to whimper. I couldn't make out what she was saying. By that time, the plane was corkscrewing down. The altimeter showed an accelerating descent. The radius of the turn decreased, which had the effect of forcing the passengers to the outside bulkhead. John, Jr. had lost control of the plane. All they could do was wait for the impact with the water."

"So you phased your son."

"I wanted to save them all, but the device strains with two people. And if I hadn't needed to include myself in the process, I would've sacrificed myself so my son's wife could live." The expression on Jack's face was a gloomy one.

"We knew you were testing the phase-shifter before you boarded the plane. I assumed you were experimenting with how many people it could phase."

"Who's we?" Jack looked at al-Rahiim in surprise.

"The Martians and I. But tell me. How did John react to all this."

"I think he was in shock. Anyone would be. His plane was ditching. He must have expected the end, but a stranger appeared, and the next thing he knew, he was alive in a similar world. Similar but for the technology."

"No trouble with downloading his consciousness?"

"All I can say is that when both of our sons woke up in the same body, they seemed okay. I wanted to stay and help them since I knew how disoriented I was when I woke up in my Hyannis home here. Perhaps it was their young minds, but once I explained things, they adapted very quickly."

"Something about the Kennedy psyche I suppose."

"I certainly hope so." Jack smiled.

"Jack, why did you come back? You know it would've been very difficult for the Agency to track you back home."

"Difficult, but not impossible. I'm not sure why, but something compelled me to return here. It's like I'm contributing more to this reality than I could ever hope to in ours."

"Can you explain what that is?" al-Rahiim asked.

Jack struggled with that awhile. He tried to come up with an answer. "No," he said finally. "But I feel some purpose here. Perhaps if you ask me again in a few years, I'll have a coherent answer."

"Why a few years?"

"I'm working toward some goal that I can't seem to put into words yet. But I think it'll come."

Al-Rahiim looked concerned before exhibiting a smile and dissolving his holographic image.

JFK, Jr. awoke with a start. *Was it a dream? Did I ditch the plane?* He looked around him. The room was at once familiar and strange. He was pretty sure he was in New York, due to the ever-present city noises. He wasn't so sure he was in his own apartment.

"Lauren?" he called out.

No answer. He got up groggily, whereupon a female voice seeming to come out of the walls startled him. What was it saying?

"Your usual Saturday breakfast, sir?"

"Wha..."

"Fresh pineapple, coffee, bacon, and wheat toast."

"Who said that?"

"Apartment Max 3000, sir. Or Suzi, as you sometimes prefer."

A computer, he thought. JFK, Jr. then realized he wasn't in his old digs. He might not even be in his right mind. Now standing, he walked around the room to examine some oddities. A picture that covered nearly all of one wall wasn't really a picture at all. It was an outdoor scene that looked startlingly like a certain corner of Montana he'd recently visited. He knew it wasn't a conventional picture since the tree branches swayed in the wind. He could actually hear the rustling. He could almost get lost in it.

The rest of the room was spare in its furnishings. That was to say, it had a bed and very little else.

And now the bed disappeared into the wall by itself. When JFK, Jr. examined the wall, he could find no evidence that there ever was an opening to accommodate the bed. Another wall became transparent moments after the bed disappeared. This wall revealed his true neighborhood outside and was in fact a window that had been opaque. The city he looked out on was undoubtedly New York, but it wasn't *his* New York. Majestically arcing monorails interwove between sleek glass spires as well as other futuristic looking skyscrapers.

Awed by this remarkable metropolis, John was startled by a noise from back inside the room. When he wheeled around, he noted a suit of clothes had appeared out of a heretofore invisible closet. The outfit looked normal enough and was even to his taste but for some unfamiliar fashion details. Contemplating the clothing, he became aware that he was dressed in pajamas. They were plain but for a New York Yankees emblem on the left side of the chest. He grinned at this. He felt compelled to touch the clothes, but lost interest as he decided to explore the rest of the apartment.

A short hall outside his room impressed him with how different it was from the bedroom. The walls were similar but they were decorated in eye-catching colors. Pictures unlike the large moving one in the bedroom hung at intervals. They were smaller, traditional sizes and didn't exhibit moving scenery. One picture was of a ship. It looked like an old clipper ship fighting mightily through heavy seas. John loved those kinds of pictures. He could almost feel he was aboard, battling the surf in order to lower the sails.

At the end of the hall was a sitting room with its own personality, like that of a library. It had book shelves made of expensive wood and big comfy chairs. This was the first time JFK, Jr. had seen the use of wood since he'd awakened. He definitely got the impression, however, that both the shelves and books were kept as some kind of display. A curiosity only.

On a glass or Plexiglas coffee table lay a device that John knew to be an e-book reader, and he was willing to bet that it was far more sophisticated than any he had seen at home.

A shadow of some sort of vehicle whizzed by the window that John only now noticed. The window glass allowed a pleasant, filtered light into the room—not too bright and not too dim. Looking out, John witnessed movement at every level of the city. Slow airborne vehicles up high, monorail cars between the buildings, and ground vehicles well beneath him. In the middle of these observations, John was overtaken by a strange sensation. He sat down in a nearby chair, and while he dealt with the feeling, all in the room and the apartment and the city became familiar to him. The mood was strange and yet at the same time calming. He felt as if a guide had been activated in his head.

"How are you doing, John?"

A stranger sat in the chair opposite him which caused John to jump to his feet again. He hadn't noticed the man entering the room. John then had the thought that the man had always been there, but beyond John's perception.

"Who are you?"

"I suppose I'm your guardian." The man grinned.

"As in angel?"

"Hardly. I must say you seem to be handling the integration at least as well as I did."

"What are you talking about?" asked John, who became visibly agitated.

"Okay. I'll explain everything to you... to both of you. But first you may get some answers by focusing on me."

"Why the hell..."

At first John resisted the suggestion, but the more he tried to look away, the more compelled he felt to continue staring. Something was happening. The stranger's features were becoming more and more familiar. Ultimately, John sat back down as he labored under the weight of an impossible realization.

"Dad?"

"Yes. Yes, son, it's me." Jack smiled warmly at his boy.

"How?"

Several hours later as the walls became opaque to greet the night, the amalgam personality known as John Kennedy, Jr. accepted the truth of their combined fathers' explanation. He/they even accepted the fact that two men could occupy one body. This new John, Jr. was a living testament to that. What John couldn't accept was his father's compulsion to go back to the universe that had nearly killed him. And Jack couldn't seem to make sense of the need to his son or to himself. He just knew he had to do it. But before that, he resolved to indulge himself for another day or so.

Jacqueline sat curled up on a swinging lounge chair on the porch of her Vineyard home. The evening was cool, so she covered herself with a shawl, making sure to tuck it in around her bare feet. At seventy years old she was still a handsome woman. Why couldn't he approach her? He rationalized that he didn't want to startle her, but that wasn't the reason.

Several times, Jack fingered the device that would allow him to phase into this plane of reality and appear to her. Those stubborn fingers just wouldn't manipulate the controls. This was a bad idea, he thought. With one more longing glance he left.

Jacqueline noticed a sudden breeze that blew some dried leaves off the porch. For some reason it caused a tear to escape down her cheek.

Early December 2000

In early December 2000, the Shadow Group of Religionists gathered again. They had scored a significant victory, but this time they held their enthusiasm in check.

"I believe that we finally have our man," stated Peter. "Thaddeus is to be congratulated."

"I'll never figure the local Americans out," admitted Thomas.

"Me, neither," added Andrew. "Who would've thought that they would choose to change such a successful paradigm and elect this Bush?"

"Ah, you underestimate their delicate sensibilities," said Thaddeus. "The middle and lower classes have embraced religious conservatism. And for that, read moral conservatism."

"Are you saying the upper classes haven't embraced the philosophy?" asked Andrew.

"They have on the surface," agreed Thaddeus, "but it's a self-serving position. They're not true believers, but as in times past, they see religion keeping the masses in check. It preserves the status quo, or in other words, their privileged position atop the socioeconomic pyramid."

"So these new 'old world' values translate to anti-Clintonism. Interestingly, it wasn't that long ago that news of his dalliances would have been off limits. That said, let's not underestimate the power of the moneyed elite. They flood the airwaves about this pariah president. They'll beat the drum of self-righteousness to convince people to vote their so-called values over their own well-being," said Bart.

"I think I can lay claim to some credit for that too," responded Thaddeus with a smug expression on his face. "Gingrich was part of our plan as you'll recall. And we calculated he would ally himself to the good Christian right."

Everyone smiled at that apparent oxymoron. Their surveillance indicated that the good Christian right weren't as good or as moral as advertised.

"Well, the unlikely patchwork that is the Republican Party has certainly been effective at getting votes from people who have no business voting Republican," conceded Bart.

"I'd love to study that phenomena," interjected John. "One of my local employees, a staunch Reagan supporter, complained of school programs being cut back during Reagan's presidency. She either wasn't able to make the connection between cutbacks and his policies or simply chose not to believe that it hurt her."

"Now you're sounding like the Agency and the scientists. Value in other realities? They can only contaminate ours. Let's remember we're going to eliminate this reality, John." Bart gave John a stern look.

John slumped back in his chair.

"Okay, now tell me why this president—Bush—can be relied on to advance our plan," Bart asked of Thaddeus.

"That's easy. He's not a thinker, not an acquirer of knowledge. He has a narrow list of truths that he never questions. His pattern of decision making is known to us. And it doesn't vary, no matter the circumstances. He's a man of very modest abilities yet believes he can manage on a grandiose scale."

Eyebrows went up all around, alongside other expressions of amazement.

"How does somebody so flawed get to be president?" prodded Phillip.

"That's easy. Family money and connections. And don't forget the Supreme Court. May the quantum field bless them. I didn't think they had it in them to publicly stop the vote count. They just couldn't have their man go down even at the risk of revealing their bias."

"Okay, so now what?" queried Bart.

"Now we continue to sow hate and aggression in the Muslim world," said Thaddeus, exuding a sense of satisfaction. "Eventually, though, we have to get them some nuclear weapons. The odds of Russia and the U.S. exchanging nuclear missiles has fallen off dramatically."

"At the moment, we're guiding our homicidal disciples in Al-Qaeda to a very visible attack on American soil. It'll bring unreasoning religious passions to play in our favor." All the Religionist members in this universe seemed pleased.

CHAPTER 24

September 15, 2001

At the Rockefeller University Hospital, Director McKay of the NSA approached a well-secured ward. He was accompanied by another man whose appearance drew hateful stares. Hospital personnel followed them with their eyes as curiosity overrode their attention to their own work. The director offered a clear view of his right eye to a retinal scanner just outside the ward. With his identity confirmed, he heard the latch on the door release. He grabbed the handle and opened the door for his companion. They entered to find themselves in front of another locked door six feet in front of them. This time a handprint granted access to a keypad in the wall. Punching in the appropriate eight-letter code allowed McKay admittance into a secret intensive care unit. A solitary nurse in a military uniform manned a small nurse's station. She was familiar with both men.

"How's our patient today?" asked the director.

"Fading in and out of consciousness but stable for now."

"Any chance he'll live?"

"Not likely. That would take another miracle." The nurse shook her head.

The director entered the sole room in the unit. On the bed lay the charred remnants of a living human being. The bed covers fell on the man's body in a way that indicated a missing left arm and leg. The burns across his face sealed half of the man's mouth. His remaining limbs were hooked up to several IV bags that for any other patient would have been discontinued days ago. Oxygen tubes had been placed in his nostrils, and his eyes periodically revealed the man's apparent pain in spite of heavy medication.

The director's companion, Imam Abdul-Fattah, went to the patient's side. The bedridden man perked up at the sight of the holy man. The director didn't speak Arabic, but it was obvious to him that the imam and patient exchanged greetings. Then, before the imam could say anything, the dying man through pulped lips forced out a story that obviously took the holy man aback.

At first the imam tried to say something to interrupt the narrative, but then he resigned himself to listening intently. After the patient finished, he fell silent, and the director seemed to fear that he'd passed on, but the equipment still indicated a pulse.

McKay and the imam left the ICU and reconvened in an empty waiting room. The holy man was obviously distressed, so the director bought him a cup of coffee and tried to settle him down. If it wasn't for the man's religious calling, the director would have offered him a deep draught of his secret flask. McKay would've cheerfully revealed his drinking habit under these extraordinary circumstances. But eventually the imam spoke.

"His name is Majed."

"One of the hijackers?"

"It would seem so."

The imam fell silent again, obviously struggling with what he'd just learned. "How could he have survived?" marveled the holy man.

"From what I've been told, it was like he surfed a wave. Somehow he was thrown clear of the plane and rode a shock wave away from the blast. Firefighters found him several blocks beyond the World Trade Center and got him into an ambulance. On the way to the hospital, he died. Or at least he was clinically dead. The EMTs revived him."

"I know that part." The imam nodded.

"He told you about his near-death experience."

"Yes."

The imam got a faraway look in his eyes but then composed himself and continued. "Allah appeared to him while he was dead."

With this statement, the imam looked into McKay's face to see how the infidel registered this information. McKay was stoic.

"You already knew this, didn't you?"

"We heard his story," confirmed McKay.

Imam Abdul-Fattah was surprised. "The whole story? How Allah preserved his life to reveal His will?"

"Do you believe it?"

"I am a faithful follower of the teachings of the prophet. There is one God, Allah. And Mohammed is his prophet."

"Can Majed be another prophet? Does the Koran allow for such a thing?"

"Majed is not a prophet," categorically stated the Muslim holy man. "He didn't reveal a prophecy. It was just a message."

"A message that wouldn't sit well with certain elements who wield the Koran for their murderous aims," mused the director.

"Mr. McKay, I have never condoned this anti-Western stance. I would not be saddened if Majed's message embarrassed our more radical brethren."

"Are you going to spread the message?"

"You know what the message is, don't you, Mr. McKay?"

"Of course. Majed was adamant that Allah was not pleased with the state of Islam. He painted a frightening image of his fellow hijackers dying the same death over and over. They were not rewarded as heroes with servants and women, but were punished in the way the Koran describes the fate of all suicides. They must relive their deaths throughout eternity. If you can believe him, he alone was spared to witness God's will and enlighten us all. I guess the question is, do you believe him?"

The imam hesitated. "I'll have to consult the Koran for guidance in this."

"You realize you don't have much time with Majed. He'll die soon."

"Yes. He knows that too. And he may be subject to the same eternal fate as his compatriots. He's not even sure that if the message got out it would save him." The imam's face gave away his sense of sadness, yet resignation.

"I guess he left it up to you," McKay told the cleric. "You could possibly save him in the afterlife. But for now I'd like to do something for the living. It seems to me that Majed's message broadcasted by the likes of me would mean little. Coming from an imam, Majed's message could save living Muslims now."

After the imam left, McKay went back into the security ward.

"Did you record the meeting between our friend and the holy man?" he asked the desk nurse.

"I'm making hard copies on disc now. Shall I distribute them?"

"Let's see what the imam does first. It'd be better if he took action as opposed to us broadcasting this without an author."

"Yes, sir."

The director went back into the room with Majed.

"How are you doing, Majed?"

"Not bad," enunciated the patient in unaccented English.

He then proceeded to remove layers of bandages and skin while his supposedly missing arm miraculously appeared from under the covers. "What did you think of my performance?"

"The most important critic is still deciding. From where I stand though, I didn't observe anything wrong. Let's see if it stands up to the imam's scrutiny."

The Others observed the director and the actor and were pleased with their handiwork and the execution of their plan by the un-knowing humans. Implanting suggestions with critical players in this reality was their best weapon against the majority of their own kind in the Martian League. They had attempted to stop the Barney Hill clone from leaving Saturn, but those type of strong-arm tactics were not their forte. They would have to achieve their purpose in other ways.

Their human ally, Colin Powell, appeared to be happy with the observed operation as well. A thoughtful man among fools, but they knew that he still wasn't totally at ease with their appearance. Humans found the size of their eyes, enlarged heads, and slight builds unnerving.

CHAPTER 25

A man with uncombed red hair, wearing a lab coat, held a test tube up to the light and examined its contents while voicing his observations to no one in particular. Another man in a suit sat on a high stool and watched the first man with an impatient air as he sipped from a Styrofoam cup of coffee. He listened to the technician but didn't hear what he wanted to hear. Finally, he lost patience and asked a blunt question.

"Well is it ready, doctor?"

The lab man started as if he was surprised to see the other man. "It's been ready for quite a while," the technician finally answered.

"Really? Ready for a while you say? Why wasn't I informed?"

"Didn't I tell you? I thought I had." Then it dawned on the scientist. "Is that why you're here? To hurry me along?"

"Something like that. Do you have the test results?"

"Better than that. I have the test results and a sample right here."

Only now did the suited government man realize that the test tube that the scientist held had nothing to do with his own project. He could feel his face reddening in anger but displaced the emotion at the prospect of seeing his idea realized.

The scientist set a large three-ring binder in front of his visitor. He also put down something that looked like a perfume atomizer bottle. Opening the notebook, the government man noticed a lot of charts, tables, and graphs. In the pocket of the notebook's front cover was a DVD. This he took to another room while ignoring the scientist.

He inserted the disc into a player and sat back to take in the information. All the statistics in the world couldn't approximate the satisfaction a person gets when observing the evidence of a successful test, a test of his own ideas. The screen came to life showing men milling around behind chain link fences under what appeared to be a tropical sunset. The men were dressed in loose fitting clothing, and all wore head coverings that were favored by devout Muslim males. The government man recognized the place as Camp X-ray in Cuba.

Two of the guards rounded up ten of the prisoners and ushered them through a door to an inside room. The point of view shifted to show the men entering a room with bare walls but for some speaker grills. The guards left and closed the heavy steel door behind them. The prisoners looked at each other with confused expressions. It was obviously not their normal routine.

Of the ten, five were in orange coveralls and five were in white. Oddly the men in orange had black bruises in the center of the foreheads. Eventually, the government man remembered that this was a sign of very devout men. The bruises were caused by repeated impacts with their hands during prayer. The government man also noted that the orange-clad men displayed a very different attitude than their companions. The man watching the video also recognized their body language as aggressive and angry, unlike the case with most religious people he knew. They were pissed off and put out. A certain arrogance was evident as well.

On the other hand, the situation intimidated their colleagues in white who were more furtive and circumspect. Some avoided eye contact with their orange-clad mates. They didn't roam around as much, preferring instead to wait for whatever was to befall them.

The observer eventually noticed that a slight mist emanated from what he thought were speaker grills. This was what he had waited for. He focused on the five men who wore orange. He knew they were dressed that way for the experiment to denote the level of their religious fanaticism. The others were more followers than anything else and not totally sold on martyrdom as a way to God. If anything they most likely had been intimidated into joining the movement.

Now the government man started to note changes. A chronometer on the screen indicated four minutes since the men had entered the room. In each case, the men in orange stopped pacing and started rubbing various muscle groups. It looked as if they were cramping up. One of them actually sat on the floor and seemed confused at what was happening to him, particularly since none of his compatriots in white showed any similar behavior. They just stared back at their stricken comrades in fear. That fear turned to horror when the affected group started to go into spasms. The screams and strange contortions of those in orange seemed to last for minutes but was actually over in about twenty seconds. Then they lay still, never to move or live or plot destruction again.

The government man removed the disc and replaced it in its case with the notebook. He didn't smile at the success of the experiment, but he did experience a great deal of inner satisfaction. Back in the room with the red-haired scientist he returned the notebook and shook hands with the man who had so irritated him throughout the development process.

"You approve of the result?" asked the technician.

"Is it as we ordered? Will non-jihadists be spared?"

"You saw for yourself. Our weapon will unerringly discriminate between violent religious fanatics and all others." With that, the scientist picked up the atomizer bottle containing the chemical weapon and sprayed it in his mouth. The G-man flinched.

"Sort of tastes like peaches."

Recovering from the surprise, the G-man gave an involuntary compliment. "Doctor, you're a braver man than I for doing that. I don't think I'd have the nerve to do what you just did."

"Don't sell yourself short. When I was making the coffee this morning, I was holding the atomizer in one hand as I inserted the filter. I must have sprayed it for a good ten seconds before realizing I was squeezing the bulb. You had one of the first cups. You'd be dead by now if you were a zealot."

"Son of a bitch!" The coffee drinker considered flattening the doctor with a haymaker before regaining control once again. "How do we know that a non-religious yet violent man wouldn't be affected?"

"If you'll look in the notebook I gave you, you'll realize that we've tested every iteration of personality. Only one thing triggers the reaction. And that is a unique chemical neurotransmitter that exists only in the brains of fanatical believers in a god. Fanatical enough to kill to promote or impose their beliefs."

"Must they be on the verge of violence to be affected?" asked the government agent.

"No, but it will speed up the effect. We placed those men that you saw in a different situation than they were used to. Stress hormones were released in their bloodstreams and that caused the mindset of the orange group to be more receptive to our chemical. Otherwise, their deaths would have taken a little longer."

The government man left the building unsure that his newfound weapon would be the total answer. He was certain that the terrorists weren't all religious fanatics. He also knew that some of their leaders adopted a religious doctrine superficially, only to manipulate young men for their own ends. In any case, he couldn't wait to loose this terror on the fanatical populations to see who and how many it weeded out.

Far away, in a chamber with rough-hewn rock walls, the interaction between the government agent and the red-haired scientist played out on the screen of a portable laptop. Robed men with covered heads squeezed together to better view the drama. Their reactions were shock, disbelief, and another emotion that would've embarrassed all of them—fear. All of the men had bruises in the middle of their foreheads.

"Is this possible?" asked one of the acolytes.

"It could be a trick," responded al-Zawahiri.

"What should we do?"

"What we always do. We will fight the infidels and win because God is on our side."

"Why did God allow them to develop such a weapon if He's on our side?"

Zawahiri slapped the underling with the back of his hand. "How dare you doubt the will of Allah! This is just another test. If we are fated to die to spread the teachings of Mohammed, then so be it."

"I beg forgiveness. Allah's will shall be done."

One of the other acolytes spoke up. "Maybe we could use this recording. Send it to al-Jazeera. That will get more Muslims on our side."

Zawahiri had already thought about the possibility. But might it also incite other Muslims to the point of making them vulnerable to the weapon? One had to be careful in dealing with such a foe. He didn't want to deliver more lives into their hands.

From yet another vantage point, the Religionists' Shadow Group watched the proceedings in the Afghan cave. They were smugly satisfied at the harvest they had sewed. Their calculus indicated that with mistrust and fear would come the war of cultures—in this case the war they incited between Islam and Christianity.

"We should have thought of this earlier instead of wasting our time on the Cold War," said Simon.

"Nothing lends itself to unreasoned hatred like religion," agreed Thaddeus.

"You mean nothing like their false religions," corrected Bart.

"Of course," said Thaddeus.

Turning to Philip, Bart asked: "How's our target reality doing? Is this one on a collision course with it yet?"

"The adjacent reality we're targeting is already in a heated religious war. Similarly to here, the more advanced West isn't threatened by Muslim military power. But some tens of thousands of people died after the so-called Islamic Freedom Fighters simultaneously detonated gas power plants throughout Christian-held lands. In retaliation, splinter groups of Christians have formed Christian terrorist organizations. They've already started a terror campaign of their own. Several hundred Muslim pilgrims have died in Mecca and Medina. And we know that more campaigns are in the works." Phillip's smile might have seemed ghoulish to all but his co-conspirators.

"Those are still small numbers. Doesn't sound like it will destroy that world."

"It doesn't have to. As long as we can instigate similar enough activity here, the parallel universes will overlap—and then *pow*. Several dozen realities will be wiped from existence, leaving ours as the one true universe." Again, that horrible smile at the thought of the death of so many.

"I look forward to that day," added the Religionist. "Until then, we can take solace in the fact that we are truly doing the work of the one true reality."

CHAPTER 26

At CIA headquarters in Langley, Virginia, George Tenet granted an audience to two men. These men were indistinguishable from the rest of the personnel in the building but for their purpose. Their office was physically located within the intelligence gathering community, but they had little interest in collecting facts. In point of fact, they were a throwback to the Ministry of Propaganda that had served the Third Reich with such blind loyalty. They gave the unpublicized aspirations of the vice president a foothold in the CIA. Their mission was to spin intelligence to prove a link between 911 and Iraq.

Sam, the more authoritative of the two, threw something onto Tenet's desk. The director didn't like the vice president and certainly didn't like his influence on his turf. Sam personified Tenet's distaste for what was going on in the intelligence community. Tenet hated that the Bush administration sought to politicize what should have been an objective function of the U.S. government. A wily veteran of political infighting, Tenet didn't let his antagonism show.

"What's this?" asked the director as he looked at it. "A comic book?"

"Take a closer look, George."

Tenet made no outward gesture to show his disgust at Sam's using his first name. After Sam's partner checked a pager that had obviously signaled him silently, he left the room. Now Tenet had only one of Cheney's minions to deal with. He took a closer look at the comic. It was in Arabic, and even though he couldn't read it, he recognized what was intended to be a superhero for Muslims.

The main character flew like Superman and wore a white leotard without a cape but with a red crescent on the chest. He also sported an Arab headdress. The director thumbed through the pages and picked up the basic story from the picture frames. Toward the end of the book it was obvious that the Arab hero had sunk a Red Cross hospital ship. The frame showed many distressed people in the water as their vessel sank. On the same page, the hero, now on a smaller ship, laughed along with several members of an Arab crew. Propaganda, Tenet realized at once.

"Where was this printed?" Tenet asked Sam.

"Jordan," said Sam. "Supposedly our ally. Is there anything else you need to know to prove the deceit of this enemy? Can we finally move on building the case for war?"

Tenet just stared at him. He couldn't believe this man took a comic as a signal for war. Indeed, the administration must be desperate to furnish reasons for invading the Middle East. Tenet merely shook his head and let Sam interpret it any way he pleased.

CHAPTER 27

February 3, 2002

Jack recreated the party atmosphere he'd provided for the lunar landing, this time at his residence on Martha's Vineyard. He marveled at how far the Boston, now New England, Patriots had come. Considering that they were the doormats of the league, he conjectured he had to be in another universe. The Keystone Cops had nothing on these guys, Jack thought. He could even remember a new head coach, Clive Rush, nearly electrocuted by a poorly grounded podium as he introduced himself to the public. An inauspicious start, Jack recalled with a grin.

Donny came over with a citron and tonic and sat next to Jack in front of the big screen plasma TV. A sharp negotiator, Donny had become one of Jack's most trusted advisors, and he knew something about football too.

"I hope you're not too disappointed with this game," Donny said.

"I don't know, Donny. I've got a feeling that the greatest show on turf may wilt against the Pats' defense."

"I just hope they make a good show of it. But it would be nice if a team called the Patriots could win the Superbowl this year. What are they, fourteen point underdogs? I think that's some kind of record." Donny chuckled and took a sip of his drink.

"Is it a bigger spread than the Jets and Colts in '69?"

"Could be, for all I know. Brady is no Namath. At least the Jets had that going for them. Wait! Here come the introductions."

The game started with the typical hype, but in a departure from tradition, the Patriots ran out as a team, bypassing the individual introductions.

"Well, that's the Patriots 1, St. Louis 0," joked Jack.

PART VII

The Campaign

Traveling the campaign trail, Senator Cody took a few moments to relax. Mrs. Cody joined him on the couch. A beautiful woman in her mid-forties who still caught his eye whenever she entered the room, she did not look happy.

"What's the matter?" he asked.

Nicole Babineaux Cody answered his question with a question. "Who is Danielle Peck?"

Ken Cody furrowed his brow at the odd question. "A singer, isn't she?"

"A country singer. Is that all you know of her?"

"Where is this leading?"

"Did you know that by shear coincidence her concerts have been following your campaign stops?" His wife stared at him.

"That's where I must've heard her name then," said Cody with perfect ease. "I bet some of the volunteers mentioned her."

"Is there anything else you want to tell me about her?"

Then it dawned on him. "You think I'm having an affair?"

His question was met with a silent stare.

"My days of running around are long behind me. I haven't been with another woman since your uncle introduced us. I'll take a lie detector test to that."

He could tell that she believed him. And he had no doubt that he could pass a lie detector test due to his rare gift of being able to split his consciousness at will. Part of his psyche believed he was faithful, in fact, while the other part acknowledged his need for sex, extramarital or otherwise.

"Now, how did you get the notion that I was cheating with this singer?" He smiled and pulled her to himself with a hug.

"The same way anyone gets notions. It starts with rumors. Then given your similar travel schedules, the fact that she's beautiful..."

"I thought you knew that I don't like country music." He smiled disarmingly.

"She sings Western too," replied Nicole sarcastically. Cody smiled.

After a longer discourse, her suspicions faded away under the strength of his denials. Later on they made up in a most delightful way. Had she known the full truth, she would've had difficulty perceiving that he still loved her. His dalliances were mostly out of a physical need with no more significance than seeing one's barber.

The next day, she revealed that the source of the rumors had been his staff.

Senator Cody summoned three of his staff workers into the office and closed the door. Two young women and a young black man—Heather, Paige, and Rashad—looked at each other nervously. They were all idealistic. What Cody didn't know was that one was true to the ideals of the Republican Party. Paige was a plant.

"I'm given to understand that one or all of you have spread malicious rumors about me. I'd like to know why," Cody told them.

"Because you've let us all down, sir. We thought you were different from other Democrats," said Paige before the others could say anything.

Both Rashad and Heather fidgeted, not having expected the bold statement from Paige.

"All right then. Let's give your disappointment a hearing. Why am I, as you put it, not different?" Cody supposed he was scowling.

In answer, Paige reached into her jeans' pocket intending to produce pictures. They would've showed the senator in a compromising position with a well-known country and Western singer. They would've that was, if she'd been able to make her hand reach into her pocket. Instead, she froze and stared at the senator for an uncomfortable length of time. Both Rashad and Heather looked at her. They'd seen the pictures and knew she had them.

"Paige?" tested Heather to see if her friend would produce the evidence.

But Paige put her hand back at her side without producing the pictures.

"I'm sorry, sir. I just came to the realization that I was fooled into believing you were unfaithful. I made a mistake. I hope you can forgive me and allow me to continue to work in your campaign." Paige looked at the ground.

Ken Cody furrowed his brow in apparent confusion. "Are you as surprised as I am, Heather, Rashad?"

"Yes, sir," said Rashad. "I don't know what to say."

"Well, what are we going to do? Why don't all three of you take the rest of the day off. Tomorrow I'll want to meet with each of you separately. And I'll want to hear good reasons why I shouldn't believe that you would undermine this campaign going forward. I'm trying to accomplish something important for our country, and I can't tackle this objective without a stable base. Trust among my staff is key to that base. Am I understood?"

"Yes, sir," said the three would-be conspirators.

Cody motioned them away. As the door closed, Niles came in through a side door. "What was that all about?"

"They thought I was having an affair."

"Cheating on my niece?"

"Can you believe it? Your niece is enough woman for any man."

"I'm glad you feel that way." Niles sat.

"What other way could I feel? Besides, who has time for that kind of extracurricular activity? I've got my hands full here."

"Don't you know it. You ready for the debate?"

"I've got data coming out of my ass. I'm as ready as I'll ever be."

Heather and Rashad confronted Paige a few minutes after they'd all left Cody's office. They pulled her into an empty conference room.

"What just happened in there?" asks Rashad of Paige.

"The man in my pictures isn't Cody."

"The man in your pictures isn't Cody?" parroted Heather. "You seemed awfully sure of it yesterday. You convinced me and Rashad that it was true even though we didn't want to believe it."

"Well it isn't. I know that now since I saw Senator Cody's collar. Did you notice it when we were in there?"

"Can't say that I did. What does that have to do with anything?" queried Rashad.

"The man in my pictures has a birthmark on his neck. It's big enough so that you should see it above a shirt collar."

"And our Cody didn't have it?"

"Right."

"Let me see those pictures again?" requested Heather.

Paige handed her the photographs. Both Rashad and Heather examined them for several seconds before Heather commented. "I don't see any... No wait now I do."

"Where?" asked Rashad as he wrinkled his brow in confusion.

Heather pointed to a spot on the photo, and for a split second Rashad was still confused until he saw what he wanted to see.

"Oh, yeah. Now I see it. Pretty noticeable. We would've seen it on the senator long before now if it were there. What a relief."

The three young politicos exited the conference room. Absentmindedly, Paige left the pictures on the desk. From another door, Jack entered and picked up the photos. He saw no birthmark. He then took the pictures to a shredder in the corner and erased them from existence as surely as they were erased from the memories of the senator's young aides.

After tidying up some paperwork, the senator left the office by himself for once and headed to a local restaurant. The fare was Thai, but upon entering he headed back to the kitchen instead of sitting at a table. Wing Fat recognized him, smiled, and performed his equivalent of a hug, namely a respectful bow.

"Can I use your phone before dinner?" asked the senator. "My cell phone batteries are dead."

Wing just pointed him to his office where his own cell phone sat on the desk. Ken Cody dialed a familiar number. A woman's voice answered. It was a beautiful voice, and it belonged to a beautiful woman.

"I was just wondering," started Cody. "Is it better to date a high-profile, big name baseball pitcher or a low profile senator."

Danielle Peck giggled. "Well, that's a no-brainer. A baseball player of course. But since Mr. Beckett, World Series hero, is not my favorite person anymore, you'll have to do. Although who could resist the excitement and intrigue of doing a senator behind everyone's back."

Now it was his turn to laugh. "Actually," Cody continued. "That's why I'm calling. Looks like we were a little careless. One of my staff suspects. Before you say anything, I've smoothed it over, but we'll have to take a little hiatus from each other for a while."

"You have more to lose than I do, but I'd love to see you in the White House," the singer said. "And I don't want to be the cause of that not happening."

"Thanks for your understanding."

"What are you doing right now?"

"I was thinking of eating and then going home. Why?"

"If you're up for a little risk, I'm at the Copley Hotel."

"When did you get in town?"

"My gal posse and I love to shop Boston and/or New York. I'm never far from your stomping grounds. Need to blow off some steam?"

"After what I just said?"

"I've known you to be very discreet in the past. It's uncanny how you can get in and out of places without being seen if you don't want to."

A strange expression crossed Cody's face. "When you're in the public eye, you develop a knack for that. You must have your ways too."

"Well, are you coming?"

"You've twisted my arm. What room are you in?"

"Room 330. It's tucked away where few people go."

"See you soon."

Later on, the country star opened the door of her room to the charming senator. She was barefoot, in jeans and a lacy tank top. Her long lustrous black hair cascaded over her shoulders. Quickly, he slid in through the opening and was encompassed by her arms around his neck. They kissed and he tried to resist losing himself long enough, at least, to voice a warning.

"This has to be the last time for a while."

"That's what you said the last time," she replied as she pulled him atop her on the bed.

CHAPTER 29

Tim Russert addressed the audience with instructions for them and the four journalists on the panel before the debate. Soon thereafter the Democratic candidates for president filed onto the stage, one by one. Senator Cody exchanged greetings first with Senator Obama and then with Senator Clinton, his worthiest opponents. Dennis Kucinich stubbornly continued his campaign in the face of diminishing voter encouragement. The first question for Senator Cody was inevitably about religion.

"Senator Cody," started the Fox journalist, "How do you address the concerns of people of faith, a huge majority in this country, that you do not share their devotion to a religious basis for leadership?"

"I'd like all voters to consider that just as political doctrine is no substitute for reality, Religion, although a historical moral beacon, cannot substitute for reason. Those who oppose me politically accuse me of not being a religious man. But as we've seen, religion is no guarantee of wisdom or compassion. I may not be a practicing Christian, but I do believe in the inescapable bonds that define the family of man. We are all connected and as such will thrive or decline given the welfare of all of us.

"Concurrently, I also believe that man cannot afford this conflict of religious doctrine. Our race faces challenges to our survival on this earth. We as a family cannot waste the lives of our young while these challenges go unmet. We need the combined effort of all peoples no matter their creed, their color, or their gender. My administration will not discriminate when we draw on those resources in our population."

"Okay, but how does that square you with a possible God and his designs for us?"

"Well, if there is a God, I'm pretty sure He wouldn't want us to cede our responsibility to anyone for making our own decisions. Given our history as a species, I think it's pretty apparent that we're meant to think for ourselves."

The crowd applauded the eloquent answer though in some cases begrudgingly. The powder keg question was handled with typical aplomb by the gifted orator from Massachusetts.

In the coming weeks, however, religion antagonist Christopher Hitchens threatened to ignite the firestorm all over again. No one disputed his inestimable journalistic skills as evidenced by his columns in *The Nation*, *Vanity Fair*, and *The Atlantic*, just to name a few, but neither political party counted him as an ally due to his patchwork of views. In apparent support of atheism he talked about the supposed hereafter. And his speech sounded all the more haughty when delivered in his native British accent.

"Another canard of religious teachings is that man's reward for living a pious life is to go to heaven where he will cease to want for anything. Now any student of human psychology can tell you that that's not the nature of man. We either strive to meet goals or we die of boredom so unless we go lobotomized into the afterlife, I can't imagine man's spirit would be satisfied by such a prospect."

Fortunately, the focus of the voting public had moved on to other, more critical national needs. Otherwise, Hitchens' support for Cody would've been a mixed blessing at best.

Several months later, Cody defeated his Democratic rivals to secure the party's nomination. The formidable political machinery of the party was at his disposal.

The Democratic Party nominee for president, Senator Ken A. Cody, addressed the floor of the Democratic Convention. He first thanked his rivals for the nomination in graceful fashion before accepting the nomination of the party. He then proceeded to incite the crowd to bouts of frenzy as he previewed his administration.

"If we want to continue to take pride in being Americans then this nation should stand for something more than improving the fortunes of the already rich. We need to define a national goal. We need a return to the policies of progress and not of stagnation and loss of class mobility. We need to invite all of our people to participate in the future. We cannot afford to let the potential of any one citizen go untapped, for the challenges of the 21st century will test us all, and in so doing, all of us must rise to those challenges.

"Every citizen must be given the tools to participate in what will be a defining moment in our history. Perhaps a defining moment for all of mankind. It is time for this nation to put aside its selfish ways and to lead the world by accepting responsibility for our fellow citizens. It is time to lift all from poverty and from ignorance. Only in this way will we as a nation be equal to the tasks that are so clearly laid before us. And only in this way can we be proud of our collective heritage and benefit from the resulting accomplishments.

"As president, I intend to devote our national energies to solving, once and for all, our reliance on fossil fuels. And by extension to cease the assault on the natural order that the burning of these fuels threatens. We can no longer deny the effects of these fuels on our world and on our wellbeing as a species.

"In addition, I intend to take a fresh look at the decades-long conflict that defines the Middle East. I believe it is past time for a balanced approach absent the old prejudices. At the same time, my administration will explore new ways to circumvent rogue groups that spurn international laws, seek to destabilize peace loving nations, and do harm to innocent civilians. We will embrace negotiations with honorable partners in good faith, but we will dedicate ourselves to the eradication of groups that base their creed on the devaluation of human life whether it's theirs or those they choose to target. For those tempted by a message of destruction, I say to you, don't be a tool for the many who would use you for their own hateful ends. Join the family of man in working toward a peaceful solution to conflict.

"My domestic policy will stop the siege on the American middle and working classes. That assault has taken the form of unfair taxes and service cuts. The so-called tax cuts of the current administration have been more than offset by rising state and local taxes as well as the increased cost of services. Internationally, the current fiscal policy has put us in a weakened position in the form of deficits both trade and budgetary. It is time for wiser, more progressive stewardship of this country's greatest strength, our engine of economic development. It is time for smart, efficient government."

In yet another mixed blessing, the liberal website MoveOn.org revealed its support for Cody's economic proposals. They set up their own debate between progressive and conservative antagonists a la Hannity and Colms on Fox News, but in the reverse, where the conservative Republican took the role of punching bag. In answer to a question about economic fairness, the progressive debater didn't allow for interruption by his opponent.

"The Republican Party benefits a small minority of the American public. That party exists solely to provide political muscle for the moneyed elite, so they can skew public discourse for their continued financial gain. To do that, they have to draw votes from those who will not benefit by their election. Consider the Republican dilemma. How do they get votes from those who will actually be hurt by their governance? They became the party of Christian or family values. Of course families will only have Christian value left once the Republican Party is done with them.

"A party can educate the public on the merits of less government. But who really benefits from less government? Hard to believe that parents of a young middle-class family would gain much from less government. Of course large corporations may rejoice at the thought of less restrictive protections for the environment and people. What other kinds of fraud is the party thinking up to glean votes from those who have no business voting for them?"

In spite of the ham handedness of this showy device, the argument resonated with the public. For the first time in decades, the American middle class accepted the premise of who the Republican Party prioritized.

During a debate with Senator McCain leading up to the general election, Cody was tested with a question on terrorism—a perceived weakness of the Democratic Party in general. The pundits expected Cody to have trouble on this issue. His response was illuminating.

"Assuming for a moment that those who take innocent lives using Islam as an excuse have a legitimate complaint, we must ask, why do they take such a violent course? Perhaps the answer is obvious, something that everyone knows. It is far easier to destroy than to build.

"This radical fringe of an otherwise civilized culture is not up to the hard work of forming diplomatic consensus. It's hard to sit across the table from someone who has an opposing viewpoint and hash out differences. It's much easier to kill, maim, and destroy what others have built. Built for the noble purpose of bettering people's lives in this existence. The hard work, the work worthy of mankind's praise is shunned in favor of the easier path, the path of indiscriminate death. The path of duping impressionable youths to throw away their lives for the sake of dubious convictions. It is a philosophy unworthy of a culture that has contributed much to the ascent of man. And it cannot go unchallenged, for it is a sickness."

Viewers of Al Arabiya, broadcast widely throughout the Middle East, were impressed with the answer. The American public reaction was mixed, but the tone bothered the Shadow Group.

Later, during a PBS interview with Charlie Rose, Cody was given the chance to expand on his vision for a new role in government.

"I am pleased to have Senator Cody at this table for the first time. Welcome."

"Thank you, Charlie. I'm happy to have been given this forum."

"Let's start with your vision of government. You're at odds with some liberals, but isn't it also fair to say that you disagree with conservatives on the role of government?"

"Well, I believe that government's purpose is to help people better their lives, unlike this administration which has wielded government as an instrument of fear to promote an ideological agenda.

"I also think that the wise and efficient running of government has been a staple in this country's epic rise. Unfortunately, that government is under attack today, an insidious attack by a disingenuous group that strips protections from the economically disadvantaged, and in effect denies this nation the potential of all its citizens.

"Government can and should be used to inspire, not to scapegoat and shrink so that the wealthiest among us may take advantage of the less fortunate."

"But can you deny that people have profited under a Republican administration? That the country has become wealthier?" asked the famous television interviewer.

"Certain people have profited, yes. But in a very disproportionate and I think self-defeating way. Look at the Clinton years.

Not only did everyone benefit by the economic expansion, the top tier did better than they have under Bush.

"But on balance I think the middle class is ill served by the Republican Party. They suppress wages and limit government beyond what is prudent to the point of cutting or even eliminating beneficial services. Except for expanding Medicare, this administration has been no friend to the working classes. And I think that example of compassionate conservatism was conceived to benefit the insurance and pharmaceutical lobbies and to win votes.

"Another consequence of Republican antipathy toward government is the inability of the weakened institutions to protect ordinary citizens from environmental and economic damage. I appreciate that American business greatly contributes to our role as the leading nation, but without oversight, their mission to reduce costs can put them at odds with the public good. I'd like to instill a model where corporate and public wellbeing each complement the other."

Another question from the host: "Does corporate and public wellbeing encompass the environment? And if so, does that mean you support the environmental agreement where nations can trade pollution credits?"

"I do support that idea. I think it's gotten a fair hearing and seems to be working in practice. It shows that it can be profitable to promote a clean environment."

"A few moments ago you talked about efficient government. But how is that progressive, if you agree with limiting government and taxes? Doesn't that sound like a conservative position?" asked Charlie Rose.

"Who can argue with efficient government, a government that would take up less of the taxpayer's resources? My position is that it simply can't be the guiding principle for all actions. When it is, either large segments of the citizenry are denied services or we hamstring ourselves with unwieldy deficits if the government continues to spend on reduced tax receipts. This administration is a case in point for that.

"But my main objection is that the Republican hierarchy sells the concept of efficient government but applies it for the benefit of the elite only. They are the ones who get the largest tax breaks while the rest of us get cuts for our children's schools, our elder care, our college assistance, and so on. This is why I'm running for president. To restore a sense of balance where all can thrive."

Ever the pleasant host, Rose, nonetheless, again challenged his guest: "You can't deny that tax increases are inevitable under your administration. Or at least you'll have to allow the Bush tax cuts to expire."

"The president, and my opponent for that matter, would love to live in a world where cutting taxes for the wealthy solves all problems. President Bush was so fixated on it that he cut the taxes at the same time he incurred massive war expenditures— unprecedented in the history of our country. I think we're all witness to the result."

"Do you believe it's possible to go back to a time where American workers can make a high wage in this new global environment? How does the American workforce compete across borders where labor is cheap?"

"Due to fiercer global competition, the standard of living of our citizens relative to international workers is under stress. And we need a healthy business community to compete. But the Republicans' answer to continued American dominance is for government to allow big business to have its way with the workforce, to export jobs, and exert downward pressure on salaries. That's the part of their 'less government' mantra you won't hear about. I say there is a smarter way, a way that takes the needs of business as well as the working class into consideration."

"And that is?"

"Progressive taxes, incentives to promote good corporate citizenship with regard to the American workforce. Also let's review our international trade agreements to get back to a level playing field. A lot of foreign workers' advantages over Americans stem from substandard worker protections and poor environmental stewardship. Tightening that up would be good for them and for us, and the huge advantage they have would be lessened enough so that in some cases it wouldn't be worth exporting a job. But finally, when those measures still result in off-shoring, we would fund the retraining for our people as opposed to putting them out to pasture."

"Someone said that the difference between the parties is that the Democrats go into public service and the Republicans go into corporate service. Is that your view?"

The candidate smiled before answering. "In my view... to be a Republican you have to be able to desensitize yourself on certain issues. Issues like poverty, like the budget deficit, the trade deficit. In other words, issues that for the short term benefit a privileged minority but weaken the nation over the long term.

"The current administration thinks the job is done when the wealthy are making money. To them it's a sign of a healthy economy, except it's at the expense of the middle classes.

"After Katrina, if you'll recall, Barbara Bush... the former first lady, caused a bit of a flap when she referred to the newly homeless citizens of New Orleans as the underprivileged. I thought that was a very telling remark since that's how the Republican Party sees the world. There's the privileged, in their ranks, and then the underprivileged."

CHAPTER 30

June 2, 2008

Jack tried to attract as little notice as possible in the waiting room of Duke University Medical Center. News of his brother Ted's malignant brain tumor compelled him to be here to lend spiritual support if nothing else. The ability to obscure one's person in the minds of observers was well tested but for family members. It was rumored that the family bond could defeat the mind-dampening effect, so Jack had to be careful. He recognized nieces, cousins, and of course Carolyn.

His daughter had grown up to be a fine woman, Jack thought, and he didn't regret that she'd chosen to avoid the family business of public service. She was visible enough in her support of causes championing the politically voiceless. The president couldn't help but shed a tear when she'd publicly endorsed Obama for president because Obama's campaign reminded her of the inspired masses JFK himself had brought to the 1960 campaign.

Now at the hospital, his daughter looked in Jack's direction, which caused him to casually turn away. At least he hoped it appeared casual. He sensed that she wanted to come over, but a nurse intercepted her with some questions. Jack moved into the hall but not before leaving his nanorobotic sentinels to monitor the room.

Picking up a magazine next door, Jack contemplated revealing himself to Senator Kennedy but thought the better of it, considering his younger brother's condition. Younger brother, he thought with irony. In spite of the age difference, Jack looked far and away the more junior of the two. It pained him to see how Teddy had aged. In spite of the Kennedy vigor, the years sat heavily on the so-called liberal lion. Jack wished he could bestow the same physical advantages he now enjoyed in this body to his entire family. Still, Ted looked no worse than others of his age and he was as engaged as any septuagenarian could be.

The doctor finally came out of the operating room. He met with the family members, which Jack observed through his microsentinels. The operation had gone well, and the senator was resting comfortably. A standard medical cliché, thought Jack. He resolved to check on his brother now and again. He left the floor just in time to avoid the curious Carolyn who had come looking for the stranger with the familiar aspect.

CHAPTER 31

Back on the campaign trail, the rhetoric heated up. Former Senator Phil Gramm appeared disgusted. The United States had never been more dominant and had benefited greatly from globalization, he stated. Since these words came from a man who actually boasted of killing the Clinton national health care plan, no one was surprised at his indifference to a public struggling with declining home values, high fuel costs, and unemployment.

"We have sort of become a nation of whiners. Misery sells newspapers," he rationalized. "Thank God the economy is not as bad as you read in the newspaper every day." Many thanked their god that Gramm never had become president.

As if the discredited neocon movement needed more publicity, an unapologetic George Will appeared on Charlie Rose and echoed Gramm's sentiments. He seemed at a loss as to what all the complaining was about. As candidate Cody had said, the Republicans thought the job was done when the wealthy were making money. In any case Gramm's publicized comments didn't help McCain's candidacy. The last thing McCain needed was a wealthy Republican surrogate making comments that suggested the party was out of touch with the average voter. As his campaign feared, the remarks draw fire. On a C-Span political talk show, an eloquent caller made comments that reverberated around the blogosphere.

"I think it's shocking that the party that claims to be the most patriotic has sold us down the river to foreign creditors with this debilitating national debt. The policy that allowed the rich to raid the treasury by way of huge tax givebacks threatens to lead this nation toward irrelevancy. Our declining global standing is a direct result of this misguided tax policy as well as foreign policy. I submit that those who have made huge fortunes take up a disproportionate share of the infrastructure and should at least pay their fair share of its upkeep."

Sarah Palin, the Republican vice presidential nominee, decried Cody as a free-spending atheist, enabling McCain to appear to stay above the fray. A looming disaster for the country, claimed Palin. He would choke off any economic growth by going back to the days of regulation.

The Democratic vice presidential nominee, Barack Obama, answered the charges with some compelling examples of the supposed virtues of an anti-regulation policy.

"Ms. Palin, do you honestly think we wouldn't have been better off if the financial sector had been regulated to prevent the latest mortgage crises? Wouldn't the institutions themselves have been saved from their own exuberance in making these high-risk loans? Loans, whose legacy is to restrict credit now and prevent new investments.

"And, Ms. Palin, don't you think the U.S. automakers would be better off now if they had embraced higher mileage standards? Instead they fought against them, and with their Republican allies in the government, American cars have the lowest miles-per-gallon standards in the world. Regulating higher efficiencies would have made them competitive with foreign suppliers. Now they're struggling to survive and laying off thousands. So remind me, Ms. Palin, why is deregulation good for the public? The business sector?"

No retort to Palin was needed, however. The country has little appetite for another Republican president, particularly with the year ending in economic crisis. The Alaska governor's disastrous media interviews strained her credibility with the voters and put the Republican ticket on the defensive.

Cody won the general election by a landslide.

PART VIII

Mission: Illumination

CHAPTER 32

The sea rocked the salvage ship back and forth as a careless parent might its infant. Spume flew up and coated the bridge's windows, and several crewman took to the toilets. The grayish green of the water suggested the Barents Sea, as opposed to the Indian Ocean off Western Australia. Those working on deck risked a queasiness that tested even the most seasoned old salt. The trick was to concentrate on one's task and try not to focus on the horizon or rough seas. Ignoring the elements was nearly impossible, however, considering the wet, windy conditions. The sounds of the creaking ship and clanging metal accompanied the shouts of sturdy seamen as they bent to their tasks amid the violent bouncing of the bow and the resultant wash of water that threatened to pull them overboard.

"This came up in a hurry," commented the helmsman.

"Just hold your course, Lieutenant," said Captain Favreau.

"Holding course, aye."

The captain, confident of his ship and crew, went below to his cabin for a long overdue conference. As he entered the room, he turned up the light as he always had to in the presence of the Others. Must have something to do with their large eyes, he thought. Once the room was illuminated, he spied two representatives of the so-called Others and a human companion of theirs.

"Enjoying the ride?" chivied Favreau. Then he hung up his hat and sat on his bunk so he could take in all three of his visitors.

The human, Jeff Staten, was the only one to grunt a response. "I've been on worse. Are we close to the position?"

Captain Favreau knew Jeff from previous meetings and was always amazed at how well Jeff got along with these Others, these Martians. Oh, they were friendly enough, even gregarious, but there was still something off-putting about them. Perhaps it was the prejudice of his physical ideal, the captain thought. Their scrawny physiques and those big heads still unnerved him. Typical alien physiology according to all the UFO nut cases he'd heard tell about. Who could have known that they were right?

Jeff, on the other hand, was someone he could easily deal with. At this point, Favreau wouldn't count him as a drinking buddy, but he shared a common bond with him, both men having been in the military. Jeff could be stone faced, even aloof, but when it came down to it, he was good with people. Could be a salesmen, thought the captain, as he'd also witnessed Jeff's powers of persuasion.

"In another hour or so we'll be at the geometric center of our planned search area," offered Favreau.

The two Martians exchanged glances with each other and then with Jeff. Some form of communication seemed to pass between them. The captain took note of this as he did the dress styles of his three guests. All wore uniforms. Jeff's was the most familiar and looked like an outfit Favreau had seen on soldiers in Iraq. Desert fatigues, perhaps. The Martians wore plain black outfits with an innocuous insignia on their slight upper arms and an insignia on their chests. But it was their heads and eyes that the captain tried to refrain from staring at.

"Captain, I think you've met one of our guests before."

Favreau had to concede that he might have, but they all looked alike to him.

"This is Vice Commandant Kel," continued Jeff as he gestured to the one on the right.

"Yes, we have met. Last year in Reykjavík."

"That's right, Captain. I'm pleased that you remember me. I know it's sometimes hard for humans to differentiate between us."

"Not in your case. I was impressed by how much Brennivín you could put away."

"Brennivín?" queried Jeff.

"A popular libation on the island," explained Kel with the Martian equivalent of a smile.

"And this," continued Jeff, "is sub-regent Xac."

Xac actually nodded, an obvious concession to human norms. "Pleased to meet you, Captain. I've heard a lot about your valiant efforts in our struggle."

"I took some convincing, but now that I understand our common dilemma, I'm more than happy to do what I can. So what are we after, anyway?"

"We're after something that may help us end religious conflict on your planet. And may also take away a tool of the Shadow Group for destroying several universes," stated Kel.

"Really! There is something at the bottom of the Indian Ocean that can do all this?"

"Not by itself," interjected Jeff. "I wish it were that easy. Do you know what germanium is?"

"An element on the periodic chart if I remember my chemistry texts," acknowledged Favreau.

"That's right. It's commonly used as a semiconductor and for transistors."

"What's the big deal about that? We seem to have plenty of those kinds of materials." Favreau shrugged.

"True. We have plenty of materials for semiconductors and transistors. What we don't have is a rare isotope of germanium that can only be produced by long exposure to gamma rays in a pristine environment like space."

Favreau had a sudden realization. "You mean an environment like Skylab was in. So that explains what we're looking for here."

"Exactly. Skylab was in orbit long enough for its germanium components to transform into what the Martians call temporalium. Still only an oddity with no useful applications by either human or Martian science. But when in a controlled implosion guided by a technology not created by either race..."

The latest in sonar technology trailed behind them on a tether and did its job efficiently without the interference of the ship's hull. They varied the depth of the torpedo-shaped device to compensate for the undulating sea bottom. Within five hundred miles of the Australian coast, the searchers were lucky enough to be on the wide continental shelf with a somewhat manageable depth of several hundred feet. Three hours later with their search only two hours old, they located a submerged debris field. The towed array sonar suggested wreckage that hadn't come from a ship's sinking.

On deck, the crew prepared cube-shaped robots to reconnoiter the bottom—Earth technology. The units were about three feet on a side and weighed several hundred pounds. These remote-controlled devices had lights and propellers, and were packed with sensors, as well as video equipment to transmit images. And unlike the similarly tethered towed array sonar units, these were artificially intelligent. They would make their own decisions about search patterns and clues to follow.

The sea was still rough, but the sky had brightened. Most of the crew were over their bouts of seasickness and worked above deck with no incidents. Jeff Staten, known to the crew (as opposed to his Martian colleagues), attached a customized device to the each of the robots. A Martian detector of the rare mineral they were after, he explained to the captain.

Lieutenant Adams shouted down from the bridge.

"Bogeys detected on radar, Captain. Fixed wing aircraft. They're approaching from the north."

"What's their ETA?"

"They'll be here in fifty-seven minutes."

"Very well. Activate Stealth Mode."

"Aye, Captain."

Jeff took in the exchange between the bridge officer and the captain when he heard the report of bogeys. He envisioned the deck being strafed or bombs exploding as they hit the water, creating temporary geysers. Before he could ask the captain about Stealth Mode, his eyes played a trick on him. Out of the corner of his right eye, the horizon changed from a moving yet sharp line, to a blurry indistinct border zone between sky and water. As a matter of fact, wherever he looked, the air had a strange, hazy quality. Ultimately, he decided the ship itself still stood out in sharp relief but everything around it was different.

"You're not the only ones with some super technical resources," said the captain as he noted Jeff's confusion.

"What is it?"

"It's Stealth Mode, a bubble of energy around the ship that's bending light. We are, for all intents and purposes, invisible."

"A cloaking device."

The captain laughed. "We have a Trekkie here. Yes, the Romulans have nothing on us."

"Great. It may take a little longer than I planned to install this device on the robots."

"A little longer is all you'll have," Favreau told him. "If those planes are sent by the other Earth's Agency, they won't be fooled for long. We're leaving a footprint that can be detected by more than just eyeballs. They'll catch on sooner or later."

"You think it's the Agency that's tracking us?"

"That's a high probability based on the Others' intelligence. Although we believe that they think we're with the Shadow Group, their enemy. They're the religious fanatics trying to collide realities. As far as we can guess, the Agency still doesn't know about the Martians or our friends, the renegade Martian group known to us as the Others."

"The Martians seem to share the Agency's agenda at maintaining the spatial distance between realities," Jeff commented. "Funny they haven't contacted Agency leadership and allied themselves to the Agency."

Favreau nodded. "The Others tell me that's because the Martians believe that even soliciting like-minded allies qualifies as tampering and may risk a collision of realities. They're here reluctantly because the Agency, in their opinion, is risking existence by simply observing. They're trying to keep the Agency in check while maintaining as small a footprint as possible in this universe."

"Interesting. And complicated. The Shadow Group would welcome our interference since they believe it'll destroy all realities but theirs."

"True. But I don't think they'd approve of our liberal ideal of bettering all lives across every reality, across existence." The captain smiled.

Both men contemplated the complex relationships between the four reality-hopping factions in silence.

"How long will you need?" asked the captain.

"About another half-hour here on deck, but who knows how long once we start searching the ocean floor."

"Well, do what you can while I try to keep the hostiles off your back."

"Captain, you don't think they know what we're after, do you?"

"That's a scary thought. I certainly hope not. But I can't imagine how they would know. This scheme is something the Others came up with independently. Unless..."

"Unless the Others have been penetrated," finished Jeff.

"Well, let's not get paranoid yet. I'm betting that they just want to stop us whether they know what we're up to or not."

"I better get back to my task at hand."

About an hour later and right on cue, two supersonic fighters roared by overhead. Captain Favreau watched as they continued on, hopefully oblivious of his ship. He issued orders for the crew to keep him informed of the aircraft's whereabouts and went below deck to check on Staten, who sat watching a video monitor with the feed from the robots. Kel and Xac, now appearing as human Navy officers, watched as well. Xac also manipulated another instrument whose design was never conceived on Earth.

"Anything yet?" asked the captain.

"Perhaps. Xac's sensor is picking up a reading but it's hard to localize. Could be radiational interference from other parts of Sky-lab. We're now searching the old-fashioned way—by establishing a search grid and checking each coordinate at close range. It's going to be slow unless we get lucky."

"Can you spare me a minute outside, Jeff?"

Outside the cabin, Favreau spoke in low tones. "How much do you know about the instrument the Martian Xac is using?"

"I don't know how it works if that's what you mean. All I know is it will give us a signal once it detects temporalium."

"So, we're relying on the Martian operator's word that the device is operating properly. And that he's using it properly."

Jeff furrowed his brow. "Of course. What are you suggesting?"

"I think you know. It seems odd that a device sent for such a critical job is having a problem with predictable conditions."

"You've been a Navy man, Captain. Is it so unusual to have equipment problems in critical situations?"

"Any experiences I've had with either Agency or Martian technology has impressed me as to how well their technology works under any conditions. They can customize almost any device for any purpose and manufacture it instantaneously by some sort of nanotech process where they build it molecule by molecule in a 3D printer. Christ, even our own technology has made great strides in reliability since Vietnam. Don't you think it's a bit odd that this device flounders in an environment it was designed for. Radiation should have been taken into account."

"You suspect the makers of the device?"

"Or the operator. We talked about the possible penetration of the Others. What if one of these Martians is a mole?"

At that moment, Xac, in his guise as a Navy officer, stuck his head out the door and announced they'd found it.

Beneath hundreds of feet of water at depths that would crush a human to pulp, the robot gathered up a sizable sample of the germanium isotope and placed it in a special container. Stowing its stash, it started to ascend but not before making a slight excursion on the way up.

The ship's crane lifted the robot from the surface and placed it on deck. Jeff ran to the device, closely followed by the captain, and examined its cubby hole for the container of temporalium. He glanced up in dismay. "It's not here."

The captain looked as if he'd expected as much. "Are you sure?"

Jeff felt around and came up empty handed.

"Check the other robot," Jeff told the sailors. "Maybe we got them mixed up."

The other robot's hold was empty too.

"Maybe it fell out," said Jeff with an exasperated sigh. "We'll just have to go down and search for more."

At that moment the drone of airplane engines made everyone look up. Large planes sporadically dropped parachuted packages from the sky. The packages, as they got closer, looked like torpedoes. Jeff's stomach constricted.

"Sonobuoys," said Favreau. "If they can't find us with light waves, as in radar, they'll do it with sound."

Jeff knew the answer to the question that had formed in his mind, but he asked it anyway. "Will your stealth bubble keep us hidden from their sonar?"

"No. Those buoys will detect our hull below the water line and triangulate on our position. I'm afraid our time is running out."

The bridge officer reported that the planes hadn't shown up on radar. Obviously, they too were equipped with stealth technology. Now, however, radar indicated fast-moving water craft approaching from the Australian mainland. Their speed and size suggested hovercraft, very probably filled with commandos, thought the captain.

"How long do we have?" he asked the radar operator.

"About two hours, sir."

"So we have that long to find this temporalium and get the hell out of here. Jeff, that container that the robot used—would it be too much to hope that it had some kind of homing device?"

"Way ahead of you, Captain. I've got a directional device that was supposedly tuned to it right here."

"And it doesn't work, right?"

"Right. But that could just mean that it's out of range. Maybe fell out of the robot's hold and is back on the ocean floor."

"Or that it was tampered with."

"All right, all right. But whether that's true or not, we still have to find it before the enemy gets here in those hovercraft."

"What do you suggest?"

"That we look for it on the ocean floor."

"Are you volunteering to go down there?" asked the captain.

"Why not? I saw the atmospheric diving suit you have on board."

"That antique? Nobody has worn that for years."

"Well, maybe it's time somebody tries it on."

The captain hesitated. He never liked the idea of sending men to their deaths. "I don't know."

"Look, we're wasting time. At least get me into the suit. If someone has a better idea in the meantime, fine. But let's start doing something."

"All right. I suppose I can't argue with that logic."

Favreau turned to his bos'n. "Get the fitters up here with that suit. We're going deep sea diving."

Almost a half-hour later, the helmet was fitted to the collar of the klunky metal suit. Jeff was all set to go. He signaled that he was ready to try on the radio. "Anybody get any bright ideas while my tailors were working?" asked Jeff through the speaker.

"I'm afraid not," responded the captain.

With that, Jeff motioned for the temporalium sensor. One of the crew placed it in his robotic hand. Jeff awkwardly moved the device so he could see the readout and gave a thumbs up. A winch raised him off the deck and over the side of the ship and then started lowering him to the water.

Once Jeff made contact with the surface, his transmitted voice announced just seven hundred feet to go. Soon, he disappeared under the waves. At about one hundred feet down, Jeff glanced at his sensor and noticed that it registered the presence of a slight amount of the substance he was after. *Good,* thought Jeff. *Maybe, if we're lucky, it'll be directly below me.*

"How are we doing, Jeff?" came a voice over his radio.

"That you, Captain?"

"Who were you expecting?"

"Hard to identify voices down here. So far, so good with the suit."

"Very well. Shout if there's a hint of trouble, and we'll winch you out of there as fast as we can. Got that?"

"Depend on it." On his way down, Jeff went over a mental checklist to be sure that all was well with the suit. He seemed to be breathing easily and he was starting to forget about his claustrophobia-producing shell and concentrate on his surroundings.

The light became very dim very quickly, and he soon turned on the suit's lights. He descended smoothly but rapidly, and he was already at a depth of two hundred and fifty feet. His descent accelerated, as he knew it would, before ultimately slowing down when he approached the sea floor.

Soon thereafter he touched down on the sandy bottom of the inky black ocean. As he moved around, each step kicked up clouds and he made sure to plan his search pattern so he wouldn't have to track back through them. He walked while monitoring his sensor. Strangely, the trace indication he'd encountered on the way down was gone now. Could the material have moved with some current? wondered Jeff. He dismissed that idea as he noted no resistance to his walking in any direction. The sea floor was calm, and he lost track of time as he did his work in what became a dreamlike state.

"Jeff, how are you making out?"

The communication had startled Jeff at first. "No sign of any of the substance yet. I thought I'd picked up something on my way down, but I'm beginning to wonder if it was my imagination."

"Do you want us to pick you up and ride with you a while? Get you over to a new search area?"

"How are we doing on time?"

"Our friends are about forty minutes away."

"Sure. I'm not doing any good here. Let's try that for a few more minutes."

Without warning Jeff felt his tether tighten. He was yanked off his feet in a not-too-gentle manner, given a ride for about a minute, and then deposited in a new search grid.

"Thanks for the ride, Captain. Although a little more notice would've been good."

"With time running out, I thought I'd skip the pleasantries. It wasn't too much of a jerk I hope."

"No more than a water-skiing start I suppose. Now that I'm here, you realize we're depending on blind luck."

"Don't waste time telling me that. Just look."

Jeff wielded his sensor as he swept it in as wide an arc as his suit permitted while still looking at the display. Had it been imagination when he'd seen the meter indicate a find on the way down? If the reading was real, how could the substance not be at the bottom and not be on the ship? And then it occurred to him. "Captain, pull me up. I think I know where our missing sample is."

As before, Jeff was jerked off the bottom. He sensed, or at least it seemed, that his ascent was much quicker than his descent. Perhaps the speed of his travel caused his next dilemma. His feet were wet and the wetness was rising. As the captain had feared, the suit wasn't totally seaworthy.

On the bridge, Captain Favreau monitored the approach of the lead hovercraft through his binoculars. Two more were behind the first, approaching at the type of speed that only a hovercraft could attain on the water.

"Well, we can't outrun them," he said aloud. "Is Stealth Mode still on?"

"Aye," responded the first mate.

"Turn it off. Perhaps the confusion of seeing us reappear will buy us a few more seconds."

At that moment, a crewman burst onto the bridge and hurried through a salute as he got Favreau's attention.

"Trouble with the atmospheric diving suit sir. It's leaking."

"Leaking! How bad?"

"The cable is pulling about one hundred extra pounds. And we've lost communication with Mr. Staten. But his radio could have shorted."

"First Mate Harris, have the doctor meet me at the winch," ordered the captain as he ran down on deck with the sailor.

"How long till Jeff is on deck?"

"About ninety seconds. Maybe less."

In a little over a minute, the winch deposited Jeff Staten in his water-filled suit onto the deck. Feverishly, men pored over the fasteners on his helmet. It seemed like an eternity, but they eventually got the head gear off, allowing the water to drain. Jeff was unconscious. His skin was cold to the touch, but his face wasn't blue.

"Get the rest of the suit off so I can work on his chest," ordered the doctor.

Several of the men employed imaginative destructive techniques with tools, torches, and so on to cut parts of the suit away more quickly, yet the seconds still ticked by.

"What are his chances, doctor?" asked the captain.

"Depends on how long he's been out. One thing that's in our favor is that his body temperature is lowered from exposure to the water."

With that, Jeff Staten's chest was exposed and the doctor administered cardio-pulmonary resuscitation. He listened and alternately pounded on the chest, worked the legs up and down, and forced air into the lungs by squeezing a bulb over the man's mouth. He did this calmly, methodically, and seemed to indicate a confidence that he could bring Jeff back. After a few repetitions, Jeff started to cough up seawater. He was going to be okay.

"Captain, we have boarders," said a seaman who had helped cut the suit off Jeff.

Indeed, the captain looked up and saw men he didn't recognize surrounding the group that hovered over Jeff Staten. Favreau had been so focused on the drama in front of him that he had become oblivious to all else, including the armed group that now leveled their guns at his crew.

As Jeff came to, he took stock of his immediate surroundings and grabbed at the sensor he had carried to the ocean floor. He nearly knocked the doctor over as he lunged at the device. The moment he got his bearings, he realized that the towed array sonar cables were being reeled in. Looking aft, he noted that the torpedo-shaped device was already being lowered to the deck as water drained off its sides. When the crewman abruptly stopped rewinding the cables, the device gently swayed about six feet above the deck. At that second, Jeff perceived the cadre of armed men threatening the crew. The captain and all within sight had their hands folded on top of their heads. Several had frightened looks on their faces. Jeff got up slowly while placing the sensor in his coverall pocket.

"Well, who have we here?" asked a familiar voice.

Jeff turned to see a former friend and current adversary, Olaf Erikson of the Varangian Guard.

"Do I know you?" questioned Jeff.

"Good one, Jeff."

The captain looked at Jeff quizzically.

"Captain Favreau," said Jeff, "we are in the presence of the captain of the Varangian Guard in the other Earth's government."

"Varangian Guard? You mean like the group that guarded the Eastern Roman Emperor?" Favreau was a history buff.

"The same group on the other Earth evolved to be an integral part of their present-day government."

"Whoa. All the parallels are mind-boggling. How do you know so much about them?" asked the captain.

At that point, Olaf laughed and interjected, "Because Jeff is one of us. Or I should say was one of us until he betrayed our charter."

Jeff shook some of the water out of his hair. "I've been convinced that our way wasn't preserving anything. And we could've been doing a lot of good but for the non-interference directive."

Jeff noted the captain's reaction to yet another Star Trek reference, the non-interference directive. *It must seem strange to him,* thought Jeff, *that I'm a fan of one of their cultural icons now that he knows*

I'm not even from his reality. If we get a chance, we'll have to have a discussion about the possibility of another universe with a Captain Kirk in it. As Jeff contemplated this frivolous exchange, he noted that Favreau's stare now contained suspicion. *I'm an alien to him,* thought Jeff.

With that, he stared back and tried to make Favreau conscious of a message. Jeff glanced at the sensor, now on the deck, and then at the towed array sonar device hanging six feet above the aft deck. Jeff was trying to tell him that the temporalium was in the suspended device. Favreau finally gave the slightest of nods to show he understood. Now Jeff wondered if Olaf and his troops knew what the prize was and what it was for.

"So shall we talk about what you've been doing out here?" chided Olaf.

"Just doing a little historical research," said the captain. "Nothing that would upset the natural separation of realities."

"Of course you were. But what's so historically interesting out here other than the wreckage of Skylab in the ocean beneath us?"

Both Jeff and Favreau remained silent.

"Did I strike a nerve? What else could you be looking for with advanced sonar technology like the device you've been towing."

Olaf walked to the back of the ship as armed men prodded the captain and Jeff to follow. The towed array sonar unit still hung and shed an occasional drip of water.

"What's so interesting about an old, poorly built space station?" wondered Olaf aloud as he looked up at the torpedo-shaped device.

"Lower this device," Olaf ordered the ship's crew.

Nobody moved so he took a pistol from his U.S. Navy-provisioned holster and fired it at the crane operator's feet. The man jerked backward as if awakened from a trance and manipulated the controls to lower the torpedo shape to the deck. While the device lowered, Olaf watched the faces of Captain Favreau and Jeff Staten. Neither man betrayed the slightest amount of interest.

"I understand this is the leading edge of underwater sensing technology on this world. Did it help you find what you were looking for? Come up with any interesting relics from Skylab?"

Favreau and Staten didn't rise to the bait.

"Maybe we should go down and have a look for ourselves?"

Jeff breathed a mental sigh of relief. Olaf didn't realize the substance was in the torpedo. But in the middle of his exhalation, he noted the Martian Other known as Xac making an appearance on deck in his human guise. He held his own temporalium sensor, and he approached Olaf. *The little bastard is going to give us away.* With no thought to his own safety, Jeff produced a knife hidden in his boot and threw it at the betraying Martian. It embedded itself squarely in the Martian's chest causing the illusional human disguise to burst like a bubble. Fully revealed, the slight frame of the Martian fell to the deck oozing bluish-green life fluid.

Jeff braced for the inevitable gunfire. None came. He looked around and couldn't find the gunmen. Olaf had disappeared as well. Rushing over to the Martian, Jeff realized that the little alien still held the sensor, except it wasn't a sensor.

"What have you done?" he demanded of the dying Xac.

"I've teleported us to the closest reality where we have no boarders."

"You mean the sensor you were holding is some kind of teleportation device."

"I had to get it as close to you and the captain as I could. Limited range." He choked out that last part.

"How can we help you?" asked the captain in dismay.

"I don't have your species' constitution. Hit the square button twice, the round one... then one more time on the sq..."

Xac lost consciousness. The captain took the device from his hand and followed the instructions. He hoped that he'd heard them all. As soon as he did, the little Martian dematerialized.

"I hope that means he teleported somewhere safe rather than disintegrated," said the captain.

"Me too," said Jeff. "I thought he was about to give us away."

"You just never know about people. Or Martians for that matter. Anyway, now what do we do? I assume we can return to our own reality. We need to get back to enact our plan."

"Getting back should be an easy matter with the technology on hand. But it may take a while to figure it out," lied Jeff. He knew that returning to their own universe could be irrelevant, and he hoped his tone didn't betray that fact to the captain. He still needed the other man's help and that help might not be as forthcoming if the captain realized that a successful mission could erase his existence from both this reality and their home one.

Jeff was willing to sacrifice himself, but he feared making that possibility clear to the captain. Favreau knew the plan but wasn't up enough on temporal mechanics to understand the danger to personal timelines.

"But do we need to bother about that now?" continued Jeff. "I'm getting the sense that this universe differs from ours only in imperceptible ways. I say we proceed with the mission here first as the priority and then tackle the problem of returning us to our own reality later."

The captain thought about that a moment before nodding his head.

"Do I have an ex and two teenaged sons here too? Maybe they're better behaved than mine at home. Well, let's proceed as you say until we can consider a return. Am I to understand that the temporalium is in the torpedo?"

With that, Jeff opened the panel on the side of the device and drew out the container that the robot had placed there.

"So if Xac didn't perpetrate this, it must have been..."

"Kel!" said Jeff.

Soon thereafter, they found Kel dead, slumped over his console. Xac had already detected the traitor and dispatched him.

CHAPTER 33

The Temporalium Experiment

Martian scientists had displayed unusual emotion at their chance discovery. A portion of the mysterious Artifact from a race that predated the Martians by billions of years became active when fed an electric current in the pico-ampere range. The frequency of the low alternating current seemed to be critical to the device's operation. It came to life and created a hologram. The scientists marveled at the detail of the image. And this hologram turned out to be meant for manipulation in controlling certain functions of the Artifact.

Sometime later, the Others commandeered a piece of this ancient probe that so fascinated the Martian public. The intelligent device had witnessed the birth of their race and possibly safeguarded it from a savagely aggressive human species in the reality that contained an ecologically viable Mars as well as Earth. The Others' inside agent, trusted by the Martian government, had no trouble smuggling a vital piece of the amazing relic back to the Others' lab.

As sophisticated as the ancient builders of the device had been, they were somewhat bereft of imagination. Scientists were reasonably certain that the ancients knew nothing of alternate realities, judging by the part of the device's memory that had been probed so far. Surprising, considering that the inferior science of Martians and Humans had long ago confirmed the existence of these other dimensions. More surprising even, considering that the hardware and technology in the ancient probe with a few minor adjustments could open portals to other realities. Nevertheless, the remarkable adaptability of the Artifact's technology galvanized the Others to embark on a bold-stroke venture that they hoped would end the conflict instantaneously. The Other's chief research scientist, Ulekbetor, conducted the final test.

"No problems so far?" asked the mysterious leader of the Others, referred to only as "the Overseer."

Ulekbetor, in an un-Martian-like gesture, turned toward him to answer. The Others' were far more demonstrative than their Martian brethren. They even considered it bad manners to avoid animated interactions. Conversely, the rest of the Martian population cultivated understated behavior.

"No problems whatsoever, Overseer. The tests have been remarkably consistent. That level of consistency by itself is scientifically significant. I, at least, expected some bugs adapting our technology to this device."

"You didn't trust to stable wormholes?"

"Can't say as I was confident, but these ancients certainly knew how to manipulate the fabric of space-time in our universe if not others. I'm just astounded that this device adapts so well to us as well as our technology. If we can imagine a place, we can go there."

"So we're ready to go."

"I can't see any reason why we would delay."

The Overseer started to imagine the consequences of what they were about to attempt. There was a possibility that Western Civilization not armed with its Christian convictions would never rise to dominate the Earth. Who knew what a new Earth would look like under those circumstances? What effect would that have on mankind? On Martian kind? But they all had debated the risks *ad nauseum*, and each alternate possibility this mission allowed was less threatening to existence itself. Even if some of them ceased to be born as a result of their little adventure, it still would be for the greater good. The safety of several universes had to take precedence, he thought.

"If you're ready, then lets proceed," instructed the Overseer, and he retreated to the gallery with several of the Others' hierarchy in attendance.

Ulekbetor nodded to the human volunteer, who walked through an opening in what appeared to be a giant, spherical bird cage. Once inside, he stepped onto the displacement pad. The inside of the cage bars were clad with temporalium. Seeing that the volunteer was in place, the Martian scientist then donned an opaque, visored helmet with the help of his aides. They made several adjustments to be sure that the fiber-optic electrodes were in contact with his skull.

When all the electrodes were positioned, nanobotic probes emanating from them penetrated the Martian's cranium without causing him pain. The filaments found the neural centers of the brain that they were designed to tap. A tone told Ulekbetor that he could start. Based on his research, he called up the appropriate desert in his mind's eye and concentrated on fleshing out the vision with his imagination. He heard the sounds, smelled the flora, felt the breezes, and tasted the dust in his mouth.

As Ulekbetor concentrated, Artifact technology complemented by contemporary Martian systems fed an electric current to a grapefruit-sized device fixed atop a four-foot-tall slender column at the center of the bird cage. The human volunteer standing very close by, inside the cage, observed no reaction as yet.

The smaller sphere at the cage's center also contained a miniscule amount of the rare germanium isotope called temporalium. On the inside of the small sphere's walls, explosive charges detonated by the applied current imploded in upon the temporalium. Operating much like an atomic bomb armed with enriched uranium, the force of the explosions compressed the atomic structure of the temporalium, which then expanded outward violently yet not destructively. Instead of a mushroom cloud, a translucent bubble of temporal energy blossomed from the small sphere, encompassing Jeff. The bubble was contained by the bird cage whose bars were lined with temporalium. Unhurt, Jeff stood stoically waiting for the next step in the procedure, a process orchestrated by the thoughts of Ulekbetor.

The gallery observed Jeff Staten, the human volunteer, slowly fading from view. Then, as if a switch had been thrown, he vanished completely along with the bubble. The effects of his actions in his new location would be felt almost instantaneously if he was successful, realized the Overseer. Or they might not even know that any of this had occurred. Or, he mused, some of them would never have even been born.

Delirious, a local man finally dropped off into welcome slumber in the shade of a rock overhang. It shielded him from the sun's unrelenting assault. In this arid landscape that was so familiar to him, he traveled deep into his self-imposed vision quest. After receiving news of the brutal slaying of his friend John, the bereaved had sought out this solitary place to gather his thoughts. Divine direction was what he desired and he hoped to create a state of mind receptive to it.

The Sabra tribe member had adopted a dangerous course in assuming the mantle of political savior of his people. It was a mantle, however, that many young men of his country either aspired to or already believed they wore. Long oral and written traditions foretold of seemingly magical heroes who'd taken on the role of savior. Such a mindset was not easily deprogrammed out of impressionable youngsters. Most grew up with the creation myth unshakably established in their minds, and no amount of reasoning created even the slightest doubt about the folklore's truthfulness. Those coming from such traditions, though, felt set apart in a positive way—special. Belonging to a chosen group engendered a certain pride, if not arrogance, and perhaps that helped the tribespeople cope with certain obvious contradictions. How could those others, living among them, enjoy infinitely more privileged lives without the true faith?

The heavy hand of the empire and its rulers oversaw and receded, depending on the whim of the emperor. The man now seeking a vision lived in a time of heavy taxation and poverty. And the situation was made that much more galling since their own sovereign, Herod Antipas, exploited the occupier's tax system for his own benefit. It was these burdens that engendered thoughts of something better, of rescue from their misery, of a hero. *Could I be that hero?* he thought.

He tossed and turned on the uncomfortable ground. In spite of his familiarity with the desert, he'd allowed himself to become dehydrated. It interfered with his thinking, his survival skills. His skin was cool and damp, and he shivered in spite of the heat. Never well covered by body excess, he had lost more weight than was healthy. Without intervention, his quest would end in a most tragic and meaningless way.

Wakened from his pitiful slumber, the seeker observed a man approaching him. Startled, his instinct was to flee, but the strange aspect of the intruder made him hesitate. The seeker was hard pressed to remember meeting a man as large as the one who approached him now. The stranger's clothes were like no others he'd seen either. His walk was as confident and purposeful as the conquerors, yet he definitely wasn't one of them. The mystery fascinated the seeker enough for him to freeze until the stranger was within striking distance.

Angrily, the local man spit out a question. "From whence do you come? And what is your business approaching me in my sleep?"

The stranger puzzled over the words momentarily, but quickly gathered himself and extended a container. "I was concerned for your safety. It's not a good idea to be out here alone," he said.

The local desert man took the strange container, somehow understanding that it held water. He drank judiciously, careful not to overdo it. Returning it to the stranger, he felt more at ease. They talked a while, each prompting the other with the typical questions men asked when meeting strangers. What was the other's name? Where was he from? And so on. Oddly the stranger, whose name was Jeff, gave the seeker answers that left him none the wiser as to the stranger's origin. An unusual man with an unusual name. One statement that Jeff made, however, put the desert local back on his guard.

"I have a message for you. One that will affect generations of people for thousands of years to come."

"A message? Who sent you? Was it God?"

"No. This will take some explaining, but I can show you better than I can put it into words."

"You are a pagan then," said Jesus, who didn't in turn receive a satisfactory answer regarding Jeff's beliefs.

With that, the stranger clasped the wrist of the desert local in a gentle yet firm grasp and manipulated a device that seemed part of his clothing. Immediately thereafter, both men ceased to be in the desert.

In dizzying fashion, the local man instantly found himself in a public bathroom with the stranger standing beside him. He started to swoon, but something prevented him, something that also becalmed him in spite of the unusual flight. The tinkle of running water could be heard in this ornate stone masonry building with the colorful mosaics on the walls. Roman, thought Jesus. And then as if the revelation made him check himself, he looked down to see himself wearing Roman style clothing. He opened his mouth to ask a question, but before he could, the answer appeared in his mind, and all it took was a touch from a device in the stranger's hand to clarify things.

Jesus wasn't in his own time or homeland. He was in Rome, the seat of the hated empire that ruled his people. This was intended as a teaching experience with the stranger as his guide. In fact, the stranger led him outside, into the daylight, where he saw a building so immense it staggered his reason.

"This is the Flavian Amphitheater," said Jeff. "It will be commonly known as the Coliseum in times to come."

"What are we doing here?"

"We're going to see a show."

"A show?"

"I think you'll find it very interesting. Please note the title of entertainment on the program schedule."

They walked over to a poster on the wall adjacent to an entryway. While pointing to a certain line in the Latin text, the stranger touched the local man again with another device whereupon he was able to read the writings.

"Lions versus... Christ-i-a-n-s!" said the local, desert man as he sounded out the last unfamiliar form of a well-known word... his last name.

"Sound familiar?" asked Jeff. "That connotation has become commonplace now about one hundred twenty years after I found you in the desert."

A huge roar went up from the inside the amphitheater. The stranger guided Jesus inside, out of the sun. Huge archways led off on either side of them, circumnavigating the interior of the structure. Stairs and smaller arches populated the spaces ahead and radiated out from the apparent center like the spokes of a wheel. Passing through these, they barely had time to adjust to the shadows before they were outside again in the seating area of the stadium. Sail-like canvasses hung between timbers that extended from the perimeter inward above the crowd and shaded most seats.

Selecting good spots for viewing, Jeff indicated that the seeker should sit to observe the festivities. Once settled, Jesus gasped at what he saw. Giant cat-like beasts chased, mauled, and gnawed at fallen victims. The scene was made all the more gruesome by the cheers from the crowd who seemed to be enjoying the bloodletting. Soon, the desert local realized his eyes were fixed on the horror in spite of its appalling aspect.

"Do you want to leave?" asked Jeff.

All the seeker could do was nod his head *yes*. The stranger led him back to the bathroom where they had previously stood.

"Why were they cheering?" The seeker appeared horrified.

"Religious prejudice. The victims are no different from those in the stands, but their beliefs are out of favor. At least for the time being."

The stranger clasped the seeker's wrist again, at which touch the same dizzying effect took place. This time they stood on the battlements of a castle looking down upon a plain of mayhem. Men in some sort of metal armor, not Roman, fought each other with swords. Red predominated the color palate of the battlefield as entrails spilled from gaping wounds. It was a dreadful sight but something about it...

"This place looks familiar," noted the seeker.

"It should. This is Jerusalem."

That comment prompted a quizzical look from the desert local.

"It's Jerusalem about one thousand years after your time."

The stranger waited a moment for that to sink in before continuing his explanation. "Remember the Christians in the Roman amphitheater? Well those Christians have enjoyed a change of fortune. They rule vast tracts of land in Europe and have carved out a Middle Eastern kingdom among the natives. Some of those natives practice a new religion called Islam and are known as Muslims. Islam is yet another religious offshoot of ancient Hebrew beliefs, with Abraham as their common ancestor."

The stranger pointed to the pitched battle going on beneath them. "Those are Muslims down there with the spired helmets. They're fighting to oust the competing religion represented by the Christians in this castle. There will be much bloodshed."

The seeker seemed astonished. "How can that be so? Our ancient beliefs aren't violent."

"Aren't they? Would you have wanted to be an Egyptian experiencing the seven plagues? The Nile allegedly turned to blood. Firstborn children died. There was pestilence, storms and infestation. Is that nonviolent?"

"The Egyptians brought it on themselves. My people were forbidden to leave to practice their rituals," protested Jesus.

"Okay. But then couldn't your god have just spirited them away? According to the Torah, he certainly had the power. Why the petty revenge?"

"Blasphemers will always be punished," asserted the seeker.

"How much punishment for these blasphemers? Is there a sliding scale? Do you think the Romans were punished? The Muslims?"

The local, appalled that he had to defend his truths, became silent and refused to argue anymore. But as he watched the carnage below, a seed of doubt started to germinate in his mind. How could God have allowed those people in the Coliseum to come to harm? How could those faithful to God fight each other?

Another touch from the stranger's hand, and the seeker was again whisked away, this time to the strangest place on his journey of sorrow. This place was like nothing he'd seen so far. The Roman amphitheater that had appeared so colossal paled by comparison to the structures in this mad, frenetic city. One had to look nearly straight up to take in the tops of these mighty dwellings.

The two men were on what Jeff called a glassed-in walkway, with walls made of a see-through substance. The mass of people on the streets below made Rome look like the meadowed outskirts of Bethlehem. Everywhere Jesus looked, he saw a moving crowd winding its way through the streets on some unguessed-at mass errand. This city seemed more like an anthill than a center of human population.

Automobiles, as Jeff called them, transported people at great speed to keep up with their calculated frenzy. *How could anyone live like this,* pondered the desert local.

"This is about two thousand years after your time. Mankind has come a long way in technical applications. Life has been made easier for a portion of the world's population, but there are still the disadvantaged and new problems never dreamed of in your time."

The local accepted the information at face value. He was too busy processing it all to do otherwise. Then his eye was drawn upward. A giant bird crossed the sky and shimmered in the sun's rays.

"That's an airplane," explained Jeff. "It's another mode of transportation used to take longer trips than cars are practical for. They can hold several hundred passengers. Sometimes people steal them and fly them elsewhere. That one that you're watching has been stolen by people who are acting in the name of god. The same god that you believe in. "

The local man watched the flying machine in fascination. He hoped to see one as it left the ground and when it returned.

"Keep watching that plane. Something interesting is about to happen."

Sure enough, the plane approached one of the more monstrous dwellings. The local wondered if it would dock with the building, like a boat, to unload its cargo. For a moment it seemed like that was exactly what the airplane was doing. But then the flying machine disappeared into the building, and the plane and the building became as one.

A tremendous orange ball of flame accompanied a booming crash, and the desert local knew something horrible had happened. Flames licked up the sides of the building, and black smoke billowed up into the sky. People in the streets screamed and some ran while others watched in horrified fascination. Debris fell from the massive tower, and the desert seeker had the sickening realization that some of the debris was actually people jumping to their deaths.

"Is this god's will?" asked Jeff.

In another shift, Jeff led the desert local to a wide, comfortable seat known as a couch. The stranger directed his attention to a window that wasn't a window at all but something called a television. Back home, local news was conveyed by official means on printed notices or by word of mouth from trusted messengers. This TV device seemed an improvement on that.

Jesus viewed images of the catastrophe he'd just witnessed. The pictures were as vivid to him as if he were there. A second building had suffered the same fate as the one he'd seen, and both had collapsed to the ground. Three thousand or so people were dead, entombed in the unimaginable mass of those colossal structures. As if that wasn't enough what he saw next chilled him to his core. People in other parts of the world, including places that he'd been familiar with, celebrated the destruction. Even women yelled, cheered, and danced in the streets.

"Remember the Muslims from our last trip to Jerusalem? No people are more devoted to god. Do they look saddened over the death of thousands of god's children?"

"Why?" Jesus stuttered out the question.

"They think god sanctioned this. Young men are looking forward to martyrdom for killing so they can have seventy-two virgins in paradise. The afterlife."

The stranger showed the seeker how to manipulate the TV controls so that he could see different aspects of the destruction. He also witnessed women in head scarves shouting their approval as they rolled their tongues to create a weird ululation. Dark-skinned men with imperfect shaves shot what Jeff called *firearms* into the air in giddy celebrations. And just in case the seeker didn't trust the device, Jeff transported him to the sites of these twisted parties. The seed of doubt in the local's mind sprouted a weed.

Jeff materialized on a dusty flatland closely surrounded by sun-baked rocky outcroppings and cliffs. The sun was high in the sky. Perhaps it was just past noon, guessed the volunteer. He reached for his canteen and took a cool draught of water. Not paying much attention to his action, he screwed the top back on the canteen while he surveyed the landscape. His visored hat helped protect his eyes from the glare, while his khaki-colored clothing helped him avoid detection by any casual observer. Little chance he'd run into anyone taking a stroll out here though, he decided—other than the one he was looking for. The man he sought should be close, if the Martian's whiz-bang teleporter was worth anything. Then, as if in answer to his thoughts, he heard a faint rustling. Spying a rocky ledge, he probed the shadows beneath it. A man lay there, sleeping fitfully.

The temporalium experiment volunteer approached the prone man, making noise enough to awaken him but hopefully not enough to startle him. The man from the other world failed in the latter, however. The sleeper awaked and bolted upright into a sitting a position, and the volunteer sensed he would have tried to run, but his strength failed him. Obviously the man was dehydrated. When he started to talk in some unrecognizable dialect, Jeff remembered to turn on the translator device given to him by the Martians.

"And what is your business approaching me in my sleep?"

The volunteer had apparently missed the first part of the dialog, but decided to answer the question he'd heard. "I was concerned for your safety. It's not a good idea to be out here alone."

He offered the sleeper a drink from his canteen while sitting beside him in the shade. Surprisingly, the man accepted the water after examining the strange container for a half a moment. He knew enough not to take too much at once and was apparently not inexperienced in surviving in this environment.

The volunteer looked the local, desert man up and down, but he was not what Jeff had expected. The local man's skin was sun baked from a lifetime of exposure. His beard was bushy and unkempt. His clothes were tattered, but that could have been from the desert ordeal he was subjecting himself to. Overall, the man was not an impressive figure. Probably only about five foot three or so, the volunteer estimated, and maybe one hundred fifteen pounds. Of course, that was even above average for this day and age. The volunteer accepted back the canteen from the local man, who seemed to be a bit more at ease with the volunteer.

"You aren't Roman?" asked the sleeper.

"No, not Roman," said the volunteer with a smile.

"I've never seen the like of the clothes you're wearing in any local village."

"I'm not from around here," agreed Jeff.

"What is your name stranger?"

"Jeff Staten. What's yours?"

"I am Jesus of Nazareth. Yours is a strange name. I don't know of a village called Staten." His face scrunched in consideration.

It occurred to Jeff that people in these parts were known by their village.

"There is no place called Staten. That's my last name. Where I come from, that's how we say our names. Would I be correct in guessing that your surname is Christ?"

Again, Jeff noted Jesus calmly accepted that his identity was found out. A conviction that one is divine can certainly anchor a psyche, marveled Jeff. No wonder religion seemed to flourish across time and place. That calm alone must have impressed enough people to adopt a belief system whether it rang true or not.

"How did you come by this knowledge?" asked Jesus.

"It's a complicated story, and I won't bore you with it. But I also know that you've been baptized recently in the River Jordan. Do you know that John has been executed?"

Jesus nodded.

"You've come out here on a vision quest thinking that privation and suffering will provide you an obvious direction for your life. You suspect that you are the chosen one. Picked by divine providence to lead your people out of misery in some mystical fashion. It's an old theme born of your ancient texts. Several people have tried to lay claim to this role, but you will eventually be taken seriously. This belief will inhibit rational behavior to the detriment of man's social development."

For the first time since he'd awakened him, Jeff noticed that Jesus was becoming perturbed. It must be a tough thing to be told that you will do a disservice to mankind, whether you believe it or not.

"Why do you say this? Aren't you a believer in God?"

This was going to be tougher than he'd thought, decided Jeff. Here was a man who had lived his life under a belief system that was unquestionable. The very thought of doubting it or any part of it was just not contemplated. This would have to be a shocking idea to anyone who grew up without a forum for critical thinking. "That question is exactly why I'm here. I have a message for you. One that will affect generations of people for thousands of years to come."

"A message? Who sent you? Was it God?"

"No. This will take some explaining but I can show you better than I can put it into words."

"You are a pagan then," said Jesus, who hadn't gotten a satisfactory answer regarding Jeff's beliefs.

Jeff clasped Jesus' wrist and manipulated the Martian-made device on his belt. The next moments seem to stretch into years as the two men shuttled through time.

After absorbing lots of strange images, Jeff and Jesus rematerialized in the shade of the rock outcropping from where they'd started. The experience must have shaken Jesus' confidence in himself and his life's purpose.

"How do you feel?" asked Jeff.

"I am well," said the desert man, who was only used to responding about his physical self as opposed to his mental moorings.

Jeff figured that Jesus didn't get that he was being asked about his state of mind. No psychobabble in this age, he thought. Jeff didn't bother to pursue it.

"Hungry?" he asked instead. "I think I've got some K-rations in this uniform somewhere."

"God will provide for all my needs."

Jeff jerked his head back up from searching through his myriad pockets. "God will provide? Didn't you understand all of what we just witnessed?"

Jesus facial expression told Jeff that he had simply come to some sort of accommodation with his strange experience. "This was a test. I've been tested like Adam and I didn't bite the fruit."

Jeff stared at Jesus, staggered that he'd made no impact on the seeker. "Okay. Provide for yourself then," said an exasperated Jeff, and he folded his arms across his chest. "Conjure up some food from this sand."

"I'm on a fast. My Lord God would not indulge my weakness."

"Would he indulge your death? If you're going to survive out here for forty days and nights, you'll need help. You'll need help to bring back the word of god. So if that's ever going to happen, get water out of these stones. Make food out of these rocks and I'll believe too."

Jesus ignored him, much to the Jeff's consternation. He'd wasted his time. By not convincing this simple desert man of the wisdom of rationality, he'd blown an opportunity to spare mankind centuries of ignorance and superstition.

Jeff dematerialized. Several weeks later, Jesus staggered out of the desert. Though somewhat the worse for his experience, he wasn't at all on the brink of death. In the town of Capernaum, Jesus happened upon Peter who was shocked at his appearance.

"What happened to you?" asked Peter as he reached for his shrunken friend. "We wondered where you were. We thought the Romans had gotten you."

"I was fasting in the desert to cleanse myself."

"Cleanse yourself?"

"With the holy spirit. And to suffer a test of God."

"What kind of test?"

"Our Israelite forefathers wandered the desert for forty years in search of a home. I honored them by spending forty days in the haunted lands."

"You could've died," exclaimed Peter.

"The word of God sustained me. I lived and passed the test in spite of the devil."

Peter's expression turned to horror, prompting Jesus to continue. "An evil one, Staten, appeared to me. He tempted me in different ways."

"Satan!" said Peter as he interpreted what must have been a mispronunciation. "What did he do?"

"He tried to convince me that there is no God. That our faith is foolish, and that it's bad for our people, all people. I was spirited away and made to see visions of a future where faith caused the deaths of many thousands. But I was strong against his lies and it angered him."

"I'm surprised he didn't kill you."

"Our God wouldn't allow that."

"So what did he do?"

"He's clever. He tried to appeal to my hunger. He wanted me to forsake the sustenance of God by having me perform miracles to sate my bodily hunger."

"You had to be hungry." Peter fasted for the high holy day every year, and even that was hard for him.

"I was. Very hungry. But my will was stronger than my hunger, and with the help of God I turned aside his temptations. He vanished in failure." Jesus smiled at having vanquished the evil one.

"I fear that others won't have your strength when it comes to facing the devil. We have to get the word out about this, and maybe people will be inspired to resist the devil's clever means," suggested Peter.

Jesus agreed. "I believe this episode is destined to be written in a new scripture. It will do just as you intend. Inspire people to resist the words of the Godless."

Peter smiled at the praise of his idea. God willing, all peoples would live by the Word of God till the end of days.

PART IX

1963 Redux

CHAPTER 34

Within the First 100 Days of the Cody Presidency

President Cody sat at his desk in the Oval Office and listened to one of his talented young advisors. In keeping with his promise to the American public, he'd selected a staff who wouldn't simply be yes men. One of the holdovers from the Bush administration was a remarkable young man named Josh Malcolm. Josh had a very compelling background as a prodigy whose designs and systems had influenced the American military and intelligence apparatus from the time he was a teenager. To call him a genius would be a gross understatement. He was also one of the few people on the planet privy to the struggle to preserve the integrity of all the parallel universes, and thus existence itself. Like Jack/JFK he was also one of the few people across all realities who had al-Rahiim's confidence.

"Mind-boggling," repeated the president.

"I think it was just a matter of priorities," said Josh in an attempt to defend his former boss.

"You're giving Bush too much credit. Was vacation time a priority? He always came across as a buffoon, but I had hoped that was just in front of cameras. How could he have possibly ignored this?" asked Cody as he dropped the file he was holding on his desk in disgust.

Josh knew the answer, but he was uncomfortable speaking ill of his former boss. The sad fact was that Bush hadn't even read it. The decider-in-chief, as he was dubbed, had little time for reports, no matter how condensed. He preferred to be spoon-fed by his aides.

"Do you think 9/11 was preventable?" queried Josh.

"Perhaps some lives if not all could have been spared if this data hadn't been ignored. Although, I think we have to accept that even if Bush had reacted to it, his follow through always left a lot to be desired. Look at Afghanistan, and closer to home New Orleans, as primary examples. Hell, he's left an awful mess for us on several fronts. Sad that a man like that could've been put in this office," said an angry Cody. He stared out the window.

"Just goes to show, anyone can rise to high office in this country with a name and a huge fortune behind him."

Cody snapped his head around for a quick rebuke until he noticed Josh smiling. "I didn't know you had a sense of humor, Josh."

"Someone once advised me to cultivate it. It's a stress reducer I hear."

"Yes, I suppose it is. And it can disarm."

The president glanced away again, as if contemplating some new thought. "I wish I could get a firsthand look at our diplomatic machinery abroad without attracting attention," he said almost to himself. "And I'd start with Iraq."

The outskirts of Baghdad were in the midst of a flare-up these days, perhaps due to the well-publicized drawdown of American troops. Some of the more violent factions among the populace abhorred the calm and took the opportunity to slake their blood thirst. JFK waited in his car at a checkpoint manned mostly by Iraqis but he also recognized one American uniform among security. Others in line got out of their cars to wait, although those lucky enough to have air conditioning remained seated. It was a hot day, and the smell of sweat permeated the air. JFK got out as well, curious to see what the reaction would be to an American citizen. He was ignored. The people had better things to devote their energies to these days. The looks on their faces reminded him of a trip he'd taken to Soviet Russia as a young man. The people had exuded a feeling of hopelessness then, as they did now, as citizens labored under an indifferent government. He hoped that would change with the new American president.

The line moved up one car as a truck pulled into the checkpoint area. A driver got out and conversed with the officers in a relaxed, unthreatening manner. JFK perceived no real danger since they seemed to know each other from previous stops. This could take a while, he thought, since a fairly cluttered flatbed had to be searched.

JFK figured that the process would've normally gone faster, but for some reason only one inspection area was open today, and that created a bottleneck. It occurred to him that since this was Friday, several of the Iraqis might have taken the day off to observe the equivalent of Sunday in Christendom.

Several more people got out of their cars. They were mostly men, and in a lot of cases decided to light up cigarettes. In one case, JFK's gaze was drawn to a young man with a particularly troubled expression. Three other older men got out of the car with him and seemed to be goading him into doing something that he half-heartedly agreed to do. The young man, several cars behind JFK, who himself was about ten cars from the checkpoint, started to walk forward.

The young Iraqi crossed over to the driver's side of the cars, and JFK noted that he wore a particularly bulky vest. Passing JFK, he took faltering steps at first, but after a while his gait became more self-confident. As he passed people waiting in line, he drew curious stares.

Eventually, the young man caught the eye of the only visible American at the checkpoint. The soldier started to reach for his rifle, but then paused. The young man with the voluminous vest veered away from the road and walked into the desert, ultimately taking a perpendicular path from the line of waiting cars.

The man's companions exchanged puzzled looks and eventually took off in pursuit of their friend, yelling his name. Ali never heeded them. He just continued on at that purposeful pace. After a while, he reached into his pocket, but didn't take his hand out. The action made his companions, now within feet of him, freeze.

Oddly the young man seemed to be carrying on a conversation with some unseen parties in front of him, but not with the men behind him. He became animated, as if he were acting out something in a play. Ali turned around finally to face his friends. He smiled and removed what looked like a game controller button from his pocket, attached to his jacket with a wire.

Expressionlessly, Ali simply pressed the button, igniting an explosion.

Ali and his friends were, each one, blown to pieces.

The concussion startled all at the checkpoint, as well as those a good distance away in the line of cars. Several more soldiers than JFK had previously counted appeared and ran toward the carnage.

Very shortly after, a Red Crescent ambulance showed up but far too late to help Ali or his so-called friends.

JFK knew that the suicide bomber thought he was among the soldiers at the checkpoint. The bomb detonated harmlessly relative to the waiting cars but not for the men with Ali, who had obviously used the gullible Muslim youth to their own ends. A certain satisfaction mixed with sorrow, as JFK regretted the loss of the young man but not of the older ones.

Sadr City's day dawned as it usually did. With a bang. Several Red Crescent emergency vehicles sped to the scene of another bombing. This Shiite section of Baghdad never wanted for turmoil. The force of this latest explosion had knocked over a couple of palm trees and shattered store fronts on the street in front of a tea shop where several local police were known to lounge. A small crater smoked with the remains of a car that had been packed with explosives. A bad smell lingered in the air, both from volatile chemicals and from human fear and hatred.

The first ambulance pulled up to the scene. Its personnel hoped that some whole people could be salvaged, as opposed to their merely having to bag bodies and parts. As soon as they stopped, the EMTs threw open the doors and rushed to the store front. Almost immediately, they succumbed to rifle fire. The tactic of attacking rescue workers hadn't gone out of favor. One of the technicians scrambled under the ambulance while the rest cowered inside the vehicle. The man underneath bled from his leg, possibly from the femoral artery. The rescuer's life was in danger if the bleeding wasn't stanched soon. No one could move, however, with the sniper at large.

Out of the smoke an American civilian walked casually to the scene. Was he mad? wondered the EMT under the ambulance. Sure enough, the stranger drew sniper fire. A few bullets missed at first, but then the gunman found his range, peppering the approaching man with deadly aim. In spite of this, however, the man still approached. He walked casually, as though out for a stroll on some holiday in Europe or America.

The sight of the uninjured interloper obviously stunned the sniper, and he released the trigger. That moment of freedom from sniper fire allowed the man beneath the ambulance to get out from under it and dive into the back for treatment from his waiting companions.

Bullets started firing again, however, and this time they seemed to be coming from several directions and from people unconcerned about exposing themselves. Several dark-skinned men with head scarves concealing most of their faces moved out onto porches and into the street as they fired at the man who had now stopped walking.

The insurgents' target presented himself with perfect calm and resolve as bullets exploded in flashes of light around him. He seemed to wear a slight smile as the efforts to take him down intensified. Eventually, another disguised man appeared with the preferred weapon of Islamist terrorists everywhere. He held a rocket-propelled grenade launcher. Taking aim, he fired. A loud concussion shook the street as the projectile exploded upon impact with the man. His body was obscured by more smoke, but as the smoke cleared onlookers were shocked to see the odd intruder standing with the same inscrutable smile on his face.

Again, the man began to walk. This time he moved away from the car-bomb blast and toward the snipers. They were nonplused and didn't know what to do until the man with the RPG launcher picked up a rifle and started firing again.

This time, though, something different happened. The American turned into an Arab wearing traditional robes, headwear, and neatly trimmed beard. As firing continued, the Arab turned into a someone whom the Shiite crowd recognized as a dead neighbor. After that, he appeared as a woman, then a well-known Sunni militia leader.

After a few more transformations the stranger disappeared altogether, leaving the observers sure that they'd just had a religious experience. Some said that the first image of an Arab man was Mohammed. No one moved as fire trucks and more ambulances arrived and started ministering to people and property. This time, the rescuers were not only unhindered but actually offered help by the same people who were firing a few moments earlier.

On a plane home from Iraq, JFK relaxed in comfort. The accommodations he now enjoyed on the second leg of his trip were a far cry from the military transport that had taken him from Baghdad to Ramstein Air Force Base in Germany. Talk about a cattle car, he thought. Conversely, his private plane held a well-stocked bar, a bed for relaxation, and most of the luxuries of home. As he drank, a full bodied apparition appeared in the swivel recliner across from him. JFK wasn't startled.

"An impressive display, Jack." commented al-Rahiim. "Like nothing you were ever trained for."

"I've learned to focus my mind-dampening techniques. Create illusions of my own design."

"None of our other operatives ever learned to do that," praised his one-time boss.

"None of your other operatives enjoyed a dual consciousness as long as I have."

"I'm amazed how well you've handled that. Remaining sane by itself was a hell of an accomplishment, never mind learning new techniques."

"It's remarkable what can be accomplished when you're at peace with yourself... yourselves," joked Jack.

"Indeed. Although I held my breath when that RPG launcher came out."

"You're not kidding. I was really just a few feet away from my illusion. No one within my influence saw the actual projectile go through the illusional me to the building behind it. I was sprayed with a lot of shrapnel. Just got some minor cuts and bruises, but I needed a lot of willpower to maintain my concentration. Fortunately, that cloud of dust obscured the illusion for a while."

"Nothing more serious than cuts and bruises?" asked al-Rahiim.

"Nothing the nanobots can't handle," Jack said, and he stood and showed the proconsul multiple puncture wounds that covered nearly half his back.

Even at that moment, evidence of the wounds were well on their way to disappearing. Another day and they'd be gone.

Jack left Iraq as a movement for peace emanated from Baghdad.

Vice President Obama wrapped up his visit to Liberia by allowing himself to be honored as an adopted son. The United States and Liberia had enjoyed good relations prior to the election, but that was elevated beyond all previous levels with the advent of the first African-American vice president. One of the things that Barack Obama brought to the Cody presidency was a gift for diplomacy. His role in the administration was like that of no other vice president. In essence, he held the same place that Kissinger had in the Nixon administration. His skills in dealing with the emerging African nations and the Muslim world were unsurpassed. His connections to both worlds were undeniable, which granted him access where earlier envoys had been denied. Cody also knew that Obama would be a capable successor in the case of his demise, and Cody would wholeheartedly support an Obama presidency once his own term was up.

September 2009

Karl Rove called in to Rush Limbaugh's radio program to add tinder to a recurring theme coming from the political right. Cody was soft on terrorism. Some of the Cheney team still embedded in the CIA had concocted a plan to use a combination of U.S. Special Forces, disaffected Persians, and moles inside the Tehran government to overthrow the Iranian theocracy. Cody, a student of history, recalled how the Bay of Pigs had affected the Kennedy presidency and how the Iraqi National Congress had affected Bush. Disastrous policy in both cases, of course. President Cody not only called a halt to the Iranian operation but went public to denounce it. If he ever enjoyed any goodwill from neoconservatives this move immediately dissipated any possible friendship.

The overall positive effect of Cody's action was to make the Iranians more receptive to overtures from the American administration. As promised, Cody reversed the Bush tactic of not speaking with adversarial governments. Even Bush, very late in his term, had reversed direction in that regard by engaging the North Koreans. Cody expanded on that particular contact, as well, to reach more substantive agreements with the North Korean regime. His international policies were slowly restoring the United States' special place and influence in the world, a fact that flew in the face of claims from the political right's lunatic fringe.

CHAPTER 35

Without al-Rahiim, the Agency descended into disarray. The praetor was a very capable woman in her own right, but had been undermined by the funk the Agency had dived into after the loss of the much-admired proconsul. Under ordinary circumstances, she might have been able to build back the organization's confidence, but the days after al-Rahiim's death were far from ordinary.

President Cody defied analysis by the Agency's computer models. It seemed his star had come from out of nowhere. None of the algorithms predicted his ascendancy, and for that reason he was immediately an object of suspicion to the Agency. By all indications, he almost certainly had help from other realities. The praetor knew he had to be dealt with, and she had just received permission to enact an unprecedented plan to do so. It would be the first time the Agency had used an adversary to meet a goal. The unwitting adversary must be led to believe it was in their best interests to neutralize Cody.

Senators Sam Brownback of Kansas and Mitch McConnell of Kentucky were both counted as strong advocates of the moneyed elite and champions for suppressing the wages of laborers to service them. Both men adopted and brilliantly wielded the language of obfuscation, as prescribed by the Republican Revolution, to convince the masses that their policies would benefit all and not just their rich patrons. The success of their campaigns resulted in their election to the Senate, where they could do the most damage to the common interest. All in all, typical work for Republican members of the government.

Now, however, Brownback and McConnell found themselves in a very unusual and dangerous dialog. Their vocal antipathy to President Cody attracted the unwanted attentions of certain unsavory characters they'd never dreamed of meeting.

Tom Delay, a former representative from Texas, sat the two senators down in his luxury suite at Deer Creek Hunting Lodge in Kentucky. Vacationing from his hectic schedule, he took the opportunity to meet with the two men whom he knew were in the area. Delay had long since been drummed out of Congress for various ethical transgressions involving lobbyists and their money, but he was still active in the Republican attack machinery. Initially, he'd been inspired to run for office since cumbersome regulations wouldn't allow him to risk poisoning people while running his extermination business. Bridling at that indignity, he'd been a rabid champion of deregulation during his career in Congress.

"Can I get you gentlemen anything?"

"I'll have a whiskey and soda," answered Brownback.

"Nothing for me," added McConnell.

Secretly, Delay didn't have much respect for McConnell. The Kentuckian always struck him as sort of a mealy mouth.

"How's retirement going?" asked Brownback as Delay fixed his drink.

"It has its ups and downs, Sam. Although this is one of the highlights. Getting away to a lakeside lodge with the great views and the excellent hunting."

"Is that why you're here?"

"Well, it's not the only reason. I've come with a proposal. Something that will make all our lives easier. Something that will serve the conservative cause."

"That sounds mysterious."

"That's actually a good characterization. It's what I first thought when I was contacted by some likeminded people. They made it plain that they have resources that will help our position."

"What are we talking here, the Mafia?" questioned Brownback.

Delay chuckled. "No, it's not the Mafia. At least they're not like any Mafia I've ever heard of. I think the best way to describe them is activist evangelicals. And with that nice segue, I'd like to introduce you to our new friend, Bart."

A thin man of slightly above-average height entered the room. He seemed much bigger than he was, though, due to his imposing manner. McConnell appeared visibly uncomfortable, but if Brownback felt ambushed, he didn't show it.

"Senators," said Delay, "this is Bartholomew. He goes by Bart to his friends."

"Hello, gentlemen," said Bart.

"How do you do?" responded Brownback.

McConnell just nodded. Both senators noted that a last name had been withheld. Then Bart spoke up as if to distract the senators from thinking too much. "Am I to assume that you gentlemen view the Cody presidency as problematic?"

"That's an understatement," chimed in Delay.

Brownback and McConnell exchanged uneasy glances, but Bart continued. "What if I told you there is a way to neutralize his presidency? What if I said we could do that for you and at the same time guarantee that there would no traceable link to us?"

"How?" asked McConnell abruptly, almost in spite of himself, but Bart's question had been so provocative.

"Several ways are available to us. Several safe, untraceable ways, I should say. And it all has to do with certain technological advantages that my group possesses. But let me give you one example by way of a small demonstration. If you would, Senators, please follow me into the next room."

McConnell, Brownback, and Delay obliged him and entered one of the suite's bedrooms. Bart pulled a nightstand out from the wall toward the center of the room. Looking around, he spotted a vase and placed it on the stand atop a couple of phone books. He ushered the men out of the room and advised them to keep an eye on the vase and on him.

He went back to the room where where they had met and positioned himself to have a water view. Then reached in a jacket pocket and removed what looked like a small radar gun. It had a barrel like a real gun, a hand grip, and a small video screen, which Bart looked at as he prepared. He pointed it at the wall separating the water-view room and the bedroom.

"Can you see the vase, gentlemen?"

They all indicated that they could upon looking left.

"And can you see me?"

Again the answer was *yes*, once they turned their heads right to take in the common room.

"Now watch the vase."

Almost immediately the vase shattered as if struck by a bullet. Even Delay was startled, and he gave indications that he had known what was coming.

"What happened?" asked Brownback.

"I just shot the vase from the other room without being able to see it."

Brownback examined the wall separating the two rooms. He was looking for a bullet hole but found none.

"You won't find any evidence that a bullet passed through the wall, gentlemen. But a bullet did shatter that vase."

"It's a cheap magic trick of some sort," said Brownback.

"It's technology," corrected Bart. "You see the bullet only materialized just prior to striking the vase. Its flight both before and after was outside normal space. It dematerialized after striking the target, and you'll find no evidence that there ever was a bullet."

McConnell came into the room and stared at the gun in Bart's hand.

"Have a look, Senator," invited Bart.

McConnell took the proffered weapon and obviously didn't know what to make of it. Bart took it back to show him the principle of operation.

"You see, you look in this viewfinder to see the object you're shooting at. It doesn't matter if solid objects are in the way or not."

McConnell could see the bedroom in the screen.

"Not only are the bullets specially manufactured, but so is the gun. They interact to target and plan the line of flight. When to be in normal space and when not to be. Once you have the object sighted, you just pull the trigger."

McConnell couldn't resist and pulled the trigger, hitting the phone in the other room. It shattered like the vase but with noisier parts ricocheting off the surrounding furniture.

"God damn it, Mitch," said Delay who was still in the bedroom. "Call your shots, will ya? We could've been hit by flying shrapnel."

"Sorry, Tom," said a sheepish McConnell.

Bart interrupted. "This was a crude demonstration based on the technologies at my disposal, but I trust it proves our resources."

"Who are you? How did you come by such gadgets?" queried Brownback.

"Let's just say that my organization is secret. And that we have goals similar to those of your ideological friends, some of whom

I've already been in contact with. We'll all get together before too long to discuss a few ideas."

After a little more preliminary conversation, Bart promised to contact them again to propose a better-thought-out plan. Both senators then bid their farewell to the former congressman and left together.

"Well, things are looking up," observed McConnell.

"Tell me you're not serious about all that," countered Brownback.

"Why not?"

"For one thing, I don't trust this Bart character. And I'm a little uneasy about his lack of a last name. And you know what it felt like to me?"

"What?" asked McConnell.

"It felt like a sting operation. Let's offer these lunatic fringe Republicans a criminal way out of their troubles and see if they bite. It's just too pat. Too convenient," Brownback told his colleague.

"I suppose you're right about that," said McConnell.

"Damn right."

"So what do we do when he comes calling again?"

"We ignore him, that's what."

McConnell nodded but in his heart he wasn't sure he could resist. The prospect of eliminating Cody's line-item vetoes of McConnell's favorite pork projects was just too attractive. It wasn't like the good old days when you could bundle all kinds of unnecessary expenditures with bills assured of passage. Now one had to be very clever in order to camouflage any extra spending. And Cody was no fool. He seemed to be able to smell pork-barrel projects. Not that he vetoed all of them, but he certainly had a bias against those that benefited the rich for no good national purpose. The senator from Kentucky had taken a lot of heat from his patrons over several such instances. *Why are we financing you?* asked one angry contributor. The thought of losing support and ultimately his seat in the Senate made McConnell's blood run cold. He, at least, would be open minded the next time he heard from Bart.

I wonder how he'd pull it off?

"The president is being watched," Jack told Niles.

"The president is always under scrutiny. You know that."

"That's not what I mean."

"Oh?"

"I mean the president is under surveillance by a hostile extra-universal group," said Jack.

"You're talking about your former colleagues, aren't you?" Niles didn't seem worried.

"Maybe. Or maybe their adversaries, more likely."

"Is this just a feeling you have or is there something more substantial?"

"The microsentinels picked up the electronic signature of a surveillance device not known to this Earth's science." Jack revealed.

"Are you sure? You can pick up a lot of electromagnetic radiation from different sources these days."

"Yes, but I'll bet none if it is phased out of our plane of existence." Jack gave an ironic smile.

"I see. You suspect it's hostile."

"All I can say is we better find out. We better start becoming proactive. I don't want a repeat of 1963 in 2010." Jack/JFK shuddered.

Nicole Babineaux woke up from a sound sleep. It was just after midnight. Groggily, she wondered what had roused her, but eventually she realized that her husband, President Ken Cody, was thrashing in the bed. He was having a nightmare.

"Ken," she whispered.

No response.

"Ken," she said somewhat more loudly while stroking his arm.

He quieted and uncharacteristically became as cool as the night breeze that gently rippled the curtains. Ken was so quiescent that Nicole feared for his health enough to check his pulse. It was steady, however, as was his breathing. Somewhat agitated, Nicole took a few moments to calm herself but eventually fell back asleep.

Two hours later, Nicole woke again. This time it wasn't thrashing that woke her although she sensed that the disturbance came from Ken's side of the bed. She felt a definite vibration... or was it a humming? Looking at her husband, she had trouble focusing in the dark. He seemed to be fine, yet she was compelled to turn on the light to be sure. In the pale glow of the night lamp, she gasped at what she saw. It was as if she were looking at an old TV broadcast where the characters on the screen were overlapped due to static ghosts caused by poor antenna reception.

Earlier in the Day

Castle Island in South Boston wasn't an island at all. It hadn't been since the 1930s when a manmade connection to the mainland had been constructed. And the "castle" part of the name wasn't quite accurate, either. The imposing structure on this peninsula was Fort Independence, a military relic left over from Colonial times. Its strategic position allowed the colonists to scan Boston Harbor for enemy ships, starting as early as 1634. Eventually, those enemy ships came from the British homeland as the War of Independence broke out. Any unfriendly vessels were subject to a pounding from heavy artillery in the form of canon fire from the fort's big guns. These days, the five-pointed granite structure served a more peaceful purpose as a public park.

The current building was the eighth fort to occupy the site and had been constructed between 1834 and 1851. It was made of monolithic granite blocks, and in some places, at the fort's base, the blocks formed oversized stairs, irresistible to the neighborhood youth for climbing. The top stair formed a wide ledge that circumnavigated the fort. Many a youngster could be seen walking the ledge in pursuit of his personal quest to complete nearly half a mile around the fort's base.

Another activity on the island appealed to people of all ages: watching the planes take off and land at nearby Logan Airport. Several harbor islands were also within view from the fort, as well as the ever-present boating activity, both commercial and recreational. The park was frequented by joggers, walkers, picnickers, and even fisherman at the pier constructed for that activity. All in all, the site was a pleasant place to wile away a sunny afternoon.

On this particular day, a ten-year-old boy walked along the ledge at the base of the fort, occasionally peering in through the barred windows. The inner rooms were dark with no internal illumination. Very little light entered the interior from window slits originally designed only for protruding gun barrels as opposed to harbor gazing. At one of the windows, however, something caught the boy's eye.

"Dad!"

The excited tone of his son's call caused the father to interrupt his conversation with a friend he'd met at the park. He jogged the dozen yards or so to his son's perch on the ledge. "What is it, Tom?"

"Someone is in there," said Tom.

In all the years the father had been coming to the park, he'd never seen the fort opened. The two massive wooden doors on the other side of the structure had a heavy iron padlock on them. It seemed unlikely that anyone would be inside. "Are you sure?"

"Yes, two men walked past the door over there. Come and look."

The father got up on the ledge and peered through the window. On the opposite side of the room was, indeed, a door whose edges on two sides admitted sunlight. The father knew that there was an internal courtyard and surmised that the door on the wall opposite the window had at one time opened up to it.

"I don't see any men, Tommy. Are you sure it wasn't some birds or something?"

"No, Dad. Men were walking past that door. I could see them in the light."

Was it young eyes or just youthful imagination? wondered the man. "Oh wait. I saw them too," he lied.

"You did?"

"Yeah. Over by the door right?"

"Yes, that's where they were. When they saw me they went through it and shut it. They must've come back. Wait'll Mom hears about this."

The father knew that Mom wouldn't approve of Tommy being up on the ledge. In some places it was high enough above the ground to threaten injury if a child fell from it. Tommy's father believed a boy should be a boy, however, and allowed the indulgence for his son. Having Tommy brag about his little adventure to his mother, however, was not part of his plan.

"Maybe we should keep this our little secret, Tom. We don't want Mom to worry, do we?"

"Right, Dad. Good idea."

With that, they started toward their car parked close enough to Sullivan's to warrant a convenient ice cream before heading home. About halfway to the parking lot, Tom's dad sensed a swelling of anxiety behind him. Turning to find out what was going on, he saw nothing except a crowd near the fort looking all around with confused expressions on their faces.

As he watched, the father noticed more and more people joining the gathering. Some people were running, but in no particular direction. The start of a collective scream built as more and more voices registered panic. Frantically, Tom's father scanned the area but could come up with no good reason for the crowd's attitude.

No sooner had the man decided this than he felt a vibration under his feet. That made him even more uneasy. He couldn't hear anything since the sound was in the infrasonic range, but it filled him with a foreboding, as if something powerful was awakening. He imagined he heard a deep bass rumbling, and as his pre-human ancestors might have, he experienced catastrophic images of earthquakes or tidal waves or volcanic eruptions. Planning to flee with his son, the sensations ceased, and everything appeared normal again.

Later That Night as President Cody Slept

The moon rose and cast a silvery light upon Fort Independence on Castle Island. Even at such a late hour, walkers typically enjoyed the park. Tonight, however, in spite of the fair weather, was different. There was a peculiar lack of human activity. Jack walked along the pathways and tried to sense what had drawn him here. The place seemed normal by all outward appearances, but something didn't feel right. Something needed his attention. And as he started to wonder what that might be, the device that the proconsul had given him vibrated in his pocket. He took it out and noted a hologram of a virtual screen that projected a six-inch-square display. Apparently the unit served several functions beyond helping him phase-shift out of reality. The screen indicated the presence of phased individuals and vehicles.

Jack instinctively turned the device around and used it like a camera. He trained it on the opening of the fort just uphill from him and maybe a hundred yards away. The holographic screen revealed a caravan of cars, invisible to anyone in this universe except for Jack, as they entered Fort Independence. After all the vehicles entered, the device's screen brought up information indicating the probability of a massive, heretofore unknown, complex inside the monolithic granite structure.

Now Jack thought he understood why the park was strangely quiet. To keep such a large contingent of vehicles and a secret base invisible to the local public, a massive phase generator would be required. Once such a device was operational, it could shed infrasonic vibrations if it wasn't isolated well enough. This must be why the park was empty. Such waves unconsciously worked on the sympathetic nervous system causing feelings of dread. All the more reason to check out the base.

The Next Day

The president traveled the country to lend support to his fellow Democrats ahead of the mid-term congressional elections. He enjoyed a celebrity's popularity as he went from city to city. Typically a shy man he did enjoy the crowds. Where he felt most uncomfortable was at state affairs that took him away from familiar turf and forced the high political equivalent of small talk on him, the G-8 summits being a prime example. Cody hated that time of year and couldn't wait for those events to conclude. They thoroughly bored him, yet he was able to call on impressive self-control to conduct himself in a courteous and stately manner.

Made from different social fabric than his predecessor, Cody resisted the urge to massage the German chancellor's neck and shoulders. And he was particularly careful never to bid farewell with the comment "good-bye from the world's biggest polluter." Perhaps he wasn't a down-to-earth fellow like the previous president, but so far the public didn't seem to mind. And that included those who purported to like an anti-intellectual leader as prescribed by the conservative ideal of government. William Buckley once said, "I would rather be governed by the first hundred names in the Boston phone book than the Harvard faculty." This early maxim in the modern conservative movement over time evolved into outright distrust of intellectual leaders. *Well, they'd hit the jackpot with Bush,* Cody thought with an internal smile.

His limo pulled up to the convention center in San Diego, where President Cody waited for the Secret Service to surround his car before he stepped out. As usual, the cheering crowds were held back by barriers and local police. Cody waved as he proceeded up the steps to his first appointment in the building with *60 Minutes* reporter Lesley Stahl.

"I think that President Bush proved that cronyism is a poor basis for governance. And I submit that cronyism is as destructive as government corruption," Cody told Stahl. "The American people would not relish a return to that system after this election."

"You're suggesting that your predecessor was corrupt?"

"I'm suggesting that certain elements of the Republican hierarchy when Bush was president made power grabbing a priority over the public good. I believe it's a matter of public record that people were appointed based on their adherence to conservative dogma as opposed to any competency they might have had. If you examine my record to date, I've valued competency, no matter the political leaning, for my appointments."

"Does that mean you would embrace conservative ideas?"

"Well, I wouldn't reject them out of hand if I saw that they made sense for working families. But let me be clear about one thing. I will not make the mistake of implementing the discredited philosophy of massive deregulation as the Republicans are promising to resurrect for this mid-term election. I won't put the country through the same kind of crises as what happened on Wall Street in 2008."

Later on that evening, Keith Olberman, newly hired at CNN, commented on the president's interview.

"I applaud the president for calling a spade a spade. With rare exceptions, the Republican Party is in business for one thing.

That is to continue to stack the deck for the over-privileged. They will do great evil to the wellbeing of the rest of us. They will adopt the lowest tactics to accomplish their purpose. And sometimes they can be very clever. Witness John McCain's congratulatory commercial when Obama was named the vice presidential candidate. It sounded friendly, but it definitely was intended to conjure fears of hip-hop artists in the White House. It was an appeal to bigotry under the guise of racial inclusiveness."

Nicole sat down with her husband on Air Force One as they jetted back to Washington.

"You look tired," she noted.

"Really? I feel fine physically. Although I won't argue that my mind has gone numb."

"Mental fatigue?"

Cody nodded.

"How did you sleep last night?"

"Pretty well. The night seemed to go by too quickly though. I felt like I'd just gone to bed when I woke up this morning."

"I wish I could say that."

"You didn't sleep?"

"I had nightmares. In one I dreamt that I looked over at you in bed and saw something strange."

Cody looked at her. After years of marriage she knew the look invited an explanation. "You were lying there asleep but there were two of you."

"Two of me?" he repeated with an amused grin.

"Sort of. One was solid. Like you are now. And the other was see-through. The see-through you overlapped the solid you. It was like you and your ghost were trying to occupy the same space."

"That is weird," said the president.

"It seemed so real. I was terrified and screamed, but then woke up to find you were right there."

"Well, let's not have any more of that. We both need our sleep for this campaign season."

"This is the hard part of the job... campaigning," she said with a sigh.

"True, but I think I'm up to it. Kind of old hat after all this time."

"I meant this was the hard part of the job for the first lady, for me. At least you get all the adulation. I just have to stand there and look supportive."

"And pretty."

"Good answer."

With that, she cuddled up next to her husband. The president and first lady fell asleep.

CHAPTER 36

Jack breached the security perimeter of the Castle Island complex that had allowed passage of several people he recognized. Using the device that al-Rahiim had given him, he phased out of his plane of reality by a sufficient number of degrees to avoid detection. Even if the enemy were phased, Jack knew they could only displace themselves by three degrees. Thanks to the proconsul's Martian connections, Jack could phase any number of degrees. He just had to be careful not to phase by so much that it put him in a different universe.

As the cars had driven into the fort, Jack recognized the likes of Senator McConnell, former vice presidential candidate Sarah Palin, Newt Gingrich, and Rupert Murdoch—the founder of Fox News or as Jack called it the 'News for Republicans' station. The group was like a who's who of the political right. There were others whom he didn't recognize, but he was willing to bet that none represented progressive politics.

Inside, Jack skulked around the complex in spite of his phased condition. He still felt it was prudent to be cautious when traipsing around the enemy's lair. He admired the architecture as he inspected the interior, and entered the various rooms and barracks. It was a shame they didn't open the building up to the public, he thought. It contained a great deal of interesting history and might even inspire school kids to pay attention in class.

The courtyard itself was empty when Jack walked the perimeter. Even the grass remained untrammeled. None of the cars or the people who entered were within sight. They couldn't have gone into the chambers, thought Jack. Some entryways were guarded by sentries but none of those openings were large enough to admit cars. Where had they gone?

With no real possibilities he could see, Jack found a stairway to the second floor. Above were the same type of rooms with the same unfinished walls as on the first floor. Back in the day, it had been considered uncouth to leave interior brick walls bare. They were either plastered over or had some other covering. Bare brick was for animals. Or, in modern times, for tres chic yuppies. Amazing how the passage of time could change status symbols.

Passing from room to room, Jack noted that the upper level hadn't been occupied in quite some time. He found no signs of habitation, unlike on the bottom floor, which some of the current occupants had obviously used. About to give up and go back downstairs, Jack thought he heard something in the next room—a voice but faint and unintelligible. Not trusting completely to his personal cloaking device, Jack moved silently to the side of the doorway and listened.

He heard no voices this time, but someone was shuffling about in there. Peaking around the corner, Jack strained to find a few clues as to what was happening. As a one-time cleaner, he still enjoyed remarkable vision, thanks to his biogenetic preparation and nanobotic enhancements. Even so, he suspected that the partial figure he saw was phased. Moonbeams, from the narrow window, passed through and negated the parts of the figure they touched. And why did the man sport a Colonial military uniform?

As Jack's eyes adjusted it looked to him as if the figure was busy with some task over an invisible counter. Eventually, Jack recognized the bricked-up remains of a stovepipe hole in the wall. Could the man be cooking on some spectral stove?

"What are you doing here?" asked the figure when he noticed Jack.

Jack froze in place. Could the apparition actually see him?

"Well?"

And then it struck Jack. He understood what he was experiencing. If only the paranormal researchers could see this. Jack was in the presence of a ghost from the Revolutionary War. Apparently to exist on the phantom plane was akin to phasing from reality, phasing in the way Jack could do to become invisible to those occupying the local reality. He stepped into the room.

"Sorry, I didn't mean to disturb you. I was just looking for some friends."

As he said this, he dialed his phase-shifter noting the figure becoming dimmer and then more solid as he adjusted in the other direction.

"Your friends? Your friends have been shaking the foundation of this fort for the past fortnight with some ungodly mechanisms. It's disrupting the routine. And if you were ever in the military, you know the importance of routine."

Jack took the rebuke in stride. "I was never in the military, but I can appreciate your position, sir."

The phantom seemed mollified. "I could tell you weren't in the military by your civilian clothes. They look strange but not like the ones your friends are wearing."

"My name is Jack, and I spoke figuratively when I said they were my friends. In point of fact, sir, they are enemies of our country. I'm gathering intelligence to report to my superiors who will decide what action should be taken."

"A spy then. Well if you are working for America then you have my blessing. I'm Captain Kenan. And I'm in temporary command of this fort till the return of Major Ashton."

"How long have you been here, Captain?"

"Since General Washington left for Long Island, New York. The third week in August I believe"

"August of 1776?"

"Of course," the captain said with disdain. After thinking about it for a moment though, he lost his certainty. "What year is it now?"

Jack saw nothing to be gained by playing along with the phantom's delusions. "It's 2010."

The captain just stared at Jack for a moment. Jack couldn't read his expression. If it was shock or incredulity, the Continental Army officer hid it well. He buttoned his coat, which Jack thought odd since the night was warm. Must be a nervous habit. For the first time, Jack took note of the uniform. The basic color for the coat was blue. The waistcoat and breeches were white. The captain fiddled with the big wooden buttons for a moment before replying to Jack's astonishing assertion. "I know."

"You know? You were conscious of time passage?" Now it was Jack's turn to be surprised.

"I've surmised that a lot of time must've passed judging by what I've seen outside the fort. Horseless carriages and ships without sails. Even flying metal birds that I suspect act like ferries with passengers. And I've noticed the flag. How the stars in the blue field have multiplied. It must be a great nation."

"Thanks to you and those like you," confirmed Jack.

"Tell me of the last centuries," pleaded Kenan. "It must've been wondrous."

"It was. Our history has been very dynamic. There was a civil war, two world wars even a cold war with minor engagements that lasted decades. I'd like to go into more detail but I'm pressed to take on a new challenge to the United States."

"The people in the fort?"

"Yes. They came in, but I can't find them."

"That's because they're underground. Building their infernal contraptions underneath this fortress."

"Underground? How do I get down there?"

"You'll have to go back to the courtyard and wait for someone to come or go. When that happens, you'll notice a hidden lift that appears to take people and those horseless carriages below."

"Thank you, Captain. I hope to do you proud."

"Just protect my country."

As Jack made his way back down to the courtyard, he wondered at the strange conversation he'd just had. He'd never suspected that ghosts could be so interactive. It reminded him of the cable television show *Ghost Hunters* that he caught himself watching on occasion. Cameras recorded the exploits of TAPS or the Atlantic Paranormal Society, which responded to people wanting validation of their paranormal experiences. Jason and Grant, the founders of TAPS, would go to the site of the alleged haunting and try to confirm or debunk the report.

Oftentimes, Jason and Grant would explain to the camera the phenomena of residual haunting. This was like a recording of some spectral event that replayed at a certain time whether there were witnesses or not. Jack wondered if those specters could be engaged in conversation too, like Captain Kenan. If Jack could generalize from his experience with the captain, the ghosts were apparently still people. They just lived on a different plane of existence. Documenting this and having researchers communicate with these people for historical perspective would be interesting. Who knew what could be learned, perhaps something that could even help people in the present.

Back outside, Jack walked to the middle of the courtyard. He looked down at the ground hoping to find some evidence of a hidden opening for an elevator, but the illusion that hid the shaft was masterful. For a moment it occurred to him that Captain Kenan's observation was a fantasy or something that he simply misinterpreted. Given the ghost's tone and body language, however, Jack trusted the dead soldier's account. Just then the gates opened to admit two headlight beams that caught Jack dead on. The light startled him for a moment, and he started to run for cover, until he remembered he was still phased. Stopping in his tracks, he turned to make sure he saw where the car went.

The next day, President Cody took time out of his schedule to visit Arlington National Cemetery. He'd been here before to silently honor those who'd made the ultimate sacrifice for their country, but this time he had a different perspective. The president was hard pressed to get a certain dream out of his thoughts. He'd awakened that morning with the definite recollection of a man from his dream that now occupied his waking consciousness. Cody didn't recall the dream precisely, but the Revolutionary War figure was very real to him. Could he have met the man in another life? *Am I the reincarnation of one of America's earliest citizens?* he wondered.

The circumstances of the vision left Cody with a definite impression of a soldier who clearly, even after centuries, loved the country he'd helped create. Cody knew that even this long after the captain's death, with this United States so vastly different than the one he knew, the long-dead hero worried over its wellbeing. The feeling the president had picked up from the man solidified in

Cody's mind what a great and noble experiment democracy had been back then. How invested those people must have been, he thought. From the perspective of that fledgling enterprise, he marveled at the historic accomplishments of this mighty republic.

Under the watchful eye of the Secret Service, Cody strolled among the headstones and markers of the oldest part of the park. A slight breeze rustled the leaves on this clear autumn day. Normally, he would revel at being outside in such weather, but now his attention was focused on scanning the names. Finally, he found what he sought. Representatives from the Revolutionary War were scarce, and he had no guarantee, but finally he looked upon the grave of Captain Ambrose Kenan, the man in his dream. President Cody's lexicon held no prayers, but he removed the flag pin from his lapel and placed it on the grave. After a moment, he saluted and returned to his limo.

CHAPTER 37

At the First National Bank of Boston, Sharon made her way back to her desk with a fresh cup of coffee. The open floor plan allowed her colleagues to note the comical disturbance at the entrance to the bank as Sharon sat down and took work from her center drawer. Eventually, she notices the unusual quiet and looked up to find several of her neighbors fixing their attention on proceedings at the front of the bank. By the time she followed their stares, a pudgy, red-faced man approached her desk.

Obviously the center of all that attention, she thought. The man sat in a waiting area just beyond her desk and cradled a box in his lap. The wooden box was about one foot on each side and was open at the top. Sharon's first reaction was one of apprehension. She was reassured, however, when she realized that the bank guards would not have allowed anyone with a dangerous package into the bank.

She got up, walked around her desk, and went over to greet the man. He shook her hand with a big smile and introduced himself as Seamus O'Malley. The bank manager motioned him to one of the guest chairs in front of her desk.

"So what can I do for you, Mr. O'Malley?" Sharon asked.

"Well, I'd like to make a deposit."

"Do you have an account with us?"

"No. No. I've just moved to America, and this is one of the first stops I've made."

"Okay," she said, and she pulled a set of new account forms from her desk. "I'm glad that you chose us as your bank. I'll just ask you a few questions from this form so we can open an account for you."

As she reached for a pen, her eyes rested on the box that her customer hadn't let out of his grasp.

"I must admit, Mr. O'Malley, you've got me curious about what's in your box."

"Oh, that's what I want to deposit. Here, let me show you." With that, he put the box down on the floor, reached in, and pulled out a pot that looked as if it was meant for baking beans in the days of the Pilgrims. He then heaved it up on her desk with a heavy thump. She took a look, and without moving her head, scanned the rest of the room to see her colleagues looking on with varying facial expressions that ranged from grins to outright belly laughs. Not knowing what else to do, she played along.

"Do I take it that this is gold?" Sharon asked.

"You do. It's a pot of gold. I've had it tested before I left the old country."

"Well, that seems prudent. Where did you get it?"

"At the end of the rainbow, of course."

"Of course."

"Now, I don't want you to think it was easy. I had to chase the little bugger who owned it from Killarney to Limerick and back down to Kerry," her customer said proudly.

"Nice job. Do you mind if our assayer authenticates these coins?"

"Not at all. I'd like to know how much they're worth in American dollars anyway."

Sharon made a quick call and waited for someone to come to her desk while she picked out about a half-dozen coins at random. They certainly seem to be gold, she thought. And she noticed some signs of age on them as well their odd shapes. A lot of them weren't perfectly round. The writing was strange too.

"That's Latin," volunteered Seamus as if reading her mind. "They're from the Roman era, you see."

The assayer showed up just in time to stifle any comment Sharon was about to make. "Ms. Bradley?" queried the assayer.

She looked up, handed him the coins, watched him depart and went back to her conversation.

"He shouldn't take too long," she assured her customer. "So you chased down a little bugger as you said. Are we talking leprechaun here?"

"Indeed, we are. Tricky little imps, you know. They've had countless thousands of years to perfect their craft. But I outsmarted this one." Mr. O'Malley smiled with the satisfaction of a job well done.

"I guess you did. Why come to America? You could've settled down in your home country and lived a nice life."

"True, but I always wanted to see America. Do you know that there are still some in Ireland who believe the streets are paved in gold here. Isn't that daft?"

In spite of herself, Sharon was starting to warm up to this obvious con man. But just then the assayer returned.

"These coins are genuine. Pure gold."

She stared at him for a moment then turned back to O'Malley. He returned her look with a quizzical expression. She got up, took the assayer by the elbow and ushered him to the back of the bank out of earshot of any customer.

"If this is some kind of joke, I think it's gone far enough."

"No joke. I know it's weird but it's no joke. These are real gold coins."

"Mayfield, get over here."

Mayfield, who was observing the happenings, obeyed and joined the twosome in the back of the bank.

"Mayfield, I saw you grinning when O'Malley came in. Did someone put this man up to this?"

"No, ma'am. Not that I know of. I just thought it was funny after I saw the guard's expression when he searched the box. I was curious to see what would happen when he brought his pot of gold over to you. I didn't think it was real. I thought he was a nut job."

With that, Sharon frowned and returned to her desk where O'Malley waited patiently. "Mr. O'Malley, do you have any identification?" Sharon asked.

"Oh, not yet. I mean I just arrived but I'm planning on getting my driver's license soon."

"You must have a passport."

"Yes, right. I forgot about that." He pulled the small booklet out of his pants pocket and handed it to her. It was somewhat the worse for wear having been in the rumpled pocket for a while, but it did have his picture and seemed quite genuine.

"All right, Mr. O'Malley, where did this really come from?"

"I got it at the American embassy in Dublin."

"I don't mean the passport. I mean the pot of gold."

O'Malley looked hurt. "I told you. It was at the end of the rainbow. Don't you believe me?"

He did seem sincere which only added to the bank manager's exasperation. "What storybook universe are you supposed to be from?"

CHAPTER 38

The next night, Jack returned to the secret installation at Castle Island. Proceeding to the hidden opening of the elevator shaft, he waited there. As before, a car's headlights illuminated the courtyard and the gates opened to admit it. Confident in his invisibility this time, Jack allowed himself to be bathed in the bluish lights of the sedan. When the car approached, Jack noted a circular opening in the ground just before him. The grass had disappeared and in its place was a circular platform that filled the opening with a dull silver sheen. Definitely not asphalt, Jack decided, and he remembered the surface of the fighter plane elevators on aircraft carriers. He hitched a ride on the platform.

On the way down, Jack noted the seams in the walls left over from the machinery that had created the shaft. The seams used the manmade creases in the native rock to reinforce the polymetal panels' joints. The walls appeared to be a smooth surface with periodic vertical seams every six feet. Definitely made by a macro-borer, Jack noted. A little too sophisticated for the science of this Earth.

Apparently the lunatic fringe of the political right was cooperating with someone from Jack's home reality.

After a while, he felt the elevator slow. Eventually, a large space revealed itself while the elevator continued to descend. The subterranean chamber had the same type of walls as the elevator shaft and was at least five stories high. Jack observed a lot of human activity on the floor, and people in some unfamiliar uniforms scurried about.

The gigantic chamber was roughly circular and its diameter seemed at least as big as a football field. The floor was made up of three concentric circles with the interior levels about a half-floor lower than its outermost adjacent one. Stairs and some ramps were spaced in equidistant intervals on the perimeter of each section, allowing passage from one level to the next. Jack guessed that the ramps were for vehicles. Railings kept people from accidentally falling off the higher levels.

In the very center of this arrangement, a hole about twenty feet in diameter was partially filled with a tall cylindrical device that Jack recognized as an unusually large portal/phase-generator. It had about five feet of space around it, except where a ramp extended from the floor to a wide opening on the device. Banks of waist-high control panels where people were seated faced the machine in a semi-circular arc.

Just then, the car that had accompanied Jack down the shaft drove off to the left and parked in a hollowed-out area outside the perimeter of the circular floor. There, the cave walls weren't as well finished, showing bare rock. A fan, obviously vented to the surface, removed the car's exhaust. Other fans that Jack couldn't see must be replacing the air, for he felt the slight breeze and smelled the freshness. While considering the engineering marvel that was this cavern, he was startled by the sound of a loud klaxon. Everyone's attention focused on the phase-generator that towered twenty feet above the ramp extending to it.

Jack sensed a vibration and knew the device had been activated. Ultimately, a shimmering figure appeared in the portal as lights surrounding it strobed on and off. The figure gradually became more solid, and after a few seconds a man materialized.

Jack was familiar with the technology, but the theatrical display was new to him. It was obviously meant to impress the locals, he thought. He was puzzled at the sheer size of the device, too. A phase-generator didn't have to take up that much room unless it had other functions as well. He wondered what else it did.

The man who had appeared walked down the slight angle of the ramp to stand on the inner floor and be greeted by several uniformed men and women. Waiting in back of that group, another few people prepared to meet the visitor, the second gathering dressed in business suits. Jack spied a few of the individuals he had seen the other night, including Newt Gingrich. The visitor or interloper soaked up the adulation, an attitude not unexpected for a Religionist—as Jack recognized Simon, the infamous Simon from his own universe, a devout man who advocated the destruction of all parallel universes except his own.

These people couldn't know Simon's true feelings about them and their world, Jack realized. Simon must be using them in some twisted plot. But Jack was also sure that the people from this universe thought they were actually using Simon and his friends. Each reality had its lunatic fringe, but now Jack understood that the fringes of two universes had formed an alliance. Not good.

With all the greetings out of the way, the group piled into a couple of waiting vehicles that resembled large golf carts. Careful not to hit other personnel, they headed off to a perimeter opening at the topmost ring. Jack followed by way of the phase-generator control consoles, so he could first get a better look at the phase-generator.

The man known as "the Architect" worked at his computer on a large wooden desk that seemed curiously out of place in this futuristic underground complex. Several floors underground, his office also sported another unusual indulgence: A very convincing window scene behind him created the illusion of a green lawn with trees and windblown foliage. An assistant who entered the office always struggled with the unusual oval floor plan. The walls curved in atypical ways for any conventional building. Of course the layout was very consistent and almost a carbon copy of the executive office at the White House. The Architect had an ego.

"Yes, what is it?" asked the Architect with mild irritation in his tone.

"An intruder, sir."

"Why are you bothering me with that?"

"This one is phased, sir."

That got the Architect's attention. He feared that his operation had been found out by those with the technology to disrupt it.

"Where is he?"

"We don't know, sir. He's using a phasing technology beyond even our patrons' detection abilities."

"Well, how the hell did you see him?"

"His shadow betrayed him. He got caught in the headlights of one of our guest cars on the ground level. I don't think he knew we could see it. He never moved to get away and rode down the elevator with the car."

"All right. He's not one of us or otherwise he would've revealed himself. And if he's spying, he must be from the left, either the left of this universe or our patrons' reality. A Democrat by any other name. I think I know how to trap one of them."

Jack finally caught up with the group as they paraded down a hall. From snatches of conversation, he picked up that the destination was a presentation room where someone called "the Architect" was expected to address the group. That nickname, or designation, sounded familiar. *Where have I heard that before?* wondered Jack. In any case, the Architect was apparently the leader of the underground conservative movement in the local universe. Whoever he was, he'd made a pact with the devil and didn't even know it.

Jack, still phased, walked among the procession and reached Simon who had hooked up with another visitor from the Religionists, Thaddeus. Jack observed both men and looked for some clue to their intentions. Both, however, stared straight ahead and said nothing while they continued on to the presentation room.

Then, as Jack maintained his observation, Simon jerked his head around to stare at Thaddeus with an amazed expression. Thaddeus just returned the look with a slight smile. They were communicating. Somehow, they were in communication on a subvocal level. Jack wasn't familiar with any such technology, but it had been a while since he was in his own universe. Technological advancement there could have come a long way since he was last home. How might Jack pick up on what they were saying now?

He took out his portable Martian-made phase-generator. Somehow he knew to use it in conjunction with his microsentinels. His microsentinels passed in front of the device, which reacted by projecting the same holo screen he'd used to see the phased visitors outside Fort Independence above. Hard to believe the old fort was connected to this underground techno-facility.

On the screen, Jack noted activity that suggested the microsentinels were being repurposed. After a few more seconds, they flew away and took up a position between Simon and Thaddeus. Now data started flowing into Jack's brain, and he put the Martian device back in his pocket. At first the message was garbled, but it eventually became clear. Apparently both men had neural implants that translated vocal, electrical impulses to signals that were transmitted to the other's brain and then translated and fed to the aural nerve center.

The two men could literally hear each other's unspoken thoughts. It took a little getting used to since conversation that is formed in our brains needs to be processed before turning into actual vocalizations, but Jack got the hang of it.

"I can't believe it's working," thought Simon to Thaddeus.

"Our huge generator, all by itself, probably wouldn't have worked. But I was confident that we could tap the local minds to make it fulfill our designs for this reality," responded Thaddeus.

"So they're unwitting agents of their own destruction."

"That's the beauty of it. You should see some of the weird stuff that our device has drawn into this reality. Stuff out of the fantasies of these local primitives."

"Well, as we know, someone's fantasy is someone else's reality in a different universe. But I'm still not clear about why it's better to bring fantastical subjects to this universe." Simon mused on this for a moment longer and the signal was muddied.

But Thaddeus responded after only a short delay. "Because the fantastic beings have to come from the farthest parallel realities. You have to go a quite a way from this universe to find the locals' imaginings to be real in another one. The more spatial distance we cover, the bigger the breach and the more destructive to the local universes. We're just being more aggressive this time. That's the way we designed the phase-portal maker."

"I'm glad we're being more aggressive about bringing down these parallel realities," answered Simon. "I thought we tiptoed around the Agency for far too long. I'd like to see them try to plug all the holes we've been making. The more myths we bring to life the better."

Frank Cobb sat on the sidewalk with his legs splayed out in front of him. His clothes were tattered and dirty, and a foul smell permeated the air around him. A scar ran from his hairline through his right eye and ended somewhere in a scraggly beard. People tried to avoid eye contact as they strode by, but they needn't have worried since Frank was blind. Without the benefit of sight in either eye, though, he still recognized the closeness of passersby due to a very keen sense of hearing. Oddly, the mine that had exploded in his face in Vietnam took his sight but left his aural capacity intact. Fortunately for him, this sense was all he needed to at least support himself in a meager fashion by panhandling. Every once in a great while, he would hear the clink of coins in the cup he held out as people went by.

Hours had passed since he'd taken up his station on the sidewalk. It was his spot to mine for the sympathies of those just getting out of work. Most of the people who were going to come by had probably already done so, and were completing their commute home. It was getting cold, and Frank clutched the rags that passed for clothing ever tighter. Living on the street wasn't lonely, however, and he knew that one of his fellow homeless people would eventually come to take him to a shelter for the night.

A slight wind blew threw his greasy hair, but the wind wasn't cold. It filled him with at least a temporary sense of wellbeing. Contemplating this, he belatedly detected the presence of a figure standing in front of him. The intruder had been silent in his approach. Somehow, Frank knew it was a man. He could sense the bearing if not the mass of the individual. Suddenly Frank felt a hand on his shoulder and knew that the stranger was leaning down. He didn't fear, however, and noting his own reaction he was puzzled by it.

Eventually, the stranger's other hand brushed Frank's face and settled on his eyes. They remained a few seconds over Frank's closed lids, and when they withdrew, Frank dropped his cup full of change. Before him, he made out a man of impressive mien. It was the first time Frank had seen anything in who knew how many decades. Frank had stopped keeping track of time ages ago.

The stranger wore his hair long and sported a very well-groomed beard. He wore a long white robe under a red toga-like garment that draped one shoulder. The white robe was cinched at the waist with a rope belt. Completing the ensemble were sandals that showed hideous wounds on both feet. His hands exhibited the same damage.

"My Lord," cried Frank, who then kissed the stranger's hands.

With the power of sight, Frank now noticed several people, homeless and otherwise, who had witnessed the miracle. They approached the two men.

The telephone rang at the police dispatcher's station. It was an anonymous call about a civil disturbance. Apparently things were getting pretty rowdy. The caller reported that a man dressed as Jesus had cured a homeless man's blindness and now a big noisy mob had gathered around them. The dispatcher took down the address and alerted the closest patrol car.

"Bob, we've got a mob disturbance down on Fifth. Would you check it out please?"

"Sure. We're about five minutes away. What's up?"

"Apparently some nut case is running around down there dressed up as Jesus. The anonymous caller said he restored the sight of some blind homeless beggar."

"A blind homeless beggar on Fifth? That sounds like Frank Cobb."

The policeman turned to his partner driving the car who nodded in assent. Both men knew the neighborhood from their years patrolling it.

"You mean there really is a blind, homeless man there?" asked the dispatcher.

"Sort of. Frank thinks he's blind. It's psychosomatic. Last week I saw him dodge a car as he crossed the road. I think it serves his purposes to convince himself he's blind so he can be more sympathetic."

By the time the police arrived, a large crowd had gathered around a stranger who apparently thought he was Jesus Christ. The troubling thing was the crowd seemed to buy into the fantasy too. Leaving the car, the police officers walked across the street toward the mob. Officer Bob noticed another homeless man he recognized, who stood beside the Lord, our God. It was Phil who habitually walked around with a cane.

Jesus laid his hands on the man and commanded him to walk without the aid of the walking stick. Phil took several halting steps, turned, and walked unsteadily back before falling to the ground in front of Jesus. "It's a miracle," Phil yelled, and the crowd cheered and applauded while others among them had to wipe tears from their cheeks.

"Did that look like a miracle to you?" asked Bob of his partner.

"Unless I'm missing something, that's no better than Phil has ever walked."

"That's what I thought."

Both men looked back at the scene. The crowd had swelled a little more since the two officers had arrived. The Messiah, back in character, preached about the Kingdom of Heaven and the ills of empire. When he saw the policemen, he pointed to them and beseeched the crowd to behold the centurions, the keepers of Caesar's ill-gotten gains.

Bob, spoke into his microphone. "Dispatch, we're going to need some backup here. And it'd be smart to bring riot gear. And, by the way, do we happen to have anybody named Pontius Pilate on patrol tonight?"

CHAPTER 39

Inside the secret Castle Island installation, Jack sat on a perch in a high alcove above the cavern floor. After overhearing the plot of the

Religionists, he anxiously awaited the appearance of the man described as the Architect, the man who championed the cause of the privileged elite—the man who had allowed himself to be seduced by the lunatic fringe of Jack's universe. Wasn't he suspicious? Didn't he sense any danger? *I suppose we believe what we want to believe,* thought Jack. It must have been irresistible to come by the power to undermine their hated rivals on the political left and maintain their destructive stranglehold on the wealth and power of the country.

The audience that gathered for his eminence, the Architect, included top political operatives as well as their patrons. Mitch McConnell, Ken Starr, Rupert Murdoch, Newt Gingrich. No shrinking violets in the bunch, yet they all seemed to defer to this as-yet-unseen leader.

Eventually, the man himself appeared. Jack did a double take. He was a lifelike version of Kuato the mutant who had sprang from the belly of a character in *Total Recall,* the Schwarzenegger movie. Of course, most people knew him as Karl Rove, Bush's Brain, the man who got George W. Bush elected twice, and therefore the man responsible for the near collapse of the United States and American democracy. What unholy plot was the Architect constructing now? Jack listened to see if he could divine the answer.

"And, with the help of our new friends, we will return to the days in which the deserving moneyed class is rewarded and the middle class will be too cowed to make demands. We will restore the muscular foreign policy our weak-willed successors abandoned. And most importantly, we will finally construct a permanent conservative majority, and Democrats will be thankful for the puny appointments that we deign to bestow upon them."

The room erupted in loud cheers. The puppet master had finally achieved something for which he always thought he needed a puppet. The spotlight was his, and he didn't require an attractive dummy to prop in front of him. He waved to the room and soaked in the adulation as he slowly left the stage.

Jack climbed down from his perch while the room emptied. *Poor fool,* he thought, as he remembered Rove's boasts. Little did Rove know he was facilitating his own demise. As much as Jack would wish destruction on the twisted neocon, he couldn't let the

Religionists' plan succeed. He decided to make his way back to the elevator while manipulating some holographic controls on his Martian device.

On the way back, Jack jogged past several conference rooms inhabited by mostly female workers. It was the first time he noticed the disproportionate gender population and it made him curious. Eventually the oddness of it slipped from his mind, and he noted the general attractiveness of the women—another oddity that all were pleasing to the eye. No uniforms here, either. Or at least not the ones that the people who worked the main floor wore. They all dressed differently with individual flair but with certain commonalities. Skirts hugged svelte waistlines, and tight blouses were the norm as well as high heels. Jack felt as if he were back in the early sixties when stewardesses were all objects of desire, no matter the airline.

Indeed, the colors of the clothing could have corresponded to the uniforms of the various airlines of the time. Some of the women also wore beret or pill-box style hats, some didn't. All skirts were the same color as the shoes which heightened the impression of an airline uniform. There were blues, blacks, greens, and so on. And strangely, by today's fashion norms, they all wore hosiery. Some of the hose matched the color of their skirts, but most were shades of tan. More importantly, the women who sported these styles were attractive blondes, brunettes, and some redheads.

Jack found himself looking into a conference room where a single woman riffled through a stack of papers on one of three long tables that were arranged in a U shape. Eventually she found what she was after, extracted the paper, and sat down to examine it. Jack was treated to an unobstructed view of the woman, who fascinated him more than the others he'd passed. Her light brown hair was cut shoulder length and the ends curled in to her very attractive face. As she sat reading, she crossed her legs, an action that caused the slit in her skirt to separate and reveal the top of a thigh-high stocking along with a tantalizing portion of skin right above it. Just then the old Frank Sinatra song *Come Fly With Me* played in Jack's inner ear.

Jack looked up and down the corridor several times before entering the room. Inside, he phased back to the local plane of existence, being careful to remain outside the woman's field of vision. Now fully visible, he picked up a few sheets of papers on another table and then created some noise to make his presence known. The woman turned around, but she wasn't startled.

"Did I miss Karl?" he asked as he held his apparently important reports.

"Yes," she said in a confident voice. "He just left the presentation room about ten minutes ago. Did you come through the phase-generator?"

She must have thought he was one of the Religionists. "Yes, I did. How did you know?"

"You don't have on a uniform or a suit."

Smart girl. And she seemed to perk up at the prospect of meeting someone from another world.

"You're observant."

"Thank you. I suppose my police academy training is good for something."

"Really. Were you on the police force?"

"No. I enjoyed the training, but the actual job didn't measure up to my vision."

"And now here you are involved with a much bigger vision."

"I just hope my contribution counts in some small way. My name is Vicki by the way."

"I'm Jack," he said as he took the hand she offered and shook it.

"I must admit, Jack, that I'm very curious about your world. They say it's like ours yet it isn't."

"Both worlds are very similar, but as you see the technology is the main difference."

"I've got a ton of questions I'd like to ask about your development. Do have time for a cup of coffee?"

This was going better than he had a right to expect. "I think I can squeeze it in."

"Great!" she said and patted his knee. Then she got up and walked over to a coffee maker. "Cream and sugar?"

"Please." He admired the way she sashayed across the floor. She sat back down and placed his cup in front of him on the long table they were seated at.

"I understand your history is different, even though the historic characters are the same."

"That's true," said Jack. He took a sip of coffee and prepared to continue. Before opening his mouth again, however, he sensed something was wrong. He was becoming light-headed and dizzy. Then, he thought of the sip of coffee he'd just taken. That was some fast-acting poison, he decided. Vicki, who seemed to know what was happening, noted him staring at his cup.

"It wasn't the coffee, Jack. It was my ring."

She showed him her palm. Jack noted a miniature spike coming out of the ring band on the palm side of the jewelry. "I injected you when I brushed your knee."

"I thought that was exceptionally affectionate."

"Still want to see Karl? He'll be here in a minute."

While they waited, she searched Jack and found his Martian-made phase-generator. The body search wasn't an unpleasant experience, but he wished she hadn't found his device. Two men showed up whom she'd apparently signaled, and they manhandled Jack up on the table. Too weak to resist, he didn't even try while they secured his wrists, ankles, and waist to the table that turned out to be more than just a table. Once he was secured, they rotated him up on it to a near vertical position and left the room, just as the Architect entered.

"You Democrats are so predictable," said Karl. "There's no denying your sexual appetites, is there?"

Vicki smiled and left the room when he said that.

"Well, at least we like women. Not men or boys," responded Jack.

Karl walked up to him and backhanded him across the face.

"Nice bitch slap, Kuato."

Rove had a puzzled look on his face at that response. Apparently not a sci-fi movie fan, thought Jack. He half expected to be slapped again, but the little puppet master thought the better of it.

"So, *you're* Jack. JFK by any other name. Or is it Jack and JFK together? Doesn't one personality subsume the other?" he asked smugly.

That put Jack on the defensive. How did Rove know that? Had the Shadow Group found out somehow and told him?

"I can tell by the look on your face that you're surprised we know. And we also know about your nanobotic enhancements. That's why you're still suffering the effects of Vicki's drug. That table you're on is like an MRI machine. The powerful magnetic field it generates neutralizes your robotic biodefenses. I realize you're biogenetically enhanced too, but your organic self alone will take longer to deal with the drug than your mechanical enhancements would. You may as well relax. You're not going anywhere for a while."

At least Rove didn't seem to know about his microsentinels, thought Jack. He had to stall Rove until he figured a way out using them.

"All right, you got me. And you seem to have the facility here to accomplish your twisted goals. Except for one glaring flaw."

"Okay, I'll play along. What is the flaw?"

"The Shadow Group, the Religionists in other words, are using you."

"Really?" said a confident Rove but Jack could tell this thought was new to him, and he found it believable.

"The Shadow Group is on the lunatic fringe of the conservatives in my universe. You know the type," sneered Jack. "Their only purpose is to purge existence of all but their own true believers. And that means destroying other parallel realities. Realities like this one."

"Assuming that's true, how would they do that?"

"They're already doing it. That machine in the middle of your main floor is creating breaches in the barriers between realities. Your world is being flooded with characters from your own myths and folklore that really exist in other universes."

"I haven't seen anything like that. And even if that's happening, how would that destroy our world?"

"Eventually this plane of existence will be so corrupted with such nonsensical doctrine that rational thought will collapse. Civilization will be thrown into a dark age full of superstition, in which all rational progress will stop. That's at best. At worst, the imbalance between the universes will cause overlapping which is another word for a Big Bang."

This term, Rove seemed to know in spite of a lack of science fiction reading. "You mean like the event that created our universe?"

"Yes. Except this would destroy all of us in favor of a new universe."

Rove sat down, but didn't take his eyes off Jack.

"Hard to accept responsibility for that kind of destruction, isn't it?" asked Jack.

"A fantastic story. But that's all it is."

"Your reaction tells me you don't find it so far fetched. I suspect you've had your doubts about these Religionists."

At that moment, a loud klaxon sounded an alarm. This sound, however, was different than the one that signified the activation of the phase-generator. This time it seemed a lot more insistent and worrisome, if one could personalize its tone. Without saying a word, Rove rushed from the room.

As soon as Rove exited, a deep bass tone accompanied a tremor. *Now what,* wondered Jack, held helpless by the restraints and the magnetic field. He couldn't see the door, but he sensed people running by it. His microsentinels confirmed his suspicions, and he considered that the complex was self-destructing. That could be in the Shadow Group's plan, Jack guessed. With a sufficient number of incursions from other realities, they would no longer need this place or their alliance with the Architect.

Another tremor rocked the complex, and this time Jack heard screams. He strained at his bonds, but to no avail. Before he could consider another plan of escape, however, Vicki rushed into his field of vision. This time she wasn't nearly as composed. In fact, she exhibited a frightened and disheveled appearance. The sleeve of her blouse was ripped, a heel of her shoe was broken, and the slit in her skirt was torn higher up her hip, although Jack suspected she'd done that to help her run better. Her chest heaved from exertion, and even in this stressful situation, Jack couldn't help but admire it. As Vicki discarded both shoes, she attacked the restraints on Jack's arms.

"I heard everything you told Rove. A group of us monitored you from another room." She indicated a painting on the wall, and Jack figured it was some kind of two-way mirror. "I always wondered about our benefactors," she continued. "Never entirely trusted their motives."

Jack undid the straps around his waist and ankles while she went behind the table to turn off the magnetic field. He sensed the free movement of the nanobots in his body when the field shut down. With all his limbs free, he raced to the table, picked up his portable phase-generator, then took Vicki by the hand and ran from the room. Outside, he noted the corridor walls periodically punctured as rock falls and gravel invaded the space. The polymetal walls had uncharacteristically failed in several places. *Must've taken a lot of force to do that,* thought Jack. He couldn't recall ever hearing about this system failing on his home world.

"Is there another elevator out of here?" he asked when he noted the way back to the entrance clogged with traffic.

Before Vicki could answer, another tremor threatened to knock her off her feet. Jack steadied her, and he gripped her hand. It made her wince but she seemed thankful, nonetheless.

"The elevator banks are all in the direction you came from. But there is an underwater exit that I don't think too many are aware of."

"It lets out under the surface of Boston Harbor?"

"Yes. But you don't have to swim or anything. There are escape pods."

Another tremor rained dust and gravel on the would-be escapees. Vicki took off running in the opposite direction of the rest of the mob. In her stocking feet she was quite fleet; surprisingly, Jack had to exert himself to keep up. Vicki took a left down a side corridor while the crowd thinned to practically nothing. This escape route must only be for the higher-ups, thought Jack. Everyone else must be intended to take their chances in the bottleneck at the elevators. It then occurred to him that the likes of Rove might have already escaped. And perhaps with one of a limited number of escape pods.

"How many of these pods are there? Could we already be too late to get one?"

"Why do you think I'm running," rasped Vicki breathlessly.

Eventually, they came to a watertight door. Vicki rotated the valve handle and yanked open the heavy metal door. They scooted inside to find themselves in an airlock. Jack could sense the air pressure rising as it obviously was meant to equalize with the next chamber. A lighted bar turned green over the inner door, which opened automatically.

Jack smelled the salty tang of sea water and could feel the increased dampness relative to the rest of the complex. A subterranean pool, held at bay by the higher air pressure, lapped at a sandy shore in this semi-circular cavern. Dripping noises echoed around the space as the damp ceilings rained condensation.

There were nine escape pods, three of which were in the process of sliding down ramps into the water. They were shaped like manta rays and had windshield-shaped portals along the leading edge. Five people could easily fit inside one as long as they didn't stand. Seated, however, the passengers seemed to have plenty of head room. Jack watched as the lead one submerged and headed toward a rock wall that must contain an underwater opening to the harbor.

Vicki pointed to another group of five conspirators who were preparing a fourth pod for the undersea route. Jack ran over and, using martial art maneuvers enhanced by his genetic and nanobotic constitution, dispatched the three people who were still on the ramp slide. Jumping on top of the pod to engage the other two, he wheeled back around at the sound of breath explosively leaving the lungs of one his first three antagonists. Vicki had finished the job of neutralizing a man whom Jack had too hastily passed over with his attack. The injured man had grabbed a large wrench and had been attempting to sneak up on him until Vicki put a stop to that.

Jack stared admiringly at his attractive companion and then was nearly thrown off his feet as the fourth pod slid into the pool. He had just enough time to jump off of it and onto the ramp.

"Let's get to number five," shouted Vicki.

He ran over to the next ramp as an alarm and lights started blaring over the airlock door. The sound wasn't as loud as the klaxon that he'd heard earlier, but it left no doubt that someone else had entered the airlock.

"They're coming," yelled Vicki, and she ran over to the airlock door, pulled off the front of a control panel near the side, and started manipulating a lighted keyboard.

In the window of the door, Jack could see several people including Rove as well as the two Religionists, Simon and Thaddeus.

"That'll hold them for a while but we should hurry," warned Vicki.

Jack found a hatch in the back of the escape pod and froze when he saw the lock. It was a typical lock used by the Agency. Opening it required a code that was constantly rotating but was always known to the agents since it was transmitted to their nanobotic receivers. Had the Shadow Group come by this technology somehow? Jack had been off the net for years. If he plugged back in to access this code, the Agency would zero in on him, know he was alive, and track his location. Talk about being stuck between a rock and a hard place, he thought.

"Hurry," yelled Vicki.

"Do you know the code to open this?" he shouted back at her.

"Only the Architect's Council knows. I thought you would've known it. They said you intercepted a lot of their protocols."

"They gave me too much credit. It's a total surprise to me that they would even have this technology."

A loud hissing came from the airlock door. Apparently the group inside decided to stop guessing at Vicki's key strokes and take the more direct approach of cutting through the door. An oxyacetylene flame poked a hole in the chromium steel and started to work its way down. Vicki became more and more agitated.

"Do you know what they'll do to us, to me, if you can't get us out of here?"

Jack looked back at the lock and then around the cavern hoping to find alternatives. His microsentinels explored the underground space at his mental command. No other exit presented itself. For a moment, Jack considered swimming out but he didn't know how deep he was under the harbor surface. And whatever his own situation, he was pretty sure Vicki wouldn't survive it.

The torch had cut about halfway around the door. They were making better progress than he'd expected. He took another look at the lock. Vicki came over and hugged him from behind. She shook from fear. Should he do it? He debated. Did he have time even if he decided to? He started to manipulate the display with finger pressure.

The hissing from the airlock door stopped. It sounded like the cutting torches had run out of gas. Jack didn't bother to look, however, as he continued the set-up process, moving certain characters to various boxes on the screen. He hoped he remembered the procedure correctly. Once all the electronic tumblers were in place, he could tap the net for the code. After he completed the reconfiguration of the symbols, his nanobotic systems would then insert the properly configured nanobots through his finger into the screen's representation of the lock. Normally the process would take less then ten seconds, but he was being careful to avoid the booby trap defenses if he remembered wrong. While he worked, the hissing restarted, and the flame reappeared to complete the last half of the opening.

"How are you doing?" queried Vicki.

"Just about ready to..."

At that second, Jack's microsentinels registered an electromagnetic detection net, not powerful enough to impede transmission and reception, but possibly sophisticated enough to read hidden signals. The timing was uncanny. As if it knew to activate just before his transmission. Jack ceased his operation and stood up.

"What are you doing?" asked an incredulous Vicki. "You were almost done."

"Have you noticed that the tremors have stopped?"

"What?"

"The tremors have stopped. We haven't felt another one since we entered the airlock."

"So what. Maybe the epicenter is too far."

"Don't you think it's odd? Tremors strong enough to break polymetal walls just yards away, and we don't even hear a whimper in here."

"What are you saying? Why are you wasting time? Rove and the others will be here soon. Can't you open the hatch to this pod?"

The torch had nearly completed its journey around the airlock door. Soon the Architect and his false allies in the Shadow Group would be able to enter the cavern. Jack stood still as if waiting for his enemies. Vicki, meanwhile, ran over to one of the unconscious men at pod four and extracted a gun. Running back to Jack's location, she stood with the gun aimed at the airlock.

"Keep working on the hatch opening," she commanded. "I'll hold them off."

Jack started clapping, which caused her to jerk her head around while still pointing the gun at Rove's entrance.

"What the hell are you doing?"

"I'm doing what I do at any good play. I'm applauding the performance."

"Are you crazy? Get to work on opening that hatch."

With that, she turned around and pointed the gun at Jack. "I'm not willing to die in this cavern even if you are. Open the hatch."

And just to emphasize her point, she fired the gun at the cavern's roof. The shot reverberated off the walls but Jack didn't flinch. "Are you going to shoot me, Vicki?"

A loud crash interrupted their conversation when the chromium steel door of the airlock fell inward. Rove and his friends stepped through. As Jack had expected, Vicki didn't fire on them. Instead, she just lowered her weapon and walked over to join them when they approached.

"How did you know?" asked a genuinely puzzled Rove.

"There was just a bit too much drama. Too much like a Bond movie. It was like the imaginings of someone who'd never been in the intelligence services but thought he knew what it was like."

Jack concealed that he'd sensed the detection net with his microsentinels. The sentinels still appeared to be a card he could keep up his sleeve. Advantage Jack.

"It seems we almost got what we wanted though. You just figured it out at the last possible second."

"You wanted the Agency's net codes."

"Of course. With them we could've brought down our only serious competitors."

"Only competitors? You mean your friends in the Shadow Group didn't tell you about the Martians?"

Rove stared at Simon and Thaddeus, who looked just as puzzled. He then glanced at the back of the group where two large muscular Marines from the U.S. Navy apparently awaited his orders. "Take our guest back to the conference room and strap him to our magnetic table. Looks like we'll have to use other means of extracting the information we want."

But as the guards approached Jack, he disappeared as though he were made of vapor. Before he vanished, however, Jack felt as surprised as anyone at his own transformation.

CHAPTER 40

The president's motorcade rolled slowly through the Back Bay Fens down Boylston Street toward Boston Common. People crowded both sides of the street to get a glimpse of the young leader and his stylish wife. They cheered wildly for the popular president, and Cody acknowledged them with smiles and waves. The early autumn day displayed a clear blue sky as well as the colorful foliage that made the region so popular this time of year. If tourists were inconvenienced by the commander-in-chief's presence, they hid it well.

Jack could see the parade in his mind's eye due to the microsentinels that shadowed the president. He admired the president's charisma, and he envied him his ability to get what he wanted. And that included extramarital sexual adventures. A risky pursuit in this puritan age, but somehow the well-scrutinized world leader seemed to indulge in total secrecy. Remarkable that he could count on the silence of his many partners. A testament to the force of his personality.

It was about 12:28 now, and the motorcade approached Boston Public Library. Jack used his micosentinels to scout the route in advance of the motorcade. People jockeyed to get the best and highest vantage points possible. The state police removed many a youngster from the trees that lined the road. Windows in older buildings that were capable of opening held numerous onlookers who stretched for a glimpse of the passing president. Unlike in Kennedy's day, the transparent bubble of the president's limo allowed a clear view while also providing protection against normal caliber rifle shots.

At 12:30 the president's motorcade crawled past the impressive edifice of the Boston Library. Moments later, an onlooker, Ralph Waterford, took advantage of the decking on the top floor of 607 Boylston to film the president. Several of his coworkers followed suit, including the newest employee, a camera buff, who'd brought his Nikon camera with the large telescoping lens. Everyone, including those who helped him set it up, was impressed with the futuristic-looking device. A weighty piece of equipment, they commented as they manhandled it into place.

The limousines inched onward. Cody and Massachusetts Governor Patrick beamed at the crowd. Ralph, on the top floor of the office building, trained his lens on the limousine as did the more serious cameraphile. Jack took in all of it, including the animated Rick Gerard, who had walked the block or so from his home to see the president. He stood beside his business manager, Niles, and waved an American flag. As was traditional, the Secret Service men jogged alongside the vehicle.

And then the explosion came. Yet it wasn't an explosion. It was the deafening report of a bazooka-like device disguised as a camera with a long-barreled lens. History repeated itself. As if in slow motion, a lethal projectile bore down on the president's party. The glass protection would mean little to the destructive force contained in the shell that hurtled toward them.

As before, in Dallas, everything seemed to slow as Jack's mental processes operated outside the dimension of time. Unlike before, however, Jack was unwilling to just be an observer. Using the device that al-Rahiim had given him, he phased out of this reality's plane. Thinking quickly, he surmised that his microsentinels would be unable to intercept the projectile and detonate it. And even if they could, the resulting explosion would still cause many deaths. So he extended the microsentinels to the incoming shell and phased the shell as well.

Then something puzzling happened. Somehow, President Cody also operated out of the dimension of time and moved to allow the shell to pass through the car floor and into the ground beneath. At a safe distance, Jack could bring it back to this reality where an underground explosion would harm no one.

How had the president done that? Jack wondered. And as in 1963, an abrupt realization burst upon his conscious mind. The president was able to do it because he, Jack/JFK, was the current president. He was Cody, and only now did he observe events from the viewpoint of their combined bodies as opposed to through the microsentinels. Jack had been in the car the whole time. JFK had invented the Cody alias and appropriated Jack's body to pull off the deception for the public. Jack had known it in one part of his mind, and yet the fact had remained hidden from another part. The result was a masterful psychosomatic splitting of his conscious. One side of his personality had deceived the other. President John F. Kennedy had used Jack's body to reassert his political aims.

Epilogue

Jack met with al-Rahiim in their usual way. The translucent holograph of the proconsul appeared to him at the White House pool.

"I'm assuming you knew about this," accused Jack.

"That you and the president were one and the same? Yes, I knew." Al-Rahiim sounded amused.

"I see."

"You don't seem nearly as upset as I thought you'd be."

"I got over that pretty quickly once I had a chat with myself. I am confused though. About two things now that I think of it. How could I swing being two people at the same time?"

"That's easy," said al-Rahiim. "Remember the device I gave you that enables you to phase-shift any number of degrees off the reality plane? Well it does more than just phase-shift. The more you used it, the more it integrated your being. It's like a mechanical symbiot."

Jack had wondered how he instinctively knew how to aim the device to see inside Castle Island. Now he didn't have to wonder.

The proconsul continued. "The device allowed your subconscious to conjure up another version of you. At first it could only do so while you were asleep. But eventually it was able to do it during your waking hours too."

"My being president seems like the biggest intervention I've ever heard of. Aren't you afraid of realities colliding?" asked Jack.

"No, not anymore."

"Really, why not?"

"Well for one, the Religionists have been trying their hardest to collide this reality with others for quite a long time now. Yes, our former Agency and the Martians have been countering, but with limited success. We can't cover it all. Many of the Religionists' plots have been successful. Yet no permanent decrease in spatial distance has occurred. It's been frustrating for them. We now know that some are questioning their creed." Al-Rahiim actually chuckled softly.

"That still doesn't explain why I've been made president."

"Jack, that was by no means a certainty at any time. The Others thought that we at least had to try for the sake of promoting the common good."

"The Others? You're working with the Others now? How do your Martian friends feel about that?"

"Let's just say I've been a double agent. I'm still working in the Martians' camp but have adopted the Others' philosophy. And Jack, the Martian cold war is just about over. My hosts have realized that it takes far more than what we thought to cause over-lapping universes and Big Bangs. As a matter of fact, the fortunes of all intelligent peoples are elevated when a group in one universe betters itself. Apparently, gravity isn't the only force that spreads to all realities. Intelligence permeates existence too. Wise leadership in any reality will benefit all life."

"So now you're in the business of promoting good societies?" Jack teased his old friend.

"At least until someone has a better idea."

At that moment, Niles entered the room and joined the conversation. Jack could usually rely on al-Rahiim's hologram disappearing when they were interrupted but this time the proconsul noted Niles' approach without alarm.

"I'm sorry, Jack," said Niles.

Jack looked from Niles to al-Rahiim and back. "You know each other?"

"We've been working together for a while now," al-Rahiim told him.

"I see," said Jack more calmly than he felt. "You're both working with the Others, aren't you?"

"I recruited al-Rahiim," explained Niles.

"You, Niles? You recruited al-Rahiim? Not the other way around? When did you find out about our extra-dimensional war?"

"When? It was November 18th, 1969 when I first became aware of it. I was enlisted by the Others soon thereafter."

Jack nearly swooned at the sound of that date and its implications. "The day my father died?"

Niles just nodded.

"Dad?" The word that Jack had rarely used escaped his lips while a tear formed in the corner of his eye.

"Sorry for the deception. I wanted to tell you. The Others cloned this body and downloaded your father on the day he died.

Considering his infirmity after the stroke, it was remarkable how aware he—or I—was."

Jack/JFK would get into it with his father later. Quickly composing himself, he considered this new development regarding the Others.

"So what role am I supposed to play in this grand scheme? What do the Others want me to do that will preserve existence?" asked a sarcastic Jack of his father.

"I know you don't like to feel manipulated, Jack, so I just subtly guided you to something you wanted to do anyway. I felt for you. I could see the angst with the disappointments of Nixon's election, Jackie remarrying, and the rise of the Republicans. Truth be told, I vicariously lived the election with you again. You seemed very happy, and I was happy for you."

Jack's demeanor suggested that he wasn't impressed with that answer.

"All right. The answer to your question is easy. Just do what you feel is right. Your governance, your philosophy, if you like, will better the prospects of a broader swath of people than previous administrations. And it should have positive implications worldwide and existentially across parallel realities."

"And I can expect no interference?"

"None, whatsoever, now that you've been elected."

"What do the Others get out of this?"

"I told you. Intelligent life across all universes benefit from a stronger social fabric in the separate realities. It's like an overmind that we're all part of. And it's growing as we do, evolving to some higher goal. It's like a rising tide lifting all boats, as our Republican colleagues used to say."

Jack blanched at hearing the opposition party's deceptive mantra. "One thing I've learned lately is that there seem to be no lack of competing ideas on preserving existence. At best, each theory is debatable. Why should any of us subscribe to one or the other?"

"Because, I believe that we make our own reality. How can a thought experiment, a daydream in the mind of Einstein spawn a truer understanding of the cosmos? Haven't you ever wondered for instance how the mind of man comes up with the Atomic Theory, or the String Theory and then the universe behaves in that way? How can some mathematical speculations on paper do that? The fabric of existence is heavily influenced by thought."

"The Greeks thought the gods governed the cosmos. Were they right?" asked Jack.

"Maybe they were... for as long as they thought that way. And maybe not. But now that we rationally examine our surroundings we shape them too. We've at least documented that the parallel realities aren't in danger of colliding based on our interference so far.

"I choose to believe we can better ourselves as an intelligent society. And I seem to remember someone saying that even though a goal is not quickly attainable, it doesn't mean we shouldn't try. Something about deciding to go to the moon in the sixties not because it was easy, but because it was hard and it would bring out the best in us. I'm paraphrasing of course."

Jack couldn't help but smile. He truly did relish the thought of a new New Frontier.

About the Author

Michael Foy is the founder and president of Publishing Search Solutions specializing in placement within the publishing industry. He lives in Massachusetts, where he enjoys kayaking, bicycling and exploring a wide array of literary subjects. His engineering background gives him a unique perspective and appreciation for speculative science fiction.

Michael started his career in 1979 as an engineer, but gravitated to publishing via the lure of creative writing. He sold an option for his first novel, *False Gods*, as a screenplay to Timothy Bogart the nephew of Peter Guber, producer of *Batman*. Michael has since published *Future Perfect*, a science fiction novel, and was an early pioneer in publishing short stories over the Internet, including the story "Solar Winds of Change," "The Adventure of the Moonstone" and "A Land to Call Our Own."

Visit him online at http://www.michaeljfoy.com.

175448UK00001B/10/P

Lightning Source UK Ltd.
Milton Keynes UK

9 780984 105304